Copyright 2022

All rights reserved. No pa... in any manner without the prior written permission of the copyright owner, except for the use of brief quotations in a book review. All characters and situations are products of the author's imagination and any resemblance to persons or situations living or dead, past or present, is purely coincidence.

I hope you have a great con weekend!

Meredith Fri

After Life
Medium at Large Book 5
by Meredith Spies
copyright 2022

HUGE THANK YOU TO:

Editing by Cate Ryan (www.cateedits.com[1])
Beta Reading by Jennifer Conklin
Cover and Promotional Art by Samantha Santana (www.amaidesigns.com[2])

---

1. http://www.cateedits.com
2. http://www.amaidesigns.com

Potential Triggers:

Mentions of assault (on page but also described, and a past event), death, death by violence (described, past event), depression, internalized ableism regarding possibly life-altering injuries, grief and grieving, murder.

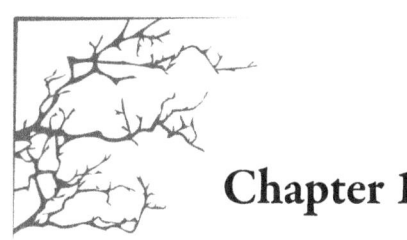

Chapter 1 – Oscar

The many etiquette classes Grandmere sent me to taught me a lot, but there was one thing they never covered: is it rude to inform your boyfriend that he's brought you to a painfully haunted town for your romantic getaway?

Julian looked so *happy*, leaning against the railing on the ferry like a golden retriever with a PhD. He even closed his eyes and tilted his face up to greet the breeze as we approached the dock. The dock where a cluster of men in various stages of raggedness waited, staring out to sea as if waiting for someone or something. Their clothes were old-fashioned—truly old-fashioned, not like my own homage to Victorian finery with the convenience of modern fabrics and cuts. No, these men were in weather-worn garb from centuries past and didn't seem to notice us at all as the ferry bumped into its slip. Julian turned his grin on me as the ferryboat captain threw a heavy rope onto the old dock, where it landed with a plop. I fought back a shiver, not at all related to the ancient seamen.

The taciturn ferryboat captain, Cap-just-Cap, as he had introduced himself on the mainland, jumped from the boat and wrapped the rope around a large metal cleat with ease. He'd said precisely three words since introducing himself (*mind your head*), and I'd almost forgotten we weren't alone until the rope sailed past.

"Isn't it beautiful?" Julian said. "It looks so peaceful. Professor Tomlinson said this end is quite secluded and perfect for a romantic getaway."

I smiled and nodded in turn, glancing at the dead men who were now drifting toward us. No, not drifting, walking, I realized, but their feet were a good inch or two above the current dock's surface, their steps following some long-gone path. "It looks very charming," I said, glancing back to see Julian looking at me with a tinge of anxiety around his eyes. He wanted this getaway to be good for us; a chance to be together without the pressures of the show crushing against us.

No, I couldn't tell him. He'd be heartbroken. The entire point of this getaway was to *get away*.

Well. And have very loud sex without having to worry about Ezra, CeCe, Harrison, the neighbors, the mail person, or random passersby overhearing.

(We're *very* enthusiastic, apparently).

Broken Palm Island and the tiny resort town of Rosie Sands had been his pick—close enough to our next filming location that we wouldn't have to rush the trip, far enough from everyone that we wouldn't have accidental meetings on the street or *just stopped by to tell you…* visits from production team members.

It was a strange feeling, really. Not necessarily a bad one, but just… strange. Being far from the people we'd been living cheek to jowl with for nearly a year.

Or longer, in the case of Ezra and myself. Even when we didn't share a hotel room or a flat, we saw one another nearly every day, and on the days we didn't, we spoke frequently via text or FaceTime.

We stepped off the ferry and onto a dock Julian declared *so cool,* but I suspected to be nothing more than barnacles holding hands in formation, and were met by a sallow, sad-looking woman in high waisted jeans and a sweater far too heavy for the weather. "Our ride," Julian murmured, looping his free arm through mine. "Sandra Cochrane. She manages the home we're staying at."

Sandra Cochrane was wide-eyed, pinch-mouthed, and near-silent. She held a piece of paper with *Weems/Fellowes* on it and stared at the ferry with a hungry gaze, fingers crumpling the edges of the paper as the ferry's horn sounded and one old man tottered onto the ramp with a plastic grocery bag, nearly worn through, dangling heavily from his wrist. As he passed, I took a peek and drew back—it was full of wet, sandy mussels. Just... sitting there. Taking the ferry to the mainland. "Is that even legal?" I asked. "Aren't there some sort of laws about transporting live animals or seafood?" Or tiny, disgusting monsters with sharp little edges and creepy little pseudopods and... ugh.

I wasn't expecting an answer, but one would've been nice.

Mussels... so creepy. Between them and barnacles, it was a wonder my skeleton didn't just leap from my body and run away whenever we went to the beach, so badly did they make my skin crawl. Which I probably should have told Julian before he made the final arrangements for this trip, but he'd been so excited when one of the fellows from University of the Upper Coast mentioned the island during one of their conversations. He'd been trying to woo Julian into applying for the lecturer position in their parapsychological research department and part of me suspected he'd mentioned it as a *wink wink nudge nudge* suggestion, but Julian had pounced on it for *us*. The idea of spending some time alone together was tantalizing and, frankly, felt like it would be a relief from the pressure and stress of the previous months.

I can handle this, I told myself. *Just stay off the beach. There's plenty to see here without hanging out on the sand all day.* I glanced at Julian and smiled. Exhibit A.

Julian tapped his cane on the dock—an affectation he picked up only a day or so before from god only knows where, but I found charming and annoying in turns. Though I suppose, given my own assortment of eccentricities and affectations, I had little room to talk.

Julian caught my eye and his grin broadened. "There's our ride," he said, grinning. "Come on. Let's grab the bags."

She jerked her chin in the direction of a rusty minivan that had been top of the line in the early nineties but seemed to be a hodge podge of replacement parts and attempts at painting over damage. "The Ford Aerostar of Theseus," Julian murmured as Sandra shoved the crumpled sign into her hip pocket and wrestled the van door open. "If no part of it was ever touched by the original owner, is it still the same minivan?"

Sandra grunted, giving the door an almighty wrench to force it open about a foot. "Here," she muttered, her voice far softer than I was expecting, a gravelly sort of whisper. "Gonna have to squish in. Nothin' else for it." She strode back to us and grabbed our suitcases—we'd sent most of our things on ahead with Ezra and Harrison, who also had custody of our filming and investigation equipment while Julian and I had our little week-long holiday. Still, the bags weren't inconsiderable. Two hard-sided cases, each holding a week's worth of clothes (okay, maybe a bit *more* than a week—I like to have options) and other items. Sandra heaved them into the cargo area effortlessly before trudging to the driver's side door and yanking it open as if it had offended her somehow.

"Well," Julian said with a tinge of unease, "this is definitely quaint."

"Does quaint mean something different in America than it does in England?" I asked, turning myself sideways to squeeze into the back seat. "Oh, god, I think I'm stuck!"

"It's your shoe. Hold on," Julian muttered, bracing his good side against the van to help me wiggle my foot loose from where it'd become wedged between the seat and the door. I popped free with a grunt, twisting to face Julian as Ms. Cochrane started the minivan with a rattling, crunching grind.

"Sorry," I said. "We need a sec here. Julian's a bit compromised."

She looked back over her shoulder and frowned at us both. "Should've gotten him in first," she pointed out. "Then he wouldn't have to be tryin' to figure out how to climb in with that cane and jake arm of his."

I winced—she was right, and guilt nipped at my heels as I scrambled forward to try to help Julian. "Here," I started, "let me—"

"No, no, it's fine! I promise," Julian swore, handing me his cane. "I'm just glad Ezra isn't here because I *know* this would end up on social media."

Julian managed to wiggle his way into the van with minimal bruising and only one low-voiced curse of aggravation, scooting to sit next to me as he slid the door shut with a mighty heave. "Sorry," I muttered. "I should've thought—"

"I didn't even think about it myself," he huffed. "It's fine. I promise. Don't let this bother you this week, okay? We're here to relax and... and get to know one another better, okay? No distractions, no filming, no work. Just us."

Ms. Cochrane made a funny, almost sad noise as she shifted the minivan into drive and pulled away from the pavement, onto the worn blacktop road in front of the ferry landing.

Julian's fingers closed around mine, tugging me a bit closer—at least as much as our worryingly loose seat belts would allow. "This place is beautiful," he murmured as we drove past a thick stand of towering trees with broad, glossy leaves and huge white flowers. A faint whiff of something lemony and herbaceous made it through the barely cracked window, followed hard by the salt-life-sharp tang of seawater and warming asphalt. The road followed the beach for most of the drive, the pale-yellow sand to our left and thick stands of palms and magnolias to our right, interspersed with salt-washed cottages and the occasional boat up on some sort of trailer or props.

Sandra muttered something under her breath as the road jinked to the right, cutting in toward the center of the island, and the town of Rosie Sands broke through the palms. "Holy crap," Julian muttered. "It's the town that time forgot."

"It's adorable," I protested gently. "It looks like a postcard from the thirties or something."

Everything was a vaguely washed-out candy hue, the sun and sea breeze doing their best to buff away anything brighter than pastels and earth tones. The buildings on the main street—possibly the only street, I realized, as we hadn't turned off the ragged asphalt drive from the ferry landing yet—were all in that round-cornered, low-slung style I'd seen in black-and-white movies when I was a boy, old American films where men wore hats all the time and the women were always sharp and quick.

I tore my gaze away to glance down at my phone, buzzing with an incoming email alert. It was from Charlotte, a distant aunt on my father's side. Her email was succinct and, frankly, a bit painful: *Oscar, I would like to apologize if my email yesterday overstepped. It must be a shock to find out I exist after so many years. If asking you to visit so soon was too forward, I'm sorry.*

Julian's hand atop mine drew me back to the moment. "Hey, this is just for us, remember?" he chided gently. "Charlotte can wait a few days."

I nodded. He was right. We'd made a promise this trip was just us, no work or outside drama. Just a chance for us to be together without anything pressing in on us. "You're right," I murmured. "It'll keep."

"Ray-Don's is the only grocery on the island. He's got everything you could need. The resort has a little quick-mart type thing, but it's limited and overpriced," Sandra said, bitterness coloring her words.

"Holy cats," I muttered as we cruised past an old-fashioned grocery store, the kind with massive displays of produce out front and handwritten signs advertising the specials instead of corporate-printed jobs. "It's like something out of *Back to the Future*."

Sandra nodded in the direction of the man standing in front of the store, carefully arranging a pyramid of sweet corn. "Ray-Don grows most of it himself," she said, nodding in the direction of a barrel-shaped man standing next to a pyramid of small watermelons. "Safer that way, he reckons, knowing what we're all eatin' and not havin' to rely on the mainland."

"Ray-Don," Julian repeated slowly. "Ray. Don."

Sandra glared in the rearview mirror. "Yeah. Ray-Don Smithers. His mother was a Noonan, one of the founding families, but married into the Smithers grocery dynasty. The Smithers folks have run the grocery here since 1911."

He nodded thoughtfully. "Ray-Don," he murmured when Sandra whipped her attention back to the road. "Like the radioactive element."

"I'm sure he has a glowing personality," I muttered.

Julian's choked laugh earned another sharp glare from Sandra as she sped the minivan past the low-slung block of pink-washed buildings bearing old-fashioned signs painted on the sides: *Delia's Baked Goods and Fresh Coffee—Get Your Day Started Right!*, *Pirate Pete's Boat Rentals and Bait*, *Wreckers Treasures Resale and Consignments*. A few people were in front of the shops, but none paid us any mind. We were there before most things were open, from the looks of it, and Sandra speeding through the small village didn't seem to bother anyone. The road took a rather sharp turn to the right, and I realized we were making a circle. "There's only the one road?"

Sandra nodded. "We don't need any more than that. All the houses and shops are on this side. The other side..."

"Is what?" Julian asked when she trailed off and fell quiet. "What's wrong with the other side?"

"Nothing. It got sold to developers after the last world war. Before that, it'd belonged to Rosie Sands for centuries, but after it got snapped up like that, it's been a tourist destination for folks into sport fishing and the like."

The rest of the ride was prickly. Sandra's eyes were fixed straight ahead, and her lips pressed into a thin line as she sped up, rocketing us toward Honey Walk, the cottage Julian had rented for the week. I had the feeling she'd just open the side door and lose us into the Atlantic on a hard turn if she could get away with it, but Sandra got us to the cottage in one piece.

One slightly carsick piece.

And when I say cottage, I'm only using that word because it was what was on the sign in front of the house. "I've seen smaller castles," I muttered. "Christ…"

Honey Walk poked out above a thick stand of trees that swayed gracefully in the sea breeze. Sandra rolled down her window and poked a code into a battered metal box by the wrought-iron gate and, a moment later, it hissed and creaked open, sliding back into glossy dark shrubs lining the front fence.

"Work on Honey Walk started in the late 1600s, but the final construction didn't take place until over a century later," Sandra said with a tinge of pride, the brusque tone of voice from the ride over dissolving under the warmth she felt for the house. She moved the minivan slowly up the drive, gravel crunching beneath the tires as she crept toward what looked like a carriage house. She slammed the car to a stop with little care for the transmission and motioned us to get out. It took some doing but Julian managed to get out without tangling his cane in the seatbelt, and I followed with an ache in my knees from the cramped back seat.

"Leave your bags," she ground out. "I'll get 'em. Follow me and I'll show you the inside."

We dutifully followed, slightly nervous ducklings in her wake as she strode up the crushed shell and gravel path and stomped up the rebuilt wooden porch. "This isn't the original, obviously." She sniffed, pausing at the door and rummaging through a heavy ring of keys from her low-slung hip bag.

"Are *those* the originals?" Julian asked, interest definitely piqued. He leaned forward, braced on his cane, as he tried to see the keys in her hand. Sandra closed her fingers around the hasps and glared.

"Yes. You'll be given your own key to the interior rooms and the exterior doors, but I ask that you leave them here," she pointed to a metal box on the porch, "if you leave the grounds for any length of time."

Julian nodded eagerly. They both turned their eyes toward me, so I joined the bobble head brigade. Sandra, apparently satisfied, unlocked the door with a heavy thunk of the lock and pushed it wide. Inside, instead of the dark cavern I'd been expecting, the foyer was an explosion of color and textures. Sleekly polished dark wood was juxtaposed with the colorful spill of light coming from a high-set stained-glass window overhead, positioned as a skylight. Bright shapes made of colorful light covered us and I couldn't help my pleased laugh. "I've always wanted to live inside a kaleidoscope," I admitted to Julian, who gave me such a tender smile I couldn't look at him for long because it made me want to tear up. "This is beautiful." Turning my hands palms-up, I grinned as they were bathed in green light from the design above.

Sandra unbent a little, pleased by our admiration of the home so far, if I had to guess. She left us to ooh and aah over the foyer while she headed back to the minivan to retrieve our bags. "This is beautiful," I repeated, and Julian smiled, dipping his chin to kiss the top of my head. "Admit it—you picked it because it's a historic home and your history-loving heart couldn't resist."

He huffed a small laugh. "Maybe. But the fact it's remote without being cut off from the world, and on the beach without being swarmed by tourists in tiny swimsuits and carrying plastic coconuts full of sugar water mixed with rum helped."

"You charmer," I teased, and he kissed me again, slower this time. I made a noise of pleased surprise and slipped my arms around his neck, returning the embrace.

Sandra's return—and the heavy thud of her dropping our bags—drove us apart. "The bedrooms are upstairs," she said, her flat tone even more pronounced. She swanned past, keys dangling from her fingers, and headed up the wide, sweeping staircase leading to the second level.

"Are you sure you can handle the stairs?" I asked quietly.

"They're shallow enough. And the PT that works with my doctor said I need to start trying them now." We gingerly picked our way up the steps after Sandra, leaving our bags behind for the time being. I cast another glance at the window as we reached the landing, pausing to admire the expansive stained-glass design. "Is it original?" I asked.

Sandra made a flustered noise, embarrassed almost. "Mostly. Part of it was damaged during a hurricane in the late 1700s." She pointed to an upper corner where a piece of glass that looked to be about the size of my hand shone bright and clear, the one uncolored piece in the image. "The original piece is long gone," she added glumly. "It can't be replaced."

Julian was practically vibrating with the need to say something—no doubt about restoration techniques or the decorative style of the glass. He navigated the next few steps on his own, slipping his arm from my loose grasp. "You're the caretaker, correct?"

Sandra nodded slowly. "Yeah. For a bit now."

"Then you're the one to ask. Have you read Doctor Colleen Sewell's paper on color preservation in antique stained-glass using nondamaging UV blocking compounds?"

Sandra's eyes widened for a moment before she set her expression into unimpressed lines and gave a sharp nod. "We were in grad school together. Haven't spoken much since I left my research position though."

Julian made an excited, happy noise suspiciously close to a purr—that's my man, a giant cat with a PhD—and started excitedly talking at Sandra about the implications of Sewell's research. Sandra unbent a bit more and started nodding. The pair of them perched atop the stairs on the narrow landing, leaving me several steps down.

My phone buzzed again. I took it out and glanced down to see a message from Ezra.

Ezra: **I'm going to assume you died on the crossing in a very tragic, Victorian way.**

Ezra: **Death due to being rained on or something equally Dickensian.**

I smirked, glancing up at Julian. He was rapt with the description Sandra was giving, despite her curt tone. I thumbed out a reply.

Me: **Not Dead Yet: A Memoir by Oscar Fellowes.**

Me: **And excuse you, my death would be Austenite, never Dickensian.**

Me: **Just ignore the fact she wrote during the Regency and my aesthetic is more Victorian.**

Ezra: **Your retro is even retro. Or something. So how is the trip?**

Me: **Good. Ish. Did you know it's perfectly legal to just carry mussels around like they're not the gods' most terrifying creatures?**

I glanced up at Julian and Sandra. She was holding forth in a surprisingly genial manner about the history of the home's restoration, and Julian seemed fascinated. My phone buzzed again to see Ezra's response, and I frowned.

Me: **Were that many laughing emojis really necessary? And there's a fucking clam emoji? WTF?**

Ezra: **I think they're oysters but yeah, totes necessary.**

Ezra: G2G in a sec. We're going to NOLA for the week! OMG!

Ezra: Harrison rented some fancy hotel room in the French Quarter. He's being all cute and shy about shit.

Ezra: **NGL I think I'm totally gonna put out.**

Me: Slag.

Ezra: **Love you too, Ozzy. Text me, yeah? Or call. Whatever. It's weird not being in the same place.**

I sent a string of hearts and weird smiling face emojis, which I guess was the thing to do because Ezra responded in kind. Then went quiet.

He was right—it *was* weird.

I looked up at Julian and offered a small smile when he glanced back down at me. *Sometimes weird is worth it, though.*

It looked like I'd be kicking my heels for a bit, I realized, so I stretched out my legs on the lower steps and leaned back on my elbows to just take a micro nap and let the sounds of their conversation buzz pleasantly in the background.

It would've been relaxing, really, if the damn ghost hadn't decided to try to scare the life out of me.

"She still on about the stained-glass?" he asked—boomed, really. I couldn't see him, but I could certainly hear him right next to my ear. "She hasn't stopped worrying about it since she got here. I swear, the first thing out of her mouth was, *oh no, that repair is terrible!*" He chuckled, and I could sense rather than see him leaning next to me, comfortable as anything. "You're the medium, right?"

I glanced up at Julian. Sandra had her arms folded and was frowning thoughtfully now as he gestured toward the window, then went in on some minutiae about the window preservation technique and how it could be applied to... something. I don't know. When Julian got going on one of his pet topics, I usually kind of zoned out a bit. Sometimes I felt a bit guilty for that, but the fact he seemed to sometimes forget I existed while he got into these conversations rankled enough to absolve me of any guilt.

Beside me, the ghost cleared his throat, their cold presence pressing closer, so I nodded.

He grunted. "Figured as much. I thought it might be him at first, but he's not quite right." The ghost chuckled. "I've met a few of your sort over the years. It gets easier to tell, once the fear wears off."

"Fear?" I murmured. "Are you afraid of mediums, then?"

He chuckled. "Not as such. More... afraid of change, perhaps."

"So, you're not about to ask me for help, then?" I asked, turning in the direction I felt his presence. "Most ghosts do."

I could hear a smile in his voice, I fancied. "I've been dead quite a while, my good man. Nothing is going to change that. Some of us have yet to learn that, I fear."

The rhythm of his speech was old-fashioned, his accent closer to mine than Julian's, and I wondered just how old this ghost was. Usually, after a time, ghosts wear thin, like fabric folded and worn one too many times. This ghost, though I couldn't see him, had such a strong presence that I was almost certain I'd feel his contours rather than a cold spot if I stuck my hand out in the direction of his voice. "Pardon me for being forward, but have you been here long?"

The ghost made a noise like a laugh, and I wondered If he was shaking his head, rolling his eyes at my rather rude question. "Long enough."

"Oscar, you okay?" Julian asked, and the coolness of the ghost beside me flared, then vanished like fog in the sun. He and Sandra both were staring down at me with wildly different expressions: Sandra's annoyed and bored, Julian's openly concerned.

"I'm fine," I assured him before he could try to come back down to me. "I was just lost in thought, staring at the glass."

Sandra's gaze narrowed, her lips pursing. "Your rooms are this way," she said briskly. "Come on. Dinner's at five, but you're on your own for the midday meal today."

Julian made some agreeable sound, but kept his worried eyes fixed on me as I trotted up the remaining steps and took his free arm. "I'm fine, really," I promised, refusing to look back even when I felt the cool pull of ghost fingers on the back of my neck, trying to get me to turn.

THE ROOM WAS SMALL but beautiful in that way only truly old places could be. Sandra pointed out the bathroom down the corridor with a muttered *obviously not original nor true to the integrity of the build* and all the cubbies and storage spaces in the room. "If you decide you don't want dinner, contact me at this number before three so I don't have to come all the way up here," she added, slapping a small calling card down on the nightstand before striding from the room like he hounds of hell were at her heels.

"Tomlinson never mentioned the place was run by a fellow anthropologist," Julian beamed, his expression freezing when he caught sight of whatever expression had settled on my face. "I, um... I apologize for getting so chatty with her downstairs. I didn't mean to make you wait on the stairs forever just so I could natter."

"It's fine," I promised, a hint of a laugh coloring my words. "At least we're here, yeah? Survived the choppy tide, I didn't throw up over the side of the boat, the island is beautiful, and we've got a house practically all to ourselves for an entire week. Just the two of us," I reminded him, hoping he took the hint.

Julian's smile was slow and warm, setting my heart racing at the familiarity of it. "Well, let's start vacation, hm?"

"I love that idea."

Julian held out his arms to me, and I all but bounced across the room to land on the bed beside him, mindful of his almost-healed injuries. Julian didn't let me fuss for more than a second, wrapping his arms around me and pushing me gently onto my back. "Hello." I grinned up at him. "Fancy meeting you here."

"What's a nice guy like you doing in a place like this?" he rejoined, making me roll my eyes at that cheesy old line.

"Well, I'm off for a bit of an extended dirty weekend, aren't I? I met this adorable, infuriating, brilliant professor who is also rather easy on the eyes, he invited me to run away with him to this island paradise and I just couldn't say no. Don't let my boyfriend know—he's the jealous sort."

Julian's cheeks were pink and eyes shining with mirth as he bent to nip my chin. "You're such an ass sometimes," he chuckled.

"Just sometimes? *Tch*. I need to up my game." I stretched up, brushing my lips against his before pressing the tip of my tongue against the corner, teasing entry. He made a happy, rumbling sound in his chest for that, relaxing back and taking me with him. Kissing without having to be mindful of a timeline was delightful, I decided.

I wanted to mention it, but that'd mean the kissing would stop while I talked and that just wouldn't do.

We were lazy with it, even though we were both hard as anything, gently, distractedly moving together as hands began to wander. Jaw, throat, chest, hair, bums... We were mapping one another with delicate, seeking touches. The room was warm to start with but grew positively muggy, both of us sweating and slick by the time Julian nudged me back so we could gulp for air. "Is it weird that making out like that is easily one of the top five sexual experiences of my life so far?"

"Definitely need to up my game," I sighed with mock-sadness. "I was sure that time between episodes one and two, when Ezra went to the museum with Harrison and we had your apartment to ourselves for a few hours, and you got the ice cubes—"

Julian's cheeks were bright pink when he pressed his fingers over my lips. "Alright, alright. I won't rank the sexy times."

I nipped his fingers till he pulled them away. "Why are you embarrassed for me to talk about our sex life in front of you?"

"I'm not!"

"You just covered my mouth," I pointed out, not unkindly. "And you're blushing."

"I'm not embarrassed. Just..." He sighed, shaking his head. "Awkward, I suppose. We've done things that former partners and I never have—" Pausing, he sighed again and let his head fall back on the pillows. "Less embarrassed and more *thinking about it turns me on and I'll absolutely come in my pants like I'm new at this*," he muttered.

I trailed my fingers down his chest, following the thin line of fine hairs that thickened just below his navel, turning into the nest of curls at the base of his still-hard cock. Julian's eyes fluttered closed, his exhalation sounding like *yes* as I wrapped my fingers around his length.

The tremendous crash downstairs was a more effective cockblock than sharing an apartment with Ezra. We both flew apart, Julian shouting in surprised pain when he rocked onto his bad hip. "What the fuck?" he demanded, scrambling to sit up.

I was less encumbered and got to my feet first, shoving my feet back into my shoes. The room wasn't huge—it took all of three steps to get to the door and fling it open. "Hello?" I called. "Sandra? Are you alright?"

Dead silence.

Julian was shrugging on his shirt when he reached the door. "Maybe something fell over."

"It sounded big," I murmured. "Come on. If something's broken, we need to let Sandra know. She seems the sort to blame us for falling masonry or the like."

Julian made a disgruntled sound and grabbed his cane from beside the door before we picked our way down the stairs.

All was as we'd left it, as far as I could tell. Sandra hadn't offered us the tour, but it didn't take much to tell the rooms—even the ones we hadn't seen before—were in order. Nothing was on the ground, no cabinets hung from the walls, no dishes broken in the kitchen. Everything was museum-neat. And very distracting for Julian. "Sorry," he muttered, dragging his attention away from the floor-to-ceiling bookshelves in what was either the home's library or a very nicely appointed study. "Just... books."

I smiled faintly, linking our fingers as he stepped out of the room, starting to reply when the soft murmur of low voices brought us both to a halt.

Tipping my head to one side, I strained to hear where they were coming from, but it was like catching fog. "It sounds like they're in there," I murmured, nodding at the study. "But..."

"It also sounds like the voices are coming from further down the hall," Julian finished. We both stood still for several long moments, the hushed rumble of voices rolling like waves, one moment beside us and the next far away, bouncing off the glossy wood walls of the corridor before coming back to the study. "I can't make out what they're saying."

"Me either," I whispered. "They sound angry, I think. Or just intense."

Julian nodded.

"You know what I have to do, right? It's a compulsion."

He groaned. "But we're on vacation," he complained.

At his pointed look, I shook my head a little and admitted, "Fine, I was thinking the same thing. Shall we?"

"After you."

We stepped back into the study. The voices fell silent. A heavy, expectant air smothered us, wrapping around us blanket-like.

The room is holding its breath, I thought, stricken by fancy. *The house is waiting.* "My name is Oscar Fellowes. This is my partner, Julian Weems." Beside me, he stiffened. I could practically hear his scrambling thoughts—*partner, what did he mean by that, oh my god, wait is boyfriend too much what*—and shot him a quelling glance. He pressed his lips into a thin line and stared straight ahead at the massive painting of a ship under full sail, secured over the room's cold stone hearth. "We don't mean to interrupt your conversation, but we couldn't help but overhear you. Is there anything I—we—can help you with?"

It didn't take much effort to open myself to the supernatural. It had been part of me for as long as I'd been alive, easy to access as breathing most of the time, but standing in the study at Honey Walk, opening to potential spirits wasn't as easy as typical for me. Instead of a small nudge, opening the metaphorical door just a crack, they flew wide, blinding me inside and out. I couldn't hear Julian's words, just his sudden sharp tone as everything blurred out and became dark and cold. The world heaved, rolling toward me, then away, sending me sprawling onto my back. Voices exploded around me, muddled and thick, only one word standing out: *Fire.*

The darkness shifted, patches growing lighter while others deepened, taking forms like people. One of them moved close to me, reaching out a hand to cup my face.

Their voice wasn't so much loud as... surrounding. It filled my head, expanding to press against the inside of my skull. *Not yet. You're not ready for me yet.*

"Oscar! Jesus Christ—" Julian's voice was too loud, too sharp. My eyes peeled open like paper with too much glue. He was leaning over me, face close to mine, pale save for the dark rings of his eyes as he stared down at me. "Can you hear me? Say something!"

"I'm okay," I said, though the way my voice slurred and muddled would paint me a liar. "Did I fall? What—"

Julian helped me sit up, wincing at his own pain but brushing off my attempt to apologize. "No, it's fine. I'll live." He pushed up awkwardly to stand as I rose, limping to rest against the heavy leather armchair near the hearth.

"Are you sure? Maybe you should lay down for a bit." His hands fluttered up, reaching for me before he tucked them away under his arms, folding them across his chest as if he wasn't on the verge of a minor freak out. "Naps are never a bad idea," he offered weakly.

I frowned. "I'm not infirm, Julian."

"No," he agreed. "But—"

"And you're not going to be able to do some of this on your own," I reminded him. "*And* we're on holiday!"

I hadn't meant to raise my voice at that end, but the way he drew back, looking abashed, made me realized I'd been almost shouting. "Sorry," I muttered. "Just... we're on holiday. The entire point was to not do this."

"So, you're willing to ignore the ghosts crashing around and having what sounds like a very stressful HR meeting?"

I nodded, albeit a bit reluctantly. "Unless it gets worse," I forced out. "Yes. The caveat being if they approach *me*, I'm not going to ignore them."

He nodded in return. "Deal. So. We just... don't investigate this."

"Mmm hmm."

"Feels weird."

"Definitely." I blew out a heavy breath and shook my head, trying to clear the thick cobwebs that were encroaching. "I need some fresh air."

Julian glanced at his watch and offered me a small, careful smile. "It's only a little past ten. Want to go into town for a bit, maybe grab lunch, do some sightseeing?"

I nodded, then paused. He'd give me a *look*, I was sure, hating being reminded of his new limits when it came to endurance and movement but needs must. "Are you sure you can manage? Maybe Sandra will let us use her van." Not bloody likely, but worth a shot in asking if Julian needed me to.

He scowled, mostly to himself. "The PT and my doctor both said I needed to walk more. It's not more than a mile into town. I'll be fine," he said with a sort of grim firmness to his tone. I held out my hands palm-out in a *no harm meant* gesture. "Let's go, before the sun gets much higher."

I let him lead the way, standing aside as he opened the door for me. Out of the corner of my eye, I saw the dark shape of someone watching from the foyer corner, gone when I turned to look at them fully.

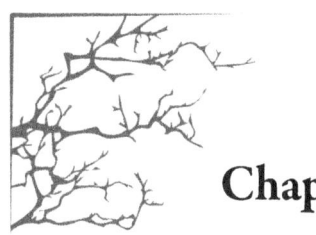

Chapter 2 – Julian

The walk into town was slower than I'd hoped or liked, but necessary. I'd been spending too much time sitting and my hip was letting me know with each step that I needed to move around more, no matter how much I hated the limp that seemed to be a permanent fixture now. *Fucking Bryan. Even beyond the grave, he managed to fuck with my life.*

Oscar strode ahead of me as we left Honey Walk, hands shoved in his coat pockets as we marched down the gravel drive toward the blacktop road. He seemed to recall my new, significantly less speedy status as soon as he reached the gate, stopping short and doing a bad job of pretending to be fascinated by the curlicues in the wrought iron as he waited for me to draw even with him. "It's fine," I muttered when he shot me a guilty glance. "I need to walk around more, anyway."

"Still," he replied, his cheeks pinking a bit as he pushed the gate open, "I shouldn't storm off just because I'm in my head like that. It's rude."

"Hm."

"Hm?"

I motioned for him to go ahead and we stepped onto the narrow path running alongside the only road in town. "Are you sure you don't want to rest?"

"Positive. I just..." He trailed off, slipping his hand through my arm as we started toward the main part of Rosie Sands. "Maybe I *am* tired," he hedged after a moment. "It's just strange being off work like this, I suppose. And not having Ezra hanging about."

I bit my tongue on that. Instead, I pointed out a cluster of primrose poking out between the bars of Honey Walk's fence. Oscar side eyed me but paused to sniff them, coming away with pollen on his nose. "Ah, that means someone wants to kiss you," I teased, laughing when he wrinkled his nose and made a face at me, looking suddenly much younger with the way his cheeks curved and the freckles across his nose stood out.

"I have a good guess who," he murmured, turning his face up toward mine and stretching up onto his toes before whispering. "I think it's Harrison."

I blinked, startled for a moment before his grin bloomed into a full-fledged laugh and he threw his arms around my neck, pulling me into a kiss. "Can you imagine," he muttered against my mouth. "Ezra would murder us both."

"That would be terrible," I replied with a solemn tilt of my head. "Who'd investigate your haunting if you're dead?"

Oscar made a thoughtful face then widened his eyes, holding up a finger in an *aha* gesture. "Quick, call CeCe! Tell her I've got a brilliant idea for a spin off, but unfortunately it can only happen after my death. A spirit medium spirit."

"You're such a dork." I laughed, kissing him again, quick and soft. The last vestige of whatever tension he'd hauled from the house at such a fast clip melting away as he looped his arm through mine again and we started our plod toward town.

Oscar stopped every once in a while to point out a cluster of flowers, or an architectural oddity on one of the older homes lining this part of the road. I knew he was giving me opportunities to rest, but the annoyance I'd expected to feel—that I'd felt when others had done it—didn't manifest with him. *Maybe it's because he's not being a dick about it,* I thought, nodding as he pretended to be rapt over a seashell-crusted mailbox painted in shades of pink and pale orange. *Or maybe I'm projecting and he's just really into ugly mailboxes.*

I wouldn't be managing any four-minute miles, not now or ever, but a thirty-minute mile wasn't bad for a guy with a bum hip. "It's not quite lunchtime yet," I said, spotting the green and white sign of Delia's Café a block away, "but if you're hungry, we could pop in there first?"

Oscar frowned; his eyes narrowed on something down the sidewalk. Two young people, teenagers if I had to guess, both with the same sandy blonde hair, were arguing outside of the grocery. Whatever they were arguing about was inaudible, but as we watched, a man came out of the store and waved them off, one of the teens stomping across the street toward Pirate Pete's Antiques and Bait, the other slinking into the grocery, taking a green apron from the man's hand. "You okay?" I asked Oscar when he kept staring even after the trio had dispersed.

"Hm? Oh. Fine. Just... Just lost in thought. Um, how hungry are you?"

He was staring down the sidewalk, his expression focused, lips pursed in an expression I'd come to recognize as *concerned but cautious*. One he tended to make when a ghost was acting up, I realized. Following his line of sight, I saw... nothing.

Well. The man from the grocery—Ray-Don—was staring back at us but other than that, not a single thing other than an empty sidewalk and some parked cars. "Oscar?"

"Oh, I was just thinking maybe a romantic walk," he said, shifting attention away from whatever it was to point to the twee wrought iron gate wound 'round with ivy (fake, I realized belatedly—far too green and shiny to be real in this climate) and a wood-burned plank reading *Virginia's Path Open Dawn to Dusk*. A narrow, sand and rock path disappeared through the gate and down a gentle incline toward the shore, past a thick stand of shrubs and trees and he frowned. "I suppose that's the nature trail?"

"I suppose so." My hip and thigh twinged in protest, but I forced a game smile. "I have to admit, romantic walks along the beach featured heavily in how I envisioned our week away together."

Oscar's cheeks pinked and he dipped his chin, the edge of his lower lip disappearing between his teeth. "That's very romantic of you," he said, his tone oddly flat. He cleared his throat and tipped me a small smile that didn't reach past the corners of his lips. "Are you sure you're up for it?"

A bitter flare of annoyance sparked beneath my breastbone but I kept that smile in place. "I wouldn't have agreed otherwise."

He nodded and, linking his fingers with mine, led us through the gate and onto the sandy path. The first hundred or so yards were easy going—wide, smooth, and free of shells and gravel. After that, though, the trail started to pitch downward toward the beach and grew narrow enough for us to go single file, gravel and whitened shells crunching under our feet. We made it to the bottom of the path without incident, and I wasn't sure if it was sheer luck or if I was just getting better with my new balance (or lack thereof). Oscar gave my fingers a squeeze and nodded toward a bench made from what looked to be large pieces of driftwood and smooth-polished boards. "Come on," he murmured, not giving me a chance to argue.

"Virginia's Overlook," I read as we reached the bench. A small brass plaque was affixed to the back, bearing that legend and the years 1801-1824. "My grandmother had a memorial bench in Hermann Park back home," I mentioned, carefully lowering myself onto the sand-speckled seat. "She said she'd rather have that than a headstone since she was more likely to have visitors that way. Really, I think she just wanted people to see the shiny plaque and think *oh, she must've been rich to get a bench here*."

Oscar was standing beside me still, staring at the path behind us. "Oscar?"

"Hm? Just... just a moment," he muttered, and hurried the few steps back to the path. I couldn't hear what he was saying, but he was frowning deeply, talking in low tones.

Because of course.

A flare of annoyance lit in my breast and for a tempting moment, I almost called out to him, said something snarky about vacation, spending time together, *no investigations*. But I swallowed the acid-burning urge to call him out, feeling guilt and a hint of shame spread through me instead. Oscar shook his head, turning back to look at me, and froze for a moment before resolutely shaking his head again at whoever was there and heading back toward the bench. "I'm sorry," he murmured, sitting gingerly beside me. "They've been following us since the pavement, trying to get my attention, and—"

"And," I sighed, "you had to. I understand."

"Do you though?"

I tilted my head, peering at his profile while he resolutely stared at the incoming tide. "I'd like to think so, at this point in our relationship. I'm not new at this, Oscar."

"But you are," he said with a trace of bitterness than made me recoil slightly. "In the grand scheme of things, you're very new at this. And I know this is meant to be *our* week but I can't ignore them. Not... not entirely," he added, wilting a little around the edges. "I want to promise you that I can, but it's impossible. It's part of who I am."

"Oscar," I murmured, "I didn't ask you to. I just asked that we don't get involved in *investigating* anything this week." Slipping my fingers around his, I waited until he looked at me before continuing. "You're right. Compared to you, I *am* new at this. Very freaking new. And maybe... maybe I don't understand everything still."

"Maybe?"

"Definitely, you pedant."

"Pot, kettle on line one."

A small smile teased the corner of his lips. Something inside me loosened a bit at the sight, a tension I hadn't been aware of releasing just a fraction, making it easier to breathe.

"The ghost," he said after a moment. "Virginia Noonan."

I felt a sharp prickle, electric and cold at the same time, down my neck. "Her path, her bench."

"Ah, that doctorate isn't just a pretty piece of paper. Well sussed."

"I will totally leave you here with the barnacles, Oscar," I grumbled, only to have him shoot to his feet and whirl around, inspecting the bench with a sharp eye.

"Are you fucking with me? There're barnacles on this thing?" He shot a baleful glare at the path and I wondered if Virginia was just as bemused as I was. "That's not funny, Julian," he snarled, seeing the bench was free of barnacles and pretty much anything other than some errant sand. "God, my skin is trying to crawl from my body!"

"You're afraid of barnacles?" I rose to my feet, doing my best not to smile at his dramatic reaction. "Seriously? They can't even move once they're cemented to something."

"They can too move," he muttered, petulant and dark. "Those little grasping mouths, those weird *frills*... They're terrible. Just waiting to eat whatever drifts past. *Ugh*! They're as bad as mussels! Mussels definitely move," he added, shooting me a glare. "I've seen videos. They *scoot* and some of them do this hop-float thing and it's *terrible*!"

"You're really upset about this," I said wonderingly. "I don't think I've ever met anyone afraid of bivalves before." Guilt nibbled at me—he was seriously unnerved and here I was trying to make jokes. "I'm sorry," I offered. "I didn't realize. If I'd known, I'd have suggested something else. Maybe a drive around the island or something." I was a little annoyed—he could've said something when I first suggested this destination, I thought, but... But I'd been in his place more than once, not wanting to admit what I'd perceived as a personal failing in front of someone I cared about. "Would it help if we went back to the street? There are no barnacles there." I winced even as I said it—it still sounded dickish, but there was no taking the words back.

Oscar glared. "Don't mock me. It's a phobia. It's not like I can help it!"

I nodded. "Of course not. I'm sorry. It's just unexpected, is all." He was still staring balefully at the very un-barnacled bench, jumping when I reached for his hand as if he fully expected a man-sized clam to have toddled up on the beach to make a play for him. "Sorry, sorry!"

"You're laughing at me," he said, narrowing his eyes. "And so are you!"

I glanced toward the trail, unable to deny the twinge of disappointment at seeing nothing more than sand, grass, and gravel. "Is she a, ah, intelligent haunt then?"

Oscar paused, shifting his gaze to me. "That's the widely used term, yes. She's very aware that she is dead. She is... sentient, I suppose is the best word for it." He paused, then, with a small sigh, added, "Sometimes I feel like you're doing a study when you ask me these things," he admitted with a rueful little smile.

"Maybe I am. A personal one, of a sort. This is new for me, so I'm doing the only thing I'm good at here and gathering information."

"A personal study sounds racier than I expect it truly is," Oscar muttered, shooting me a baleful glance.

"It can be," I chuckled. "I mean, it'd be an entirely different methodology. And for the record, I haven't been intentionally making a study of your methods since we left Bettina. I... It's just habits sometimes," I admitted. "I'm trying to understand, to learn."

He rolled his eyes, the tension receding from his posture just a bit. "If you have questions, ask. But I can't promise I'll know the answer. And if you want to make notes on *me*, tell me first."

My face warmed. "I'll do better."

"That's all I ask." He sighed, then glanced "Now. Virginia. She's 'intelligent,'" he said after a brief pause, air quotes practically neon and flashing. "She doesn't want us—me, specifically—down on the sands. She says it's too dangerous. That..." He trailed off, staring at something—someone, rather—beside me. "Her body was never here, but it's where she died."

"How does that work?" I murmured.

"I have no idea, Julian. I'm not... I'm not an expert." Raking his fingers through his hair, he watched the ghost—Virginia, I reminded myself, because she did have a name after all—as she apparently moved away from us, toward the incoming tide yards away. After a long few moments, he shifted his attention back to me. "I apologize," he rasped. "I shouldn't have snapped at you. I've been distracted lately, upset about the entire situation with," he made a gesture at his head, one I took to mean his abilities, "and then the show is not at all what I'd been lead to believe it'd be and..." he ran out of steam on a sigh. "I apologize." He finally let me catch his hand, so I wove our fingers together, tugging him closer on the soft sand..

"This isn't exactly how I pictured our romantic beach walk," I admitted. "In fact, if I'd known about your phobia—"

"No," he cut me off. "It's... it's ridiculous, I know." He shrugged again, glancing back at the path and frowning. "She's very determined," he said. "She's worked herself into a state about me going to the beach."

"You, specifically," I noted. "Not us. Just you." My fingers itched for my phone and the notes app there. The compulsion to make notes, to start a research project, was great. Ever since my experiences with Reg, with freaking Boo Con, I'd been dying (well... no pun intended there) to start in earnest, but the sheer breadth of the potential project was daunting. *You know people you can ask about this,* a niggling little voice reminded me. *Professionals even. Just answer Pro-*

fessor Tomlinson's email. Or call Professor Demmings back—he's left you two messages this week about the position.

Oscar nudged me, smirking and dragging me out of my incipient spiral. "Jealous?"

"Terribly," I sighed. "I don't know how I can go on like this. Alas, alack, et cetera."

"Arse," he grumbled, but smiled as he tugged me closer for a quick kiss. "Also, she's taken her wailing to the water. We can make a break for it if you'd like."

I hesitated. "Would you?"

He looked toward the water, seeing Virginia. "I think so, yes."

"If you're certain..."

His expression was amused, but it didn't quite sit right on his face. "I thought you said no investigating this week."

"I thought *we* agreed on it," I rejoined sharply.

"I'm just confirming our agreement," he snapped. "And no investigating means no investigating. So I'll leave her be. She told me what she wanted to tell me. And I offered to help her, but she said..." He paused, glancing back at Virginia, back toward the lines of sea foam and rushing water. "She said she's tried so many times to make someone hear her. I'm the first who's actually listened."

WITH SOME UNSPOKEN agreement, we abandoned our beach walk and went back up the trail to the sidewalk. I grimaced through most of it, trying to take as much of my weight as possible on my good leg but even with the help of the cane, the trail was too pitched and too soft for me to make it up without some more pain flaring to life in my bad hip. I was unable to stop the hiss and grunt of discomfort when we finally reached the pavement and I could adjust my weight better. Oscar darted me a guilty glance, but I tucked his hand beneath my arm and motioned toward Delia's Café. "Looks like the path is clear," I noted.

He nodded. "Um. I must admit something. Earlier, when those teenagers were arguing, there was a ghost between us and them."

"Virginia?" I asked. "We're at the head of 'her' path."

He shook his head. "No. A man. He wasn't happy about… Well. I'm not sure. He didn't speak to me. He was down by the grocery." Frowning, Oscar stared at the empty sidewalk ahead of us. "It's not terribly often I find a ghost to be discomfiting, but this one was."

I sighed inwardly. My hip was killing me, I was actually fairly hungry, and my head was starting to throb after a long morning of travel and now the emotional roller coaster with Oscar running hot and cold. But I bit my tongue hard before speaking, holding back an exasperated sigh I'd have thought nothing about less than a year ago. "Do you want to go back to Honey Walk?" I offered. "This romantic walk is kind of a shambles. Maybe head back, get some lunch, rest up, and start over later? Or tomorrow?"

Oscar's frown deepened. "No. I'm spoiling things, aren't I? Don't lie to me—I know I am. Come on, ignore my maudlin turn. Let's go to this café then, get something in our bellies, then decide what to do next. This is a charming town," he said, tugging me forward. "I bet there're all sorts of things we can check out before heading back for the evening."

I let him lead me along but I couldn't miss the way his gaze darted back toward the spot where he said the ghost had been, or the way he tensed as we reached the café door.

He hung back as I pulled it open, the electronic tone of the door chime sharp and grating on the quiet street. "Oscar?"

"Sorry," he muttered, looking past me again. "Pardon." He ducked past me and I had the distinct feeling he hadn't been apologizing to me.

The café was empty, a sign hung above the counter declaring: *Order Here, Seat Yourself, We'll Find You When It's Ready*. Oscar wavered for a moment, but I motioned for him to grab us a table while I made my way to the counter. Racks of brochures—mostly for mainland attractions but a few for things like Tibbins Quay, the Broken Palm Island Museum and Cultural Center, and Pirate Pete's Shipwreck Tours were clustered on one end of the rack near the door. Magazines of the dull and respectable variety lined another rack by the counter, all about seasonal crafts, deep sea fishing, or nature and wildlife. They were sun-faded on the edges and gave the place an abandoned air with their curling edges and publication dates from a year past. "Do you see anything you'd like?" I called to Oscar, pointing to the menu board above the counter. A few letters were missing here and there, the plastic pieces no doubt long gone, but it was easy enough to see the café specialized in coffees, smoothies, and sandwiches as well as a few burgers.

"Anything," he said. "Anything and a lemonade."

I turned back to the counter just as a woman pushed through the doors that led to the kitchen, looking entirely nonplussed with our presence. "Welcome," she said in a polite but distracted sort of tone. "What can I get for y'all?"

I placed our order—chicken salad sandwiches, chips, and lemonade seemed like a good bet—and she gave me a ticket with a muttered *be right out* and disappeared back into the kitchen. Joining Oscar at the booth he'd picked—situated in the window overlooking the road—shrugged. "The surlier the staff, the better the food in my experience."

"I think that's just a trick our brains pull on us to ensure we don't complain about the food in establishments where there's a high chance they'll spit in it."

The door chimed, and we both craned our necks to see who was coming in. The two teenagers we'd seen arguing earlier ambled in, one shaking a cup full of ice and slurping noisily as they leaned on the counter. "Delia," the other one called loudly. "Ray-Don sent us over to get his order!"

The woman who'd taken my order strode out of the kitchen, scowling. "Ray-Don can get it his own damn self. You two have school today!"

"Nuh uh," the cup rattler protested. "It's an in-service day for the teachers."

"That's a load of shit," Delia snapped. "You're the only two I've seen out today and if it were in-service day I'd be up to my ears in kids from the quay slumming it for cheap coffee."

"Come *on*," the other one whined. "It's useless. We'll just get our GEDs this summer, you know?"

Delia shook her finger in their faces. "Last time," she ground out. "Tell Ray-Don he enables this bullshit again, I'll kick his ass myself!." Delia turned and strode back into the kitchen, cursing not so under her breath.

"Ugh." Cup rattler sank down on one of the red vinyl covered stools at the counter while her counterpart turned to lean on their elbows, apparently attempting to channel every too-cool teenaged character in the movies since 1950.

Oscar realized we'd been clocked before I did. "Shit," he sighed on a soft breath. "Smile. We've been recognized."

The elbow-leaned shoved away from the counter and crossed to our booth in just a few long-legged strides. "I know who you are," they said, pointing at Oscar. "Holy shit. Are you here to investigate the museum? Oh! Or West Beach? Holy shit! Marilla! Look who it is!"

Marilla—the cup rattler—turned, shrugged, looked away then did a double take. "Oh. My. God. Oscar *Fellowes*! Ohmygod, is Ezra Baxter here too? I love his camera work and ohmygod, he's so cute!"

Oscar winced at the sharp squeal of his surname. "Hello," he said affably. "Ah, we're just here enjoying a bit of a holiday, just me and Julian. Ezra's on his own trip with... a friend," he added, answering the leaner's question. "It's lovely to know we have fans here."

Marilla snorted. "No one comes here on *holiday*," she said, imitating Oscar's accent on the last word. "Seriously. Not unless you're like, wannabe rich and even then you go to Tibbins Quay. Rosie Sands is a ghost town." She paused, then snorted. "Literally."

Her companion nodded, eyes wide as he stared at Oscar avidly. "I'm Kelly. Total old dude name, I know, but, I mean... Oscar, right?" He chuckled. "You know that feel, am I right?"

"I suppose so," Oscar murmured, clearing his throat. He shot me a desperate glance—one even I could interpret as *make it stop please*.

"So if y'all aren't in class, what are you up to?" I asked, drawing Kelly's glare.

"Nothing," he sighed. "Waiting for Ray-Don's food. Dude, seriously though. How do you get started in the biz? Oh! I bet you get a *ton* of cash, huh? Like all those people who wanna talk to grandma and shit?"

"Kelly! Christ, dude," Marilla groaned. "It's not all about money, you dick."

Delia emerged from the kitchen with a large paper bag just as the café door swung open to admit Ray-Don, the owner of the grocery next door. "What the hell's taking y'all so long? Gotta go kill the cow yourselves?"

Kelly folded in on himself and Marilla rolled her eyes as Ray-Don shot them a glare. "Order up," Delia chirped through gritted teeth. "Ray-Don, a word?"

"Ain't got time for that, Delia. Gotta do a run out to the site before the storm hits." He nodded at us, adding, "If you see Sandra before I do, let her know I'll be by to help batten down the place before dark-thirty."

"It's just a watch," she said, throwing up her hands. Marilla and Kelly exchanged looks and started easing toward the door.

"Hey! You got ten minutes to get to the boat," Ray-Don snapped. "We don't got a lot of time to finish before the storm moves everything around."

"Ray-Don!" Kelly erupted excitedly. "Do you know who we got in town? Those guys from *Bump in the Night!* Well, most of 'em anyway!" He was practically vibrating as he pointed at us. Oscar gave a weak wave and I offered a brisk nod. "Maybe they'll talk to—"

"Ten minutes," Ray-Don interjected. "Get your butts in gear, you two."

Kelly groaned. "Imma find y'all later," he promised. "Come on, Marilla."

"Ugh," Marilla groaned, rattling her cup again as she and Kelly slunk out of the café, Kelly shooting Oscar one last, hopeful glance.

Delia shot a look our way. "Your food'll be out in a sec. Apologies for the"—she glanced at Ray-Don— "theatrics."

Ray-Don rolled his eyes skyward as Delia swanned back into the kitchen. "He right, though?" he asked as soon as the door closed behind her again. "You here to talk to some, er, ghosts?"

"We're here on vacation," I said firmly. "Oscar's not holding any séances this week."

If I could've been flayed alive by the power of a look, Oscar would've accomplished it in that moment. "Julian." His tone was quelling. My face heated under the glare he shot me before he turned back to Ray-Don. "Is there someone you're looking for, Ray-Don? Or maybe someone you hope is looking for you?"

Ray-Don shook his head as Delia emerged from the kitchen with a tray holding our food. "Just curious is all. You talk to 'em, huh? All the time?"

Oscar fell into a very basic, somewhat stilted conversation with Ray-Don as Delia deposited our plates and drinks, then the three of them got into a discussion of the island's alleged hauntings. "It's not much," Delia protested. "I mean, you can't swing a cat in the South without hitting some long-dead lady in white or a grunch or something, but we're a bit proud of our local legends."

Ray-Don made a choked, growly noise and shook his head once at her. A *shut up damn it* gesture, if I ever saw one.

"Julian booked our stay here," Oscar said, barely glancing at me. "He didn't mention any local hauntings to me."

"I wasn't particularly looking for any when I planned the trip," I muttered. "Since we're *on vacation*."

Delia's expression flickered between prurient interest and awkward embarrassment. "Oh! Vacation! Well, have you checked out these?" She rushed to the rack near the door and grabbed a handful of brochures. "Virginia's Path goes 'round this half of the island and has a few sites of historical interest along it. Oh! And there's the Rosie Sands Historical Museum," she added another to the stack. "It's in the old Noonan House—they were Ray-Don's people, but his great-grandmother married a Jennings, so she didn't get house—and it's got a surprising amount of artifacts and local history. Some of the rooms are done up like back in the day, too."

Ray-Don grunted. "My mom's people were Noonans," he repeated. "One of the families that founded Broken Palm."

Delia and Ray-Don fixed us both with an expectant look, like we were supposed to know the significance of that. So I nodded and made interested noises, unable to stop myself from shooting a worried glance at Oscar. He smiled and flipped open one of the brochures, ignoring me entirely. "No ghost tours then?"

Delia and Ray-Don exchanged another look. "Ah, no. Just the legends."

"Such as?" Oscar asked, flashing them both one of his infamous charming smiles. "I'm sure you can glean that I'm a bit of an enthusiast when it comes to this sort of thing."

"Oh. Well. Ah, there's Virginia," Delia offered, gesturing weakly toward the café door. "People have reported seeing her ghost on the walk there. She—"

"Was lost at sea," Ray-Don supplied. Oscar's eye twitched and his lips tightened at Ray-Don's lie, but he kept his smile firmly in place. Ray-Don took that as his cue to continue. "Yeah, she was on the old ferry that ran between here and the mainland. Drowned when it sank midway."

Oscar's smile was so tight, it must've hurt. "How tragic. And she haunts the path there. Who else?"

Delia cleared her throat, folding her hands across her middle like she was trying to protect herself when she replied. "Well, some folks say Jeremiah Tibbins himself haunts Honey Walk. Isn't that where you're staying?"

I nodded. "Sandra Cochrane's been very accommodating," I fibbed.

Ray-Don grunted. "She's real... enthusiastic about the history here."

Delia's smile was so big it was scary. "I bet she'd have all sorts of things to tell y'all. So do the ghosts you talk to... do they ever, like... tell you things?"

Oscar's attention narrowed to laser-like intensity. Even I sat up a bit more at that. "Like what?" I asked. "He speaks with them so obviously they're talking to him."

Oscar's foot hit my bad leg with more force than I thought absolutely necessary, but he didn't even glance at me when I made an embarrassing sort of squeaking sound. "Julian is still new at this and lacks tact." Oscar smiled. "What he means is, is there something particular you're worried about, Delia? Someone you miss, a message you're hoping to hear?"

She shook her head as Ray-Don made a disgruntled, disagreeable sound. "No, no, no," she protested. "I'm just wondering if they ever, I don't know, tell you something weird."

Oscar leaned in conspiratorially and stage whispered, "I once had a monk from the sixteenth century give me the monastery's secret mead recipe."

Ray-Don's watch beeped, making Delia jump. "Well. That was kind of him, huh? Who says the dead can't be accommodating. Not me, that's who. Delia, thanks for lunch. I'll stop by later to help get the storm shutters done on your place."

"It's just a hurricane watch," she muttered, hesitating by our table as Ray-Don strode out, the door chime signaling his departure as a small cluster of older ladies in matching Tibbins Quay visors scooted in. "Sorry, gentlemen. Let me know if y'all need anything else."

Delia hurried back behind the counter and started seeing to her new customers. I picked up my sandwich and took a bite as I glared at Oscar, reaching down to rub my shin. "Ow?"

"Julian," he murmured, "please..."

Checking to make sure no one was overtly listening in, he leaned toward me and hissed, "I can't *not* be a medium, Julian. Even on holiday."

"I never said—"

"You acted like a prat about me seeing ghosts just now. I thought you..." He closed his eyes, setting his sandwich aside before opening his eyes to level a baleful, hurt glare in my direction. "I thought you were past that, honestly. And I don't know how to feel right now."

"You love me but you don't like me."

"At the moment, yes."

The group at the counter shuffled over to a nearby booth. Oscar looked up at me, then at the door, and sighed. "There's a ghost on the sidewalk. He keeps coming through the door then going back outside. He's agitated. He kept me company at the house, while you were busy talking with Sandra about that stained-glass."

"Oscar—"

"Don't worry," he said, sliding out from the booth. "I won't waste your time talking to him since that's not what we do on holiday."

"All I said was no investigating, and you agreed," I growled, slipping out to stand next to him and setting some bills on the table for Delia's tip. "I never said no ghosts period."

Oscar worked his jaw like the words in his mouth were hard, then nodded. "So you did. But I wonder if you understand the difference between what I do on camera and what I do every other moment of the day."

"Don't act like I don't," I muttered, taking his elbow in one hand and my cane in the other, leading him to the café door. "You know I've changed since we first met."

"Yes. Now ghosts are academically fascinating."

"What?"

Oscar opened the door and held it for me, his attention fixed on the sidewalk as I edged past. "I think maybe I do need that nap after all," he announced. "Shall we walk back or would you rather call Sandra for a ride?"

A thousand things threatened to spill out, most of them things I'd regret. So I clenched my jaw and nodded once, curtly. "Let's walk back."

The trip back was quiet; Oscar slipped ahead of me and not looking back until we reached the house.

WHEN WE REACHED HONEY Walk, Sandra's minivan was gone and the house quiet and dark. Oscar headed up the stairs with a barely mumbled comment about resting, leaving me in the foyer, at a loss. "Hey," I called after him. "Oscar—"

"Not right now," he sighed. "Just... not right now, alright?"

He didn't wait for a response.

"Shit. Goddamnit. Shit." I wanted to kick something but, with the way my luck had been running, I'd break my good foot and end up in the hospital for some reason.

A haunted hospital, no doubt.

With nothing else to do, I took myself to the study and stretched out on the settee, leaving my shoes by the door and my socks tucked inside. I sighed—my feet were a bit swollen, my body still adjusting to its new normal and creating all sorts of exciting new reactions to things I took for granted just a few months ago, like long walks or being able to sit in a car for more than an hour at a time and not be in pain.

Pity party, table for one.

I could faintly hear Oscar's voice from above, filtering through the vents no doubt, and hoped he was talking to Ezra. *Maybe it'll put him in a better mood if he is. Maybe we can sort this out later if he's not so touchy...*

I must have dozed a bit because Sandra's sudden presence at my side startled me. One moment I was alone, the next she was towering over my supine form. "Make sure you don't get your dirty socks and shoes on the soft furnishings," she warned. "You have a comfortable bed upstairs, by the way. No need to use the study for a bedroom."

I sat up, blinking away a trace of grogginess as I focused on her unsmiling face. "Oscar's using the bedroom to make some personal calls," I extemporized. "Thought I'd give him some privacy."

She made a thoughtful sound in her throat and then, after a moment's hesitation, sat in the armchair across from the settee. "I, um, wanted to ask you about your work. And since you're on your own for a moment, I thought now would be a good time."

"Oh, sure. Well. Right now I'm not doing much in the way of academics, if that's what you're after. I've been doing the show for several months now."

She waved that off. "It's not often I get a chance to talk about the real nitty gritty of things here. The handful of tourists we get, they ooh and aah over the rooms and ask about silly things like how people used the bathroom without indoor plumbing. It's rare for someone who has an actual background in a complementary area to my own comes through here."

"You sound like you miss academia."

She stiffened. "I'm sure you know how it is. Once an academic, always an academic."

"True." I sighed. "I wish I could go back."

"Why did you leave?" she asked.

I scoffed. "There was a scandal. Dated the wrong guy. What about you?"

"It's a long story. Started after my partner died. It was sudden but not a surprise."

"Oscar tells me all deaths are, whether they're expected or not. In my limited experience, I have to agree."

She nodded, starting at her fingers where they were knotted in her lap. "Your boyfriend... does he really speak with the dead?"

"Yeah. He does."

She nodded. "Back when I worked at the university, some of the other folks in my department, they thought they could but nothing much came of it. I just wondered..."

Oscar's footsteps sounded overhead as he moved toward the stairs, and Sandra's expression shuttered once more. "Well. I suppose I should start dinner. I'd gone into town for supplies. Must've just missed y'all heading back."

I started to point out there was no way she could've missed us, since there was just the one road in and out of the little town, but kept my mouth shut as Oscar stepped into the study and drew up short, seeing Sandra sitting with me. "Hey," I said. "We were just talking about our former academic lives."

Sandra rose to her feet, smoothing her hands over her rumpled linen shirt and giving me a brisk nod. "It's nice to share with someone who knows," she said. "I'd like to talk more with you about our shared interests later?"

"Sure. I'd love that."

Oscar's lips tightened, but he gave her a polite nod as she headed for the kitchen. "Sorry, didn't mean to interrupt," he murmured, slipping in to sit on the settee next to me.

"It's fine. We were just chit-chatting."

He nodded, worrying his lower lip with his teeth. "I, ah, called Ezra," he said after a moment. "He and Harrison are apparently having a lovely time in New Orleans."

"Not sober, huh?"

A tiny smile broke through. "Just a bit tipsy. We talked about that email from Charlotte, offering to send me some family pictures I'd never seen."

"Ah. And what did Ezra say about that?" This formality between us was making me itch. I wanted to shake him a little. I wanted to scream, something to break the tension and rattle everything loose. But instead, I folded my hands on my bent knee so I didn't reach for him and waited.

"He said go for it. Which is basically the same thing you said," he murmured. "I..." he huffed. "Damn it. Can we talk? Really talk?"

"I think we need to."

He nodded again. "I... earlier, What I said about not liking you? Um. That wasn't good of me. I didn't mean that."

I gave in to my urge to touch him, reaching across the short but incredible distance between us to lay my hand atop his. "It's okay if you did," I whispered. "I'd understand it, even. Sometimes I'm an ass. And I think... I think I can see how I fucked up."

"I think it might've been a bit of a mutual fuck up." He sighed. "I was... No, I *am* feeling a little wrongfooted here. I'm not sure how to *be* without the context of the show these days. For so long, the only way I defined myself was as a medium, as who I was taught to be. I've been *on* all the time, ever since I was old enough to follow Grandmere's directions. Some days I don't know how much of me is Oscar and how much is Oscar Fellowes, Renowned Medium. When Ezra and I were making those videos, before it even became a channel, it felt safe, you know? I knew how to be this person, how to be Oscar Fellowes the Medium. And I didn't have to worry about the world being a strange place to me. When Ezra had the idea to make it a show, I was more into it than I wanted to admit. Every day has been either an investigation, a séance, or preparing for them. And this week is the very first time I've been outside of that context in a long while. I felt like maybe you... like maybe you wanted me to not be Oscar Fellowes."

"Who else would I want you to be?" I rasped. "I love you, Oscar. You. Not whoever your odd little fan club thinks you are, not the face you put on for the cameras." Taking a chance, I reached out and laid my hand on his knee. He stiffened for a moment, then relaxed under my touch. "You've been really stressed lately. And I wish I could help but you're not letting me in. And I know that we're really new here but still... I love you, Oscar, and I want to be part of your life."

"That's the problem." He sighed. "I keep thinking, once you get a real feeling for my life, you'll run screaming back to yours."

"And you don't want to be part of mine?"

"I didn't say that," he groaned. "It's just... I don't fit with yours, do I? Outside of the show or our time away from the real world, I'm not the sort of person you'd take around your friends from university, am

I? I'm not a scholarly sort, and I don't have some grand background in the sciences or research or—"

"Or," I cut him off, leaning in to brush a kiss against his temple. He closed his eyes and shuddered against my embrace, making relief flare to life in my chest. "Or it doesn't matter. Seriously. When was the last time you saw me hanging out with a bunch of egg heads, huh?"

"Egg heads?" he snorted. "Seriously?"

"I'm trying to defuse a tense situation with disarming humor. Is it working?"

"Not really."

"Well. How about with kissing? Does that help?"

"Maybe."

"Well," I asked, tugging on his fingers as I struggled to my feet. "Maybe we should go diffuse the tension further upstairs?"

He grinned. "I think that is an excellent idea."

WE MISSED DINNER. I had the feeling Sandra was annoyed about it, judging by the solid door-slam around eight. Neither of us cared much, Oscar snickering against my collarbone when I suggested I put on my robe and go make us a snack some time later.

"I think I'll survive till breakfast," he murmured. "Getting out of bed right now would make all that tension come back and we'd have to start all over."

"Oh no," I deadpanned. "No, anything but more sex with my boyfriend. Noooo..."

He laughed and moved to straddle my hips carefully, both of us sinking into long, slow kisses until sleep became too much of a necessity.

I'm not sure what woke me, but the room was quiet when I opened my eyes. Quiet darkness filled the room, but something felt wrong.

Someone was staring at me. It wasn't Oscar. He was breathing steadily, albeit a bit wheezily, beside me on my right, his legs tucked up and arms flung out in childlike luxuriance, as if he had the space to himself and trying to clothesline me in his sleep wasn't a thing.

So it wasn't him at all. But someone was definitely staring at me. I could feel it in the stillness beside me on the left, between the bed and the window overlooking the back gardens. They were quiet, unmoving. I kept my eyes closed and strained my ears, trying to pick up on some indication of who—or what—it was. *It's a dream*, I told myself. *Not an uncommon occurrence, to wake from dreams sure whatever was in your mind was real for a few moments after waking. Hell, night terrors are a thing and those definitely feel real, real enough for people to think they're being haunted or even physically attacked sometimes.*

But night terrors and dream remnants didn't last this long, did they?

Oscar snuffled, coughed, and shifted, his arms jerking as he tried to roll without untucking his legs. His hand flailed and caught my chin, making me wince. The stillness beside me erupted, a rustle of fabric and thump of steps with a rush of air as whoever it was moved, heading for the bedroom door. I rolled out from under Oscar's arm to his muted, sleepy protest. "Hey!" I said sharply. The figure in the doorway stopped. They were facing away from me, I thought—hard to tell in the dark, even with the moonlight and faint glow of the backyard security light trickling through the warped window glass. "What do you want?" I demanded. "Put your hands where I can see them, okay? I don't want anyone to get hurt."

"Julian?" Oscar murmured. "What's going on?"

The figure moved then, disappearing into the dark of the corridor. "Shit! Stay here," I ordered Oscar, who was slowly coming more awake. "Someone was in the room. Don't go anywhere."

"Julian! Wait!"

I grabbed my cane and was off, in as much as I could manage, after whoever it was. Behind me, Oscar was cursing at the bedsheets as he tried to untangle himself, but I didn't slow down. "Hey!" Whoever was ahead of me was quiet on the stairs, their steps not making the old wood creak or even thumping on the risers. They must be the most light-footed person in existence, or... Well. Or.

I was considerably slower than they were, navigating the stairs in the dark. When I reached the bottom, I paused. The front door was closed, and surely I would have heard that one being shut even as far behind them as I was. That left the kitchen door, I decided, turning to head toward the back of the house.

"Julian! Stop!" Oscar panted, galloping to the top of steps, still tugging on his sleep pants.

"See if you can get Sandra on the phone," I said. "Her number's on the card on my side of the bed, on the nightstand. I doubt this island has a responsive emergency number this time of night."

"Goddamnit, Julian!" he snapped, sounding angrier than I'd ever heard him. The kitchen door thumped, and I huffed a breath. "Please?"

"If you die, I swear to god I will summon you and annoy you for the rest of eternity," he snarled, turning to run back to our room for the phone. I strode to the kitchen and nearly slipped on a wet patch that hadn't been there earlier—a slick spot like oil or grease, between the sink and the small table where we'd eaten earlier. Fumbling for the light switch, I hissed as the overheads glared to life. The patch was clear, glossy, and thick, more like some sort of mucilage or slime than the spilled grease I assumed it to be. It wasn't a lot, just enough to be an issue if you weren't expecting it. It made the soles of my slippers feel slick and my cane slide as I tried to ease past it, to the kitchen door bouncing gently in the stiff offshore breeze that cut through the back garden.

Gingerly, I pushed the door wide and stepped onto the small back porch. The garden was dark, the sodium glow of the security light doing little to illuminate the space beyond a small glowing sphere next to the house. *Should've grabbed my phone. I can't see for shit out here.* The moonlight was enough to pick out the flagstone path that led from the porch and into the garden, so I moved forward quietly, listening for whomever had been in the house. Only the rush and sigh of the ocean—not nearly as far away as I'd thought from the sound of things—and the rustle of the constant breeze could be heard. If someone was out there, they could be tapdancing on the flagstones ahead of me and I'd never hear them. Not until I got too close. Still, because I'm a dumbass with a PhD, I followed the path into the garden. The high walls around the property meant that, if someone had taken off out of the back door, they either had to have a ladder waiting to scale the wall, or they'd be stuck back there until they could go back through the house and get out the front door.

Or they just happen to be staying at the cottage on the back of the property and don't have to try to escape at all. I thought hard about what I'd seen—could it have been Sandra? The figure had been tall—taller than me, or nearly so. And big. But that didn't mean anything really—size could be misinterpreted due to lighting, disorientation, or even the use of disguise.

But why would she disguise herself to come stare at us sleep?

Is this some weird fetish thing? Or something that's going to get us our own Dateline *special and a memorial bench on the beach one day?*

"Hey!" Oscar's panting voice carried softly from the porch, startling me from my increasingly gruesome thoughts. "Sandra didn't answer, and there's definitely no emergency number here." He jogged up beside me, bare toes curling on the cool flagstone, and shivered. "Christ, why is it so cold?"

I glanced at him and smirked. "Because you're mostly naked. Not that I mind." He made a face at me, rubbing hands up and down his arms. Asking him to go back inside to get warm would go over as well as a lead balloon, so I gestured to the stone path. "I was going to see if I could find whoever it was, or where they got in."

Oscar nodded, untucking his arms to show me his phone, turning the little flashlight on. "Together, or divide and conquer?"

I hesitated, and he rolled his eyes, smiling a little. "I'll go around the house, you go to Sandra's? Shout if something happens?"

I nodded. "Meet back in ten?"

"Fifteen," he offered. "And if I don't see you on the porch by then, I'll"—he shook his head— "do something suitably dramatic."

I gave him a quick kiss on the side of his mouth. "Be careful, okay?"

"I'm not the one who nearly got murdered less than a month ago," he pointed out, worry tinging his tone. Before I could protest or assure him I'd be fine, he held the phone out to me. "There's enough light around the house for me to see where I'm going. You take this."

We split up, Oscar jogging back to the porch before following it out of sight along the back of the house, and me turning to follow the flagstone path. The breeze stirred the overgrown plants, each rustle of leaves and stems making me tense up, sure it was whoever had been standing over us. The path wound through thick green stands of cabbage palmetto and smooth hydrangea before jinking down a small drop. The weak light of the phone barely pierced the darkness, the glossy leaves of clematis plants and something thorny and viny swallowing any shine the weak LED could provide. The path narrowed, the flagstones replaced by rough-hewn rock that looked worn by time and unsteady to walk on. I picked my way along the path carefully, wincing when one of the thorny plants caught my bare forearm, leaving itching pinpricks as I pulled free. I hissed in annoyance, jerking back when another of the vines scraped my ankle and calf through my sleep pants. The sudden movement sent me slipping on the stones, flailing out with my cane as if it could stop my fall.

"The hell you doing?" Sandra hissed in the dark, her surprisingly strong hands closing around my upper arms and jerking me upright before I could go sliding down the stones to whatever lay beyond the attack berries. "It's the middle of the goddamn night!"

She glared at me in the phone's light, still fully dressed despite the late hour. Around knee level, I heard the soft huff of an annoyed dog. "Lenny, heel," she muttered. "I asked you a question," she said, whipping her attention back on me. "You trying to cause problems, Doctor Weems? Sneak in some filming for your show? The people here deserve respect, do you hear me? If you're going to disturb their rest—"

"Whoa, whoa! Hold on! We tried to call you but Oscar said you didn't answer. Someone was in the house earlier—I woke up to them staring at me while we slept. Oscar's looking around the outside of the house to see if he can find where they got in. I'm looking out here in the garden to see if I can find where they got out."

Sandra's expression shuttered. "There's no way anyone got in," she said, tight-lipped. "Lenny would've lost his shit if someone was skulking around in the dark."

I glanced down to see the bored-looking Airedale inspecting one of the steppingstones. "I'm sure he would've, but the fact remains we saw someone."

She grunted softly. "Maybe you did. But I've been walking Lenny for the past half hour and there's been no one in the gardens but me. Me an' the Tibbins family." She jerked her chin at a dark spot between a stand of palmetto and what resolved itself to be a small gazebo as my eyes adjusted to the dark. "Celeste and Thomas have been here since the late seventeenth century. The rest came later."

I turned the phone in the direction she indicated. A cluster of small, round-topped headstones like so many jagged teeth stood just feet away, hidden by the night and the weather-worn color of the stones. "There's a graveyard," I murmured. "The original owners, I'm assuming?"

She nodded. "Thomas insisted on being buried here instead of on the mainland, and Celeste couldn't stand to be away from him. The others are their kids, grandkids, and so on. Except for Jeremiah. He's..." She glanced up at me, her expression—which had been soft a moment before, tensed back up and she shook her head. "Well, Jeremiah's not here. His nephew, Tobias, became the heir to the family fortune and is buried here, with his wife and children."

"How many graves are there?"

She shrugged. "Fifty, that I know of. This is just the old graveyard. The new graveyard is past the cottage, overlooking the inlet where the ships used to come." She fumbled something out of her sweater pocket and a moment later, bright blue LED light flooded the space around us. The graveyard was small, old, and honestly, the most amazing thing I'd seen in days (okay, so not counting the ghosts—I was still having very definite feelings to work through about ghosts). "Most of them are in the new one. This one here was made when it was still just them and the Noonans on the island."

"The Noonans?"

She nodded. "They owned the land that'd become Tibbins Quay. Funny how that worked out." Swinging the light up to illuminate the path behind me, she jerked her chin in greeting. "Mr. Fellowes."

Oscar gave a small wave and crossed his arms over his bare chest, tiptoe-jogging toward us in his fuzzy slippers. "Good evening, Ms. Cochrane. Lovely night for it."

She quirked a brow. "Seems so, for both of you to be out and half-dressed."

Oscar chuckled, coming to stand next to me. "Julian told you about our little incident, I take it?"

Sandra nodded. "I've been outside for a while now, walking Lenny, and haven't seen a thing."

Oscar's glance darted toward the graves, then back at me. "Ah, am I correct in guessing you've decided what you'd like to do in the morning, love?"

I blushed. "Sandra was explaining that the Tibbins family is buried here and also in a newer site in the back of the property."

"Except Jeremiah," Oscar murmured, his gaze unfocused. "He's..." He paused, snapping his attention to Sandra, who'd gone pale, clutching Lenny's leash like a lifeline. "I'm sorry. Speaking out of turn again. Sometimes I forget that not everyone is comfortable with my abilities."

Sandra sniffed, tugging the hem of her sweater down and straightening her spine. "It's fine. You're not the first person I've met who has the Sight."

"The Sight," he repeated. "You sound as if you have some familiarity yourself."

She shrugged. "I'm a scientist," she said, and I knew without looking that Oscar was fighting back a smirk—how often had that been my protest to any suggestion of the paranormal? "I'm a scientist," she repeated, a bit more softly, "but I'm very open minded." At her feet, Lenny made a noise of doggy boredom, seeming to draw Sandra out of whatever reverie she was slipping into. "Well. I can assure you there's been no one out here. Maybe it was a dream? Sleep paralysis, perhaps?"

I nodded, face hot. "Maybe so. I'm sorry for keeping you from your morning."

Oscar took my elbow and we picked our way back toward the house, Sandra's eyes hard on our back until we were out of the reach of her flashlight's beam.

When we stepped back into the kitchen, Oscar tugged me to a halt. "Look," he murmured, pointing to the slick spot on the floor.

Or rather, where it had been.

"Dry as a bone," Oscar said. "I came back through the house before going to find you. The spot was gone."

"I hate myself for asking this but did you save any?"

Oscar snorted softly. "It was already gone by the time I came back through here."

"So," I said slowly. "What are we thinking here?"

"Possibly... ectoplasm?" Oscar winced as he said it. "I know, I know—it's ridiculous. I've never, in my entire life, seen it. And I've seen hundreds of spirits, ghosts, what-have-you. Not a single time was there ectoplasm involved."

"I haven't done a huge amount of research but anything I've found regarding ectoplasm with regards to paranormal events has been about how it's a hoax, or how to make it, or how it was used in spiritualist circles to rook clients." *But you know people who have done quite a lot of research... People who've been asking you to send in your CV and material, to set up a meeting with them...*

Shut up, inner monologue. You're not helping here.

It was Oscar who suggested it, surprising me. "Well, it's not long till sunrise," he sighed. "I don't know if I can get back to sleep."

"Me either. I think I might read a bit."

He nodded, looping his arm through mine and leaning his head on my shoulder. "I know we said no investigating," he murmured. "But I'm starting to think we might not have a choice."

"There's always a choice." I sighed, though the tiny spark of excitement dancing in my veins couldn't be denied. "We could just close our eyes and ears, enjoy the rest of the week and any time we hear footsteps in the night or see a shadow looming over us, we pretend it's nothing and go on about our day."

"True," he allowed, slipping his other arm around my middle. "But do you want to do that?"

"No."

"Me either."

Chapter 3 – Oscar

Taking my tea on the front porch was a surprisingly lovely indulgence. The temperatures were much lower that morning than they'd been the previous day. Julian suggested it might be due to Hurricane Nelson, far offshore but doing a fine job of pushing cooler air ahead of itself. "Are you sure we'll be okay?" I'd asked over breakfast, hating the tremor in my voice. "Sandra mentioned the ferry wasn't running due to some high swells. A hurricane sounds terrifying, to be honest. We don't have much of that back home."

"I've been through..." He paused, staring out over the garden for a moment. "Oh, god, maybe six? They can be terrifying, true, but this place has stood for over four hundred years and weathered more than one hurricane just fine. Besides, Sandra is doing a supply run and we checked the forecast this morning, remember? It's not going to be worse than a category one, and that's if it even hits the island. There's still plenty of time for it to hook back out to sea or decide to bother some other spot on the seacoast instead."

I'd nodded, pretending to be assuaged by that, but really I was low key terrified. All I could think of was the fact we were surrounded by the sea, and the ferry would be shut down for the duration of the hurricane watch.

So I did what almost any Brit would do in a time of great internal conflict. I made a cup of tea and retreated to a comfortable chair. In this case, the chair was on the porch and overlooking a tangle of bright yellow flowers on a glossy green vine wrapping around the porch's pillar.

"Mr. Fellowes."

"Oh!"

"Sorry," Sandra murmured, stepping from the house onto the porch beside me. "I thought you'd heard me open the door." She rubbed her hands over her bare arms briskly and offered me a stiff smile. "A bit cool this morning, all things considered."

I nodded. Small talk about weather, a cup of tea, an overcast sky... It was practically home. "The storm and all."

She smiled tightly. "Yeah. First time?"

I nodded again, feeling like one of Ezra's bobble head dolls. "Not a lot of call for hurricane preparedness in England."

"Suppose not." She slid into the chair next to mine, a wood rocker that had so many coats of varnish it felt like satin and propped her feet against the porch rail. "I didn't know who y'all were when you first checked in," she said suddenly. "Thought you looked familiar but just kind of figured it was one of those cases where you had a face like that, you know?"

"Ah, yes?"

"But this morning, Ray-Don mentioned those kids who help him with the salvage business, Mary and Kerry—"

"Marilla and Kelly."

"Whatever. Said they wouldn't shut up about you two. It got me thinking..." She fidgeted with the end of her plait and resolutely stared out at the yard, refusing to look at me. "You really see them? Not cold reading or leading a mark. You truly see ghosts and interact with them."

I nodded. "Every day, for as long as I can recall." There was a canned speech I had prepared for these moments, but Sandra didn't strike me as the sort to sit through the carefully practiced, honed statements about my abilities and the show. Not without some cutting comments at least, and it was too early in the morning for me to handle sarcasm with aplomb.

Maybe another cup or two of tea first.

"And the ghosts... they talk to you."

I waited. It wasn't a question but more like she was working through something, deciding which way to jump with her new knowledge.

Deciding whether it was worth the risk to ask me what she really wanted to know.

"Do they come to you, the ghosts? Or do you have to... summon them, somehow?"

A small smile tugged at my lips. She reminded me a bit of Julian, asking such specific questions. "Usually people ask if I'm like the kid in that movie. Or if I can 'bust' ghosts."

"People are idiots," she said, tone flat and brooking no argument.

Very definitely reminding me of Julian, at least when I first met him. "The ghosts sometimes come to me," I said. "Other times, they don't even seem to notice me. Or they hide from me. I don't force a ghost to communicate, not unless the need is dire, and even then I can count on one hand with fingers left over how many times I've done that."

She hesitated then, daring a sharp glance my way before turning her attention back to the tangled vines on the pillars. "Honey Walk is a very old house, Mr. Fellowes."

I nodded. "There's a man here. Seems quite fond of the place. I didn't get his name, but he spoke to me yesterday, under the stained-glass."

She dropped her feet and sat up. "Jeremiah Tibbins."

"Like I said, I'm not sure of—"

"No. That's who it was." She sounded a shade breathless. "I'm sure of it. This house was built by his ancestor, and the Tibbins family has lived here consistently until... Well, until relatively recently." She looked as if she might burst, her cheeks turning pink with excitement as she leaned toward me. "How does it work, your mediumship? Are you clairaudient? Clairvoyant? Do you channel? Are there particular rituals you need to do in order to get into the mindset, or does it require psychotropics first? Some mediums need to enter an altered state with the use of chemicals, but I wasn't sure if you were one of them. I admit I only saw a few clips this morning but what I did see was compelling."

"Ah. Well, I don't need any assistance, so to speak. And I'm a bit of everything, really. It runs in my family. We all have the ability to some degree or another." Charlotte's email flashed briefly to the forefront of my thoughts—*We're all blessed with this strangeness, Oscar. Embracing it is the only way to ensure you are not controlled by it but rather the other way 'round,* she'd written. *Your grandmother fought it.* "Some of us more than others."

"That's pretty amazing, Mr. Fellowes. Have you ever worked with a parapsychologist? There's a team at the University of the Upper Coast—"

"Oh, Professor Tomlinson, right?" I sat up, setting my tea to the side. "They've been asking Julian to submit his CV for some guest lecturer position."

Sandra's nascent smile faded. "Oh?"

"Mmm. We met them at Boo Con last week and Julian was singing their praises. I've never worked with a parapsychologist myself, but I've heard good things about that group. Julian's an anthropologist by training and vocation, and they seemed very keen about the fact his area of specialty has to do with burial practices and death rituals."

Sandra's expression shifted from bland to sour in a heartbeat. "Excuse me. I left the coffee on."

She shoved to her feet and was back through the door so fast I wondered, for a moment, if I'd just hallucinated the entire visit.

I grabbed my cup of tea and followed her gingerly. "Sandra? I seem to have upset you and I apologize. Might I ask what exactly it was so I can avoid it?"

Sandra stood at the stove, determinedly not looking at me as she grabbed the old-fashioned coffee pot off the back burner. I frowned—there was a fancy pod coffee machine on the counter that Julian had been using so why was she dealing with that antique?

"Sandra, I don't know what I said—"

"Pardon me, Mr. Fellowes," she muttered, turning with the heavy pot held in her gloved hands. "This is hot, and I don't want to spill it on the original flooring." I held up my hands, standing back to let her pass.

She carried the pot to the stone sink and, wordlessly, grabbed a thick white mug from the cabinet in front of her and poured the contents of the pot into it. It wasn't coffee but a chartreuse-colored brew that smelled like licorice and something green with a hint of iron.

Smells like grass and blood, a morbid little part of my brain noted. She pushed the mug to one side and started decanting the rest of the brew into a stoneware teapot.

"What's going on?" Julian muttered. I shook my head and shrugged.

"I see you enjoy tea," she said suddenly, turning to hand me the fresh mug. "This is a local herbal blend. Used to be real popular for a good while here. Tea was hard to come by, and coffee expensive. The locals used to brew this from some of the native plants in the area. Supposed to be relaxing."

I gingerly accepted the mug. "Um, thank you?"

"Let me know if it needs to be stronger, Mr. Fellowes. I hope it's suitable."

"I'm sure it will be."

She nodded once, sharply, and turned her flinty glare to Julian. "You can get your own coffee."

I wasn't sure but I think she muttered *bastard* under her breath as she grabbed her keys and strode from the kitchen.

The back door slammed in her wake. After a moment, she opened, hissed for Lenny, who had been sleeping under the table, and slammed it again once the dog scrambled after her.

"What the fuck?" Julian muttered. "You saw that too, right?"

I nodded, eyeing my cup warily before nudging it toward Julian. He smirked, pushing his mug of tea toward me. "I doubt they're poisoned," I offered. "If they were, why bother with being polite?"

"Maybe treating us like veal? Soften us up then," he made a throat slicing motion, complete with sound effects.

Whatever face I was making, it amused Julian no end. He chuckled, nudging my ankle with his sock-clad toes. I rolled my eyes and said, "I doubt she wants us dead, but she *was* rather excited to show you the cemetery at oh-god-o'clock this morning. Really, I should say last night since it was barely past midnight. Nothing before dawn should be morning. Maybe that improved her mood. She got the chance to talk to a like-minded person about something she enjoys?" As much as it pained me to defend her, it seemed possibly true.

Julian wobbled his head to side to side—*maybe, maybe not*. "My hinky detector is going off around her," he said. "I'm not one hundred percent sure it *wasn't* her in our room last night."

I sighed—truth be told, I wasn't either but the idea of her creeping in to watch us sleep scared me more than anything dead ever would. "You're absolutely certain you weren't having some sleep paralysis thing?" I asked.

"What's that saying about couples that have been together a while? They start to look alike? Does that happen for mediums and skeptics, too? We take on one another's traits?" He took a bracing sip of his coffee and grimaced. "Christ, I think I found what they use to stain the exterior of the house."

I saluted him with my tea. "My tea is wonderful, so at least one of us is having a nice breakfast." Taking another sip, I couldn't help the slight grimace that crossed my face. "Alright, I lied. It needs more sugar. It's a bit tannic."

He snorted, spearing a piece of sausage with his fork. "I was thinking we should go into town this morning. I'd like to see that museum Delia mentioned yesterday. Maybe give that romantic walk another try? This time in town and not on the beach?"

"Are you sure it's safe?" I asked. "The hurricane is still due to hit, isn't it? What would we do if we got caught out? I—"

Julian smiled, reached across and grabbed my hand to give my fingers a gentle squeeze. "It's okay, Oscar. I promise. It's still a good way's out, and the island is small. Even if it suddenly got some sort of super jet boost or something and hit within the next few hours, we could get back here before getting washed out to sea." The look on my face made him blanch and sputter an apology. "Sorry, bad joke. We won't get washed out to sea. Seriously. Just some wind and a bit of rain if it gets here sooner than expected."

I pursed my lips as I considered. Hurricane aside, the idea of another walk was honestly a bit boring, but I knew Julian was all about the historic sites, and I really did want to spend alone time with him. I could never fathom the couples who took separate vacations or booked a romantic getaway only to spend the entire time doing things without one another. I didn't expect to live in Julian's pocket but the entire point of this sort of holiday was to spend time together. Romantically. Hence the phrase. But the thought of spending all or even a large part of the day wandering the same few blocks of main street and dodging the ghosts there made my head give a weak throb of warning. "Maybe check out the other end of the island for lunch instead of coming back here?"

Julian smirked. "Afraid of Sandra?"

"She's very mercurial."

"That's a tactful way of saying bitchy."

"Well. You said it, not me."

Julian shrugged, chewing for a moment before swallowing to reply. "She's prickly, but she *is* the manager here. So, whatever her problem is, she's apparently still making an effort to run the place for guests."

"I wonder if she gets many. This place isn't exactly on the map for tourism unless you're heading to Tibbins Quay."

Julian hummed thoughtfully. "Hm. I hadn't really thought of it. The chief attraction of this place was the lack of heavy tourist traffic."

"Which is what drew you to it, hm?" When he gave me a half-roll of his eyes, I chuckled. "If you were looking for a quiet, low-pressure getaway, there're bound to be others who are, too. And they'd probably enjoy a nice walk on the beach as well."

"You make me sound so oatmeal," he muttered, stabbing another sausage.

"Warm, comforting, delicious?"

He used the breakfast meat to point at me. "Boring. Bland."

"We have very different experiences with oatmeal."

"Oatmeal's only good if you put a ton of sugar or something with it." He frowned at his plate. "Do I need to add more... sugar? To this?"

"To your breakfast?"

"Don't be precious," he grumbled. "I mean, am I too boring? Or... bland, or—"

His faltering insecurity made my chest ache. Sometimes it was easy to forget that, as much as our lives had meshed so thoroughly over the past year, we were still strangers in some ways, or, at best, acquaintances in others. When the pressure and flash of filming and investigating weren't looming, who were we with one another?

That's why you're here, you knob, I reminded myself. To find out.

"I think that oatmeal is one of my favorite things," I said. "And too much sugar ruins the flavor."

He set his fork down, flashing me a glance that was a mixture of shy and cautious. "You have terrible metaphors."

I grinned. "But I still love oatmeal."

"ARE YOU SURE WE SHOULD be out?" I asked. The sky wasn't dark but some thick gray clouds were drifting in, and a dark line on the horizon looked very upsetting.

"It's fine. We've got plenty of time. Probably won't even see rain till tonight. Besides," he said, waving me through the gate at the museum ahead of him, "it's a small island. It won't take us long to get back to the house if we have to make a run for it."

The Rosie Sands Museum was easy enough to find, being the only large home in the town proper. It had a view of the curving eastern shore of Broken Palm, perched as it was on a jutting cliff that gave the home an impression of floating over the beach if you looked at it just right. The remaining yard and gardens were fenced off with a classic wrought iron number, complete with pointy staves, and a tasteful little wooden sign proclaimed:

The Charles and Eliza Noonan Home, Est 1698.
THE ROSIE SANDS HISTORICAL MUSEUM AND CULTURAL CENTER.

The hours of operation were added on an additional little wooden plaque hanging beneath the sign, creaking gently in the breeze. "This place is *massive*," Julian muttered as we stepped through the waist-high gate.

"And haunted," I sing-songed, following him up the path.

He snorted softly. "I'm starting to think that's pretty much everywhere we go. Wait... is it?"

I shrugged, smiling slyly. "I couldn't really say. I've been places where I've not encountered a ghost, but it doesn't mean they weren't there. Or hadn't been. Or won't be."

"I think you're trying to confuse me."

"That's my plan. Addle you so badly you bend to my wicked ways."

He smirked, stopping as we reached the museum door. "If you want me to bend for you, all you have to do is ask…"

"*Later*."

He chuckled, opening the door to let me in first. A small sign just inside, propped on a wooden easel, announced all tours were self-guided and donations were gladly accepted, docents available if you call in advance or on Thursdays between two and five p.m.

"Damn, it's Monday." Julian sighed. "Well, let's be nosy, shall we?"

He made a beeline for the row of dour-looking portraits lining the foyer wall. I hadn't been kidding when I said the place was haunted—I could feel it as soon as we were near.

"Oh, cool! There's a whole display about stained glass at Honey Walk! They mention the break in 1797. Huh." He paused. "I hope Sandra had it reinforced. That was only a Cat 1."

The buzzing pull of a ghost had curled around my awareness and tugged, wanting my attention. Now, in the foyer, the buzzing was nearly tangible, making the hairs on my arms stand on end as Julian peered at the nameplates on some of the pictures, muttering (to himself? To me? Who knew?) about whatever he was finding there.

"I'm here," I murmured. "I'm listening."

She was difficult to see with the sun shining through the high windows, but I could just make out the petite form of a woman in a blue gown, the style they called an at-home dress some centuries back. She was washed out, barely visible in the daylight glare, but she was strong. At least for the moment. "I've waited for ages." She sighed. "Are you telling the truth? You can hear me?"

"And see you," I promised. "My name is Oscar Fellowes. What's your name, madam?"

She laughed softly. "Madam. And your accent. You sound a bit like my father, when I was a girl." She moved closer to me, one hand reaching for me and the other clutched at her waist. "You're a very handsome fellow."

"Ah, thank you. I didn't get your name?"

She paused, the cool brush of her fingertips along my face shocking in the otherwise warm home. "My apologies. It's just been so very long since anyone's truly heard me. I'm Mrs. Charles Noonan. Eliza. I suppose there's no use standing on formality now, is there?"

She sounded dejected, small. Lost. "There is, if you wish."

"It... It might be nice," she murmured. "It's been so long."

"Well, Mrs. Noonan, you have a lovely home." I was aware of Julian moving through the foyer, focused on something in one of the glass-topped cases. He either didn't hear me murmuring with Mrs. Noonan or was doing a very good job of ignoring us for the moment. "How long have you been here, if I might be so bold?"

She shook her head, her pale eyes closing. "I'm not certain. After a while, I started drifting in and out. I would lose track of time and people... They change so much. One moment, they are familiar faces, familiar clothing and food and sounds and names, the next they're so strange. Wrong. Why am I still here, Mr. Fellowes? I thought there was an eternal reward waiting for me. That's what Reverend Malthaus preached. Is it"—she moved even closer, the chill of her shot through me, making my bones ache, but I stood still, letting her drift— "is it because I wasn't supposed to die? Did they cause me to linger?"

"Most people I've met in your situation feel they passed too soon," I began, but she cut me off with a sharp shake of her head and a spectral foot-stomp.

"No, Mr. Fellowes, I wasn't supposed to die, period. What they did... they took me from my body, Mr. Fellowes. I saw them. I saw them! They forced me out, all because Charles—" She broke off in a sob that pulsed with energy, all of her rage and sorrow and fear coalescing into a physical force that rattled the plain metal chandelier overhead and made the windows shake. Julian jerked around to face me, his eyes wide. I held up my hand to stay him and he hesitated, then nodded once. "What they're doing is so wrong, Mr. Fellowes. I thought perhaps it was over. It's been so many years since I've seen them do it but now..." She trailed off, fading fast. "Now they're trying again."

"Mrs. Noonan," I said sharply. "Madam, wait!"

It was futile, I knew, but still...

"Oscar?" Julian murmured. "Are you okay?"

I nodded. "I think I need some air though."

He cast one last, longing look at the foyer—we hadn't even seen the rest of the museum. Guilt washed over me, and I started to back away. "I'll just step onto the porch," I murmured. "You can—"

"No," he insisted. "We can come back tomorrow. Ah, I know! Want to have a picnic on the beach? Fresh air, food, and I'll make sure it's barnacle and mussel-free?"

I huffed a small laugh. "Let's do that. I'll tell you about Mrs. Noonan as we go."

WE OPTED TO AVOID DELIA'S Café—I knew it was because it now had bad memories attached to it for the both of us, but Julian proclaimed picnics meant nibbling and we needed to just grab some prepared veggie trays and maybe cold cuts and cheese rather than heavy sandwiches and burgers, steering us to the grocery store instead. A few cars were parked in the tightly angled spots along the pavement but inside the store, it was a (ha) ghost town. Soft music played overhead, something country-western sounding and too quiet to make out the words, and someone out of sight was using a floor buffer from the sound of things.

"Christ, this is some liminal shit here," Julian muttered as the doors slid closed behind us. "Come on, before something comes out of the cold storage to drag us into a Stephen King novel."

"It's quaint," I hissed. "You're just spoiled by those huge HEB stores back in Texas."

"Maybe," he muttered, heading for the small produce section. "It's been ages since I've been in a store like this. It reminds me of the grocery stores near where my mother's parents lived, in West Texas, when I was little."

The produce section was all wooden baskets on graduated risers and the aisles beyond were about chest-high to Julian, nothing like the towering, sprawling shops we'd gone to in other cities when we needed to grab a few things. He made a soft noise of discovery and tugged me toward a small glass-front refrigerator where several ready-made plastic boxes of cut vegetables and fruit waited. "Any preference?"

"Dealer's choice."

We moved through the store, Julian selecting a few things to go in the hand basket he'd picked up, including some bottles of water and one slightly dusty bottle of wine. "Looks a bit picked over," I murmured.

"The hurricane's gonna make landfall in the next day or so," Ray-Don said, startling us. He came around the end of the aisle, strolling to where we'd been picking out the wine for our little outing. "Just announced officially a few hours ago, Nelson's been bumped up to a cat two." He stopped a few feet away and rocked back on his heels, hands shoved deep in his jeans pockets as he regarded us. "Didn't you hear me tellin' Delia that yesterday?"

"Ah, must've missed it," Julian murmured. "I should try to get hold of Sandra, see if we need to get supplies or if she has some at the house already."

"You stayin' at Honey Walk?" Ray-Don nodded to himself, not waiting for our reply. "You're good. She was in here this mornin', stocking up on water and what-not. You sound like you're from down here," he nodded at Julian. "You know how to ride out a hurricane?"

"I'm from Southeast Texas, and yes," he assured Ray-Don. "I rode out Rita when I was just a kid, and Harvey a few years ago now. I know the drill."

"Most of it's gonna get the mainland but, well, we're a small island here, not far off the coast." He shrugged. "We've weathered worse over the years."

"Have you lived here long, then?" I asked. The way he was staring at us made me uneasy, like he was waiting for us to do something wrong so he could pounce. I edged closer to Julian.

"My family's been here since the beginning. The Noonans," he added proudly. "Well, my mom's people, anyway. My dad's, they were latecomers. Didn't get here till the late 1800s. But the island's been good to us, even after everything that happened back in the day, when Jeremiah Tibbins lost his fool mind and sold off so much of the land."

"Ah." Julian moved closer to me now, linking our fingers. Ray-Don's eyes tracked the movement of our hands and he frowned, sucking on his teeth in apparent displeasure. "Well. It must be really something to be part of a place's history like that. My family doesn't have such deep roots where we live now."

"Mine does," I offered, "but we're mostly dead so it's just me and I'm rather a tumbleweed at the moment."

"Invasive and a threat to the locals?" Ray-Don asked ingenuously.

"Ah..."

Julian cleared his throat. "Well. I think we're set, Oscar. Time to check out!"

Ray-Don grunted and edged past us, heading for the single register at the front of the store. We exchanged nervous glances and followed him. He took the basket from Julian without asking and started scanning the items, shooting us keen looks every few seconds. "So, where y'all heading? Looks like a picnic here."

"We were definitely considering it," I said.

"West Beach is nice. There's a cove there. In the spring it's absolutely covered in these," he made a vague gesture with a pack of cold cuts, "viny plant things. When it dried out in the summer, they used to use 'em for the fires. Supposed to make it smell real nice, I guess. The folks here used to have these big gatherings there. Bonfires and all. Used to go every year when I was kid but..." He shrugged. "Kind of fell off over the last decade or so."

Julian's expression shifted and I could tell he was remembering something. "The cove... Is it by any chance below the Noonan House?"

"Well, yes it is," Ray-Don said slowly. "How'd you know that already?"

"We were at the museum earlier," Julian said. "They had all these old pictures up in a gallery in what I think was a study at one time. A few of the older ones had bonfires and looked like a festival or something. One of them was labeled *Noonan's Cove, 1922.*"

Ray-Don's eyes narrowed, and he set the food down with extreme gentleness. "Now, Doctor Weems, it ain't nice to go digging through other people's secrets."

"It was a picture in a public museum," I said. "He didn't go rummaging around in someone's locked room for it."

Ray-Don sniffed. "Maybe so, but those sorts of things, they're not meant for outsiders. They're private. Special." He picked up the food and started scanning again, quiet now and not looking at us as he rang up the total.

Julian pulled some bills from his wallet and handed them to Ray-Don, his expression troubled and more than a little annoyed. "Well, enjoy your day, Ray-Don."

Ray-Don nodded. "Y'all be careful. Don't go getting into something you can't get out of."

We hurried from the store and headed toward the beach path across the road. By unspoken agreement, we avoided Virginia's Path and opted for the less scenic walk down to West Beach. The cove wasn't hard to get to, a ridge of flat-topped rocks serving as a sort of low wall and a natural set of steps to reach the protected bit of beach. Despite the stiff breeze and gathering clouds on the horizon, the little cove was calm, protected on three sides by the tall rock cliffs in a rough V-shape. The beach itself was surprisingly hard-packed, not at all soft and sandy as the rest of the shore seemed to be. Julian made a face, turning in a slow circle as he took it all in. "You're making your thinky face," I murmured, taking the grocery bag from his free hand and heading for a nice, flat spot near the apex of the V. "Come on. You told me this was a romantic getaway. Romance me, Doctor Weems."

He snorted, following me at a slower pace. The sand might be hard-packed but it was still difficult to navigate for him, so I changed direction and headed for part of the low stone ridge, where it started to slope upward into the rock face. Julian shot me a sideways look but didn't comment, the both of us sinking to sit on the knee-high flat stones and spreading the picnic between us. "It feels like we're the only people on earth right now," he murmured. "I think I like it."

"If we were the last people on earth, what would you do?"

"I mean, honestly?" He shrugged. "Scream, cry, freak out. Then I'd end up like that episode of *Twilight Zone* where the guy decides to read all the books he never got to read and his glasses break."

"You wear contacts."

Julian sighed dramatically. "And one day I'd run out of my prescription and since we're the last ones on earth and neither of us knows how to make contacts, I'd be out of luck."

"I'd read to you," I promised, pressing against his side as he chuckled. "So long as you talked to me. I like hearing your voice when you wax rhapsodic about something you're passionate about."

"Dear Diary," he intoned, "I finally met a guy who likes it when I word vomit about my special interests."

I laughed, reaching up to kiss his jaw. "Shut up, you prat."

Julian poked my side, making me yelp, and reached past me to grab a carrot stick. "Do you think this place looks very different at high tide?" he asked suddenly.

I smiled, popping a cherry tomato into my mouth and watching the gray waves roll in as the tide changed direction. "I'm guessing that you saw something about Noonan's Cove, and your thinky face was you comparing what you were seeing to what was written."

He huffed. "I'm trying to be romantic here, damn it. Work with me. But yeah, a little."

Laughing, I leaned in for a kiss, tasting the tang of red grapes on his tongue as he deepened the embrace. The quiet of the cove, the absolute lack of anyone demanding our time or attention, was a heady combination, damn near an aphrodisiac. As I pulled away from the kiss, Julian made a small noise of protest that turned into pleased surprise when I knelt on the hard sand, pushing his legs gently apart. "This isn't exactly private," he whispered.

"It's private enough for now."

"Fuck."

"We'll see how the day goes." I laughed, helping him fumble his trousers open, nudging his hands away to pull out his hardening cock myself. "Let me," I urged when he reached down to hold himself. "Just let me, alright?"

He nodded, leaning back on his hands as I took him into my mouth. It wasn't the most elegant of blowjobs—despite my outward bravado, I had no illusions about the fact we *were* in public, and the little cove wasn't exactly the best kept secret on the island. Julian gasped as I sucked just the head of his cock, tracing my tongue along the seeping slit before taking him deeper, slipping my fingers into his pants to cup his balls, making him lean further back, silently asking me for more. I was only too happy to oblige, angling to take more of him in, and more still, until the coarse curls at the base of his cock were brushing my chin.

"Christ, Oscar," he breathed. "This is going to be really embarrassing soon. Just... oh, god, more. *Please.*"

And because I am a very obliging sort, I did just as he asked. Julian did his best to bite back his gasps and cries as I did *my* best to make him fail in that endeavor. The slick salt bitter taste of him on my tongue sent a sharp spike of arousal to my own aching cock and I knew if I didn't take matters in hand soon, I'd either have the very worst case of blue balls or embarrass myself and have to walk back to the house with sticky, cold trousers and pants. Which *might* be a little hot, but I tabled that thought for another time. Right now, I wanted to come, and I knew Julian was close. When he realized that I had pulled myself out of my trousers and was stroking myself in time with my tongue on his prick, he made a deliciously pained sound, tangling his fingers in my hair with barely a gasp of warning.

Feeling the warm burst of release on my tongue set me off, and I groaned around him, feeling his prick pulse and thicken in my mouth as I spent on the sand, not stopping until I was too sensitive to bear another stroke, until Julian hissed and gently pushed me away from cleaning his spent cock with my tongue.

We righted our clothing, and I climbed back up to sit beside him again, both of us catching our breath as the water crept closer and our food sat forgotten between us. "Well," he said after several minutes. "That wasn't the picnic I had in mind, but I think I prefer it to the cold cuts."

I snorted, reaching for the little bowls of vegetables as Julian scooped up the drinks and plastic ware.

"Not very filling though, was it?" I teased.

"I didn't hear any complaints a few minutes ago."

I grinned. "And you won't. Ah, shit, my shoes are wet!"

"Damn it, okay, come on, let's get going before we're completely waterlogged."

WE MADE IT BACK TO Honey Walk just as the first fat drops of rain began to fall. It wasn't the hurricane but some outer band of storm, the advance guard promising more later. We'd just ducked into the foyer when Sandra came barreling out of the kitchen, making a beeline for Julian. "Doctor Weems, may I have a moment of your time?"

"We're busy," Julian replied curtly. "Maybe later."

"I see. Well. I'd like to apologize for my earlier demeanor regarding your potential guest lecturing position and..." She paused, sniffed, glanced away. "I'd like to request your opinion on a monograph I'm working on. It's in a rather delicate stage and as you are an expert on mortuary practices in early American settlements, I thought, perhaps..."

Julian made a flustered sound and looked askance at me. I hesitated, then shrugged. "Go on then," I said. "You want to do it, go for it." I wanted to remind him that this romantic getaway was his idea, and maybe our ideas of romance differed but mine did not include being ignored for the sake of academia. Being in my feelings about that job offer of his wasn't going to help either one of us though so I swallowed it down for the time being and gestured to the stairs. "I owe Ezra a call, anyway. I'll be back down later."

Julian started to reply but Sandra took his elbow and tugged him toward the library. "I found your paper on intentional saponification of the dead via burial practices in—"

"Godspeed," I muttered as he library door closed behind them, and I headed for our room.

Ezra answered on the third ring. "Oscar!" he cried. "I flashed someone for beads and it's not even Mardi Gras!"

"I think our next episode is going to be investigating the ghost of your liver seeking vengeance for the cruelties visited upon it in life."

"Aw, you love me," he sing-songed. "And I'm not drunk. Just well lubricated *and* in a good mood. Harrison took me to this place that sells pralines. *Just* pralines. So many kinds of pralines."

"Never mind your liver," I muttered. "It's your pancreas that'll haunt you. I take it you're having fun though?"

"Mmm hmm. It's been wonderful. Even when I'm sober." He laughed. "We've been to a few museums in the area, and a cruise on the river in an actual paddle wheeler. Harrison's got some conference call he can't get out of so he's out on the balcony now but I'm on the bed and oh my god my feet hurt." He paused for breath, then sighed. "How're you, Oz? I must admit, I was a bit disappointed in your lack of texting, but Harrison's been keeping me distracted so I forgive you."

"Well, thank you," I laughed. "I miss you, you prat." The admission, while not a surprise, was definitely one I hadn't meant to make aloud. My face felt warm at that, and Ezra's startled silence made me want to just cover my head with a pillow.

"I miss you too," he said gruffly. "Harrison kept asking me if I'd make him bring me to that island of yours yesterday," he said with a small chuckle. "He was worried I'd wither up and blow away without you in proximity."

"Ah, well, here we are. Alive and well and in one piece. Well. Two pieces. Tell me about the trip so far and spare me no details. The last time we were in New Orleans was to meet with Jacob. I'm hoping this trip isn't as fraught."

"Did you know," Ezra said, stretching out on the bed, the rustle of sheets clearly audible, "there's actually a streetcar named Desire?"

"After the movie or is the movie named after it?"

"No clue, mate. But I got to ride on it last night."

We fell into an easy chatter and for a few minutes it felt like there was no distance between us at all. It was only when Harrison returned to the room and Ezra told me to 'hang on a tick' that I felt a sort of glum sadness creep in around my seams. It wasn't jealousy—I was thrilled he and Harrison were getting on. Ezra truly cared about the man, and he seemed to return the sentiment. Ezra, I knew, needed someone who wasn't me in his life. And logically I knew that didn't diminish our bond, but I couldn't help but feel a little strange that he was there, and I was in South Carolina, and we weren't in one another's pockets like we'd been for years.

And he didn't seem bothered at all.

But do you want him to be? I mused as he had a muffled conversation with Harrison. *Or do you just want the reassurance he still loves you too?*

"Hey," Ezra said breathlessly. "Harrison made reservations for some fancy place, so I need to go get suited and booted. Call you tonight?"

"I'll be around," I said. "Don't forget your manners."

"Never. Oh! Wait a sec—are you guys staying through the hurricane then? I saw on the news one was heading right for you. Are you going to head back to the mainland or—"

"We're riding it out," I said. At his dismayed noise, I clicked my tongue softly. "Oi, I'm in good hands. Julian's been through these sorts of storms, and this house has been here for centuries, through more of these things than I can count. We'll be okay."

"If you get washed out to sea, I'm never forgiving you."

"Understandable. Now go scrub up. Harrison's never seen you looking nice."

"Oi!"

"Love you, you arse."

"Your mum loves me."

"Dude!"

He hung up, cackling. I felt lighter, having talked to him for a bit, and was glad for it. While Julian and I seemed to be back on our feet, a dose of Ezra went that much further toward making me feel like myself. Shrugging out of my waistcoat and cravat, and, feeling a bit fancy, slipping a banyan over my untucked shirt, I headed downstairs to find Julian. It didn't take very long—I just went where the books were. "Hey," I called softly as I pushed open the study door. "Are you free?"

He looked up from the small book he'd been studying, a look of relief crossing his face and making me feel a tad guilty. "Oscar. I thought maybe you wanted some time on your own so I just..." He shrugged. "Sorry?"

"It's okay," I murmured, easing into the room and closing the door behind me. "Um, about earlier..."

"I'm sorry," he blurted. "I should've told Sandra to leave us alone and I'd talk to her at a different time. When we came back," he said, standing to move around the desk and close the distance between us, "I really want to just go upstairs with you and"—he sighed, face coloring in endearing embarrassment—"hold you, actually. Just take some time to actually be together without anything else pressing."

I nodded slowly. "I was hurt," I admitted, holding up a hand when Julian started to speak again. "Let me finish, okay? I was hurt and it sucks, and I just want you to know that, alright?"

He nodded, casting his eyes down and looking miserable.

"Oi, listen though, I'm not telling you not to talk to her or whatever. I just... I just want to feel like you see me too, alright?"

His gaze snapped up. "I see you," he whispered. "I always see you, Oscar."

The kiss was bittersweet at first, both of us still smarting, but it melted into something warmer, lovely and close as we stood in the study doorway, just kissing and swaying together until the clatter of dishes told us Sandra was making dinner and our affectionate pursuits would need to wait a bit longer. "Come on," he smiled against my temple. "Let's eat so we can have energy for later."

AFTER DINNER, WE RETREATED to the study. Julian stretched out on the sofa in front of the driftwood fire, his feet propped on the arm while he thumbed through *Rites and Rituals of the Carolina Seacoast Wreckers*. "This is so weird," he muttered. "I wonder if I can find a copy on eBay or something when we leave here. I'd love to add it to my collection."

"What is it?" I murmured.

"It's a book about the folkways of the island's original colonists. It was sitting on the desk in the library room," he said, flipping another page. "It's fascinating! A combination of farm records, folklore, and looks like some religious stuff."

"Sounds right up your alley," I yawned. Something about the sea air and the lack of any metaphorical fires to put out made me exceedingly sleepy. I could barely keep my eyes open despite the fact I'd gotten plenty of sleep the night before. The mug of tea Sandra made for me cooled on the spindle-legged end table beside me as I tried to thumb through my private social media (which, to be fair, was just to follow Ezra's accounts and now Lisa and Jesse). My eyes were heavy and gritty, similar to how I felt when I had a cold. "Are you feeling alright?"

I glanced up to find Julian giving me a concerned look, brows drawn down and lips twisted in a thoughtful frown.

"Fine," I said. "Just very tired all of a sudden." The sound of thunder rolling in over the sea was a deep, monstrous sort of growl. "Probably just the change in weather," I offered, seizing a possible reason. *Swear to whichever god is listening, if I'm sick on this getaway, I'll be very blasphemous once I find out which one of you is on shift today.*

Julian was talking, but his words were warm tar, slow and thick as they drifted between us. My eyes wouldn't stay open, even when his tone sharpened and the sound of him struggling to his feet from the overstuffed chair broke through the warm cocoon of sleep tugging at me. I felt floaty, warm and safe. A vague thought—*is this what babies feel like in utero*—crossed my mind before it was replaced with just the simple sensations of warmth and nothingness. Slowly, my body grew heavy again but in a way that wasn't usual for me. My gravity was off, I thought wildly. All traces of comfortable warmth evaporated as sensation rushed at me in one all-consuming wave, making me gasp and thrash against the blanket over me until finally, finally, I could convince my eyes to open.

This isn't my room.

My body felt different. Wrong. No, I realized—just wrong for *me*.

And *me* wasn't who I was.

Instead of the over-warm study where the thunder rattled the windows and the promise of rain seeped in on muggy little currents of air through the cracks in the molding, I was in a brightly lit bedroom under the cold blast of a window air conditioning unit. The room smelled of wet wool with a hint of mildew laced with gardenia or something else very floral and lush. I was cold, my limbs bare and sweat-dappled.

Where's my waistcoat? My shirt? My legs were covered, which made me feel less exposed, but those were definitely not my trousers.

"Where the hell did I get jeans?" I muttered. My voice was light but raspy, startling me.

"Whose accent is this?"

American—or maybe Canadian? It was hard for me to tell. Definitely not my own dulcet tones, that was for certain. I pushed myself into a sitting position and winced as everything moved strangely. My body was too long, thin in ways I usually wasn't.

And I knew, knew in my bones (well, whoever's bones these were), that I was not in my own body.

And what the fuck was I supposed to do about that?

Gingerly, my heart racing so badly I felt nauseated, I got to my feet and looked down. Jeans, white tank top, thick gray socks... I blinked and everything snapped together. Rushing to the dresser to peer in the mirror set over it, a panicked laugh bubbled from my chest.

"Sandra. What the actual fuck. How..."

Touching my (her) face, hair, hands, it all felt so real. I've been having weird dreams lately. This has to be one of them.

Thunder rolled long and heavy, the lights flickering in the bedroom.

Is this her cottage? Or at least what I'm assuming her cottage looks like? I did a slow turn, taking everything in. If this was a dream, it was sharp and vivid. Dust limned the blinds over the tiny window, a generic lamp sat on a pressboard nightstand beside a plain, neatly made bed save for where my (her) body had wrinkled the sheets on one edge.

Dog toys sat half-chewed and grubby in a basket by the closed door.

A mug of tea steamed gently beside the lamp, a small one-cup teapot over a candle-warmed stand simmering nearby. I took a few cautious steps toward it, bending to sniff. It smelled grassy, dirty, medicinal.

That was the smell, I realized, or at least part of it. Whatever it was, was strong.

Do I usually smell in my dreams? I thought that was impossible. Julian would know.

Thunder rumbled again, louder and lower this time. The power shuddered. "Don't you even think about it," I muttered. Patting myself (herself) down, I checked for a phone and found none. Maybe somewhere in the house, I thought.

But if this is a dream, wake up. There. Just wake up. End it.

It wasn't often I was stricken by how ridiculous my profession—no, my life—could be but I was definitely experiencing a moment of clarity regarding the level of banana-pants weirdness at that moment.

The power flickered again, then blinked out entirely. A flash of lightening illuminated the room for just a second, making everything washed out blue and white. Lenny started howling outside the bedroom door.

"Shit, Goddamnit, fuck!"

Sandra's voice—definitely not mine—was shrill with my nerves. Fine, I wasn't waking up, I'd try to walk to the house. Maybe a change of scenery would snap me out of this.

When are you going to accept what's happening, Oscar?

This isn't a dream.

I padded to the door and opened it, hoping for some nonsensical dreamscape. My third form sport class, aisle six in the Tesco near Ezra's parents' place. Disneyland. Instead, it was just a storm-darkened hall with a nervous dog dancing at my feet.

Lenny was whimpering, half-rising to put his paws on my legs when suddenly he froze and dropped into a low crouch, baring his teeth. "It's okay," I said, hoping he'd believe Sandra's voice. "It's just... It's me. I'm nice. Here!" I stepped back, keeping my eyes on him as I bent to rummage in the toy basket, coming up with a well-chewed thing shaped like a dumbbell. "Here! This looks like you enjoy it!"

Lenny snarled.

"Easy there, boy," someone else said, his voice startlingly familiar.

"What are you doing here?" I demanded. The ghost from the stairs, the one who'd followed me into town, was smiling at me, ruffling Lenny's fur and Lenny seemed—no, Lenny definitely—felt his touch. Seeing me in the doorway, though, the ghost's smile fell and was replaced by a deep, angry scowl.

The ghost looked up and froze. "You're not Sandra. Where's Sandra? What've you done to her?"

"Nothing. I'm still trying to convince myself that I'm dreaming." I offered a small smile and he scowled, those laugh lines turning into something angry and grim. "I literally woke up here. I was in the main house, in the study—"

"You're staying there with your friend."

The slight emphasis he put on *friend* told me he knew very well what Julian and I were to one another, even if he didn't want to say it. "Yes."

He stared hard at me, lips pressed into such a thin line they practically disappeared into his beard. "Sandra..." He sighed after a moment, closing his eyes. "How long?" he asked, gesturing at me.

"I don't know."

The storm rattled the windows some more, and the power gave a hopeful pulse before fading out once more. Lenny whimpered, stretching for the ghost to pat him. "How can you interact with him?" I asked. "Most of the time, animals seem afraid of spirits."

Jeremiah shook his head sharply, scowling at something in the dark past me. "She's never managed this before. It was for pretend, yeah? Fantasy-like. I never thought..." He snapped his gaze back to mine. "Is she..."

"I have no idea." The thought of her in my body like I was in hers made me sick, hot-cold sweat breaking out all over and stomach cramping with nausea. "How do I make this stop? You said she's tried this before. What is it? Is it... is it some sort of hypnotism?"

The man narrowed his eyes, peering at me like he couldn't believe what I was saying. "She did this without your participation?"

"Well, other than the fact I'm apparently participating..."

He rolled his eyes. "This isn't how it is supposed to work," he muttered. He reached out, his fingers cold and frictionless, just points of ice where they touched my face. "This isn't hers to use," he whispered to himself. "This isn't—"

Everything felt both too heavy and too hot at the same time. I was alone in the study, under two crocheted blankets and a thin throw I'd last seen on our bed upstairs. The fire was blazing, making the room a sauna. The power was out and the storm I'd heard in my—dream?—seemed even louder here.

Julian's face loomed over me as I shifted onto my back. "Christ, you scared the hell out of me. I tried to call Sandra but there was no answer. I think we need to get you to a doctor. You were out so hard, and just shaking like you couldn't get warm."

I grabbed his fingers where they moved restlessly against my arm. "I'm..." Pausing, I made a decision. "I'm not fine. Fuck. Let me up."

He scooted back as I threw off the covers and sat up, immediately starting to work on unbuttoning my shirt to cool off. "When did you last see Sandra?"

"The same time you did," he said, frowning. "When we went to have dinner, and she was putting away the pots and pans she'd used."

I nodded. "Okay. Good. Good." The room was slowly swimming into focus, and I noticed my coffee mug on the table. I'd had a few sips before dozing off, I recalled. "Did you have any of your tea?" I asked sharply. "Even a sip?"

Julian nodded. "Finished the whole thing an hour or so ago, before you dozed off. Oscar, what's going on?"

I closed my eyes. "Right. So. Forgive me for this but when you say your eyes are open to more things now, how open are we talking?"

"I mean... I've had ghost experiences I couldn't explain away, so that's on the table. But if you're about to tell me you're having Bigfoot's lovechild then I'm going to tell you that you need professional help."

"I think that might be easier than this," I muttered. "In that little book, does it say anything about... possession by the living?"

Julian's lips quirked and he shook his head. "I'm sorry, what?"

I told him what had just happened, at least how I think it happened, even the dog's reaction, the details of Sandra's room... "Was I acting oddly?" I asked. "Maybe saying something? Doing something I wouldn't do?"

"I covered you up and built the fire because you were shaking so hard your teeth were chattering. I couldn't wake you up. I tried to call Sandra when I couldn't find her in the house to find out how to get you to the mainland when the ferry isn't running, but she didn't answer..." Julian sat back against the arm of the sofa, my head in his lap. "You didn't have a fever, but it was as if you were having a febrile seizure or something."

I shook my head, the urge to curl up and freak out a bit stronger than I expected. It was easy to dismiss it as an illness, some strange sleep issue, anything but what I knew in my core that it was. Closing my eyes, I bumped my head against Julian's shoulder, thinking hard and fast. It wasn't a lie, really, when I said, "I'm just very tired. I'm sorry, Julian. I'm not sure what's gotten into me."

He nodded, still openly concerned as he reached up to stroke my hair back from my face. "I want to find Sandra, see if there's a doctor on the other end of the island we can call, maybe."

"No." When Julian looked like he was going to protest, I added, "Not yet. Please. If I'm still feeling like this later... We can call someone."

Julian stopped stroking my hair and instead gently cupped my chin, tipping my face up toward his. "Oscar, talk to me. What's going on?"

For the first time in a long time, I hated my ability, hated dealing with ghosts, hated being different from most people. *I just wanted a damn week away with my boyfriend! Can't I just have a few normal days?* Cupping his hand where it rested on my face, I shifted to press a kiss to his palm before admitting, "I don't know."

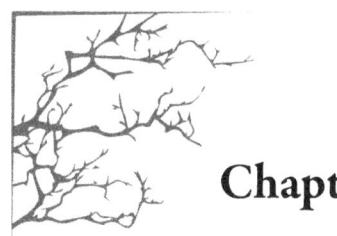

Chapter 4 – Julian

Despite our best efforts to the contrary, the evening was unsettling and felt brittle somehow. Oscar had rallied from his odd spell and made himself a cup of the herbal tea from the bag Sandra had left on the kitchen counter for him, but he hadn't taken more than a sip or two after returning to the study. We were clingier than usual, neither of us wanting to move far from the other.

Oscar had retreated into himself a bit, and I was restless. We decided to settle in the study for the evening, the storm outside ebbing and flowing around the island and lending the entire scene a rather gloomy, foreboding air.

"We first met during a storm," Oscar murmured, resting his head against my arm.

I nodded. "Remnants of a hurricane, even."

He smiled softly, though it was more anxious than romantic. "I wonder if that's some sort of omen for us."

"I think it could only be a good one," I protested.

Outside, a stiff gust of wind made something crack and snap—probably, I realized, one of the old palms out front. Oscar tensed, relaxing only when the creaking stopped and the wind seemed to fade just a bit.

If I was one to be swayed by signs and portents, I'd have been nervous. As it was, I was nervous for entirely different reasons. The window of time to leave the island was rapidly closing. As it was, the ferry was no longer running due to the increased swells, but emergency evacuations were still possible via the Coast Guard. Oscar *seemed* fine, hours after the weirdness, but I couldn't shake the feeling that whatever had happened wasn't a one-off. He swore he was alright but I couldn't shake the anxiety that had settled into my bones after his spell earlier. So I gritted my teeth and faked it, picking up a book from the library room that caught my eye, something that promised a bit of local history and weirdness, and took up my post on the settee in the study while Oscar read something on his phone, the two of us falling into familiar, warm quiet for quite a while. Occasionally, he'd giggle, or make a sound of surprise, and shoot me a heated glance when whatever he was reading got racy, and I pretended not to notice so he could have the thrill of pouncing later (not that we'd done this before—Oscar did love a good sneaky pounce). I dove back into the odd little book I'd found in the library. I'd only read a few chapters of it but it was compelling, drawing me in until I stopped noticing Oscar's increasing glances and heated sounds.

"It makes no sense."

Oscar fixed me with a distinctly unimpressed glare, and I corrected to, "In this context, it makes no sense. This is definitely folklore, but it's specific to this island. *Just* this island. It was uninhabited before the first colonizers arrived in the area, and then only a handful came out here because the indigenous people on the mainland said it was unlivable." I flipped to the fragile flyleaf, the map of the island, and turned the book so he could see it more easily. "This is from... Okay, looks like 1698? Maybe 1699? Hard to read the handwriting honestly. No fresh water sources, the tides are rough and drastic thanks to the offshore drop on this end," I tapped the spot that would later become Tibbins Quay, "and this end where Rosie Sands is," I paused, closed my eyes, and exhaled with the world-weariness of a man who was over just about everything. "Haunted."

Oscar's snort was nearly elephantine. "Julian, my darling, that didn't come up in your research before booking the trip?"

My cheeks warmed. "Honestly, no. Not one single mention of ghost, specters, spirits... not even a tourist-friendly pirate captain looking for his lost treasure." I flipped to the first chapter with careful fingers. "This first part is archaic in the language but whoever had this reprinted kept it faithful rather than attempting to modernize it. It's not terribly oblique but there're some parts..." I trailed off, shaking my head. "Even if this isn't the original, it's still well in the realm of antique and it's definitely rare. I tried searching it up on the Library of Congress then widened to an international search and there's no record of it ever existing."

"That's not unusual though," Oscar said. "Especially with older or niche books. If someone wrote the first one just for themselves, and later a descendant wanted a copy, hoping to save something of dear old grandad's when the original finally fell apart... It might never have been sold widely."

I nodded. "I know, I know. But the fuckery comes in with this. *Chapter One: On Blood and Sand to Rouse The Spirit,*" I read aloud. "Firstly, a fire must be built of the vines that run yellow-sapped in summer. Ensure it is hot enough to burst the body of the plant and cause the sap to burn with thick smoke and sweet scent."

Oscar furrowed his brow, leaning forward to peer at the book. "Do what now?"

"It goes on from there." I reached out and gave my phone a nudge in his direction. "I've summarized some of the first few chapters in my notes but," I shook my head, "there's so much. Some of this, I have to admit, I'm not quite grasping. I studied a bit of Southern folk magic practices but only as they pertained to death and burial practices in specific regions. This is not only out of my wheelhouse, it's in an entirely different boat."

Oscar picked up my phone and read the note I had open. "*Chapter Five: Vessels of Flesh Chosen by Man.*" He sat back, folding his hands across his lap, staring into space for a long moment. "Okay, nope. I cannot fathom a single reason that title wouldn't be unsettling."

"It gets better." I turned the pages to the one that had caught my eye. "This is a sigil." Oscar leaned forward again to peer at the book, a whiff of his sandalwood and berry and salt-air scent distracting me for just a moment. He knew, judging by the smirk he shot me.

"We're still on holiday, don't forget."

"Couldn't if I tried." I responded sweetly, biting down on the snarky response I wanted to throw his way, a reminder that he'd been making friends with the resident ghost apparently, while we were on our holiday.

Oscar snorted but didn't comment further on that topic.

He made a pleased little noise. "I don't recognize this. Not even in part. Granted, I don't work with sigils myself, but many mediums do, and many of our clients fall into using things like that for their own reasons. Does it mean anything to you?"

"It doesn't look like anything I've seen before, but that doesn't mean much. The thing is, though," I said, turning to the next page. Another sigil, a mirror of the previous one, took up half the page with thick black lines and delicate scrawls that looked like waves. "This is a grimoire. A spell book. Or something like it. And whoever wrote it was determined to raise the dead."

Oscar stared at me wide-eyed for a long moment before bursting into a cackle. "Pull the other one, there's bells on!"

"I know, it's ridiculous but the fact remains, this is what it's for. Here, the passage beneath the first one. Loosely, it says *to call on the ocean's lost, mark out this sigil where the sand pinks at dawn. Mark with the blood of your heart and burn with salted flame.*" I turned to the second sigil. "And this one is sort of a reversal, from what I can tell. *Send them back to the sea lest their desire for the shore root them in place.*"

"Why would anyone want to summon the dead from the ocean?" Oscar asked, wrinkling his nose. "Unless," he continued, tone thoughtful, "they were specific dead. People they'd lost to an accident in the water. A shipwreck, maybe?"

I shook my head, paging ahead, past lists of ingredients for protection charms and imprecations about the correct times and days to perform this particular bit of work. "In chapter two, the author describes Broken Palm Island before people settled here full time. It wasn't considered habitable due to the lack of resources and what the author claims were *rank spirits and dark movements among the nightshadows, the ocean too bitter and hungry for those not prepared to draw on her secrets.*" I glanced up at him. "Rank spirits could be something like rotting vegetation, or maybe just the smell of the shore and cove at low tide. Dead fish, seaweed, who knows."

"You said folklore. It's folklore? This sounds more like someone fancied themselves to be a witch of sorts."

Scooting closer, I opened to a page about midway through the book. "Here. The author describes creatures who live on the island. Now, there are the standard things like crabs, sand fleas, birds. But, they go on to describe something like... like..." I trailed off, shaking my head. "I can't think of something to compare it to. While cryptids are not uncommon in American folklore, they tend to fall into regional lines. At least before the internet became a thing. Now you have people from California claiming they saw the Flatwoods Monster and New Yorkers crying Chupacabra."

"I'm starting to think I should've paid more attention to that folklore podcast Ezra found," Oscar murmured. "What did the author claim lived here?"

I shrugged, starting to pace the narrow confines of the room as I spoke, falling into professor mode almost without thinking. "This is the weirdest part. They call them wreckers, which at first I assumed meant they were *wreckers*, like actual people but living rough or maybe the author was being denigrating over perceived social class disparity. But wreckers weren't active here like they were in Florida, at least from what I recall."

He wrinkled his nose in thought. "Wreckers? Is that what it sounds like?"

"The stories go that wreckers would lure ships to run aground, then loot them. Piracy without the overhead of having to outfit and maintain a ship."

"Piracy on a budget."

I smirked. "Something like that. Actual wreckers would originally help salvage shipwrecks in exchange for a portion of the cargo, but as the stories go, some people figured why wait for a disaster to occur. Make it happen. There're tales of fires set on beaches to draw ships to the shallows, that sort of thing. The veracity of the more salacious tales is debated—everyone loves a good story and making up something daring and a little scary to tell visitors may have given rise to the legends of wreckers especially along the Florida coast. Original wreckers were legitimate and didn't create the shipwrecks themselves."

"Well," Oscar sighed. "Pirates have always been a thing, eh? People love the idea..."

I hummed in agreement. "There's an area off the coast here known as the Graveyard of the Atlantic due to how many ships wrecked there over the years. Secondly, this island, at least according to the maps and the geological and oceanographic surveys I was able to pull up online, lacks reefs or any sort of submerged dangers that would lead to wrecking. Third—"

"Love, how many points do you have?" Oscar asked, a small smile tugging his lips. "Is it more than five? If so, I think I'd like some tea first."

I mock-huffed, unable to stop the warm little bubble of amusement at his teasing. *Damn it, I love him*, I thought, and nearly distracted myself from the matter at hand with my goofy grinning up at him. "This is the last one on this topic," I promised. "But if you're gonna make a pot, I'll take some." He stuck his tongue out, startling a laugh out of me. "Well, third thing is: the book refers to Wreckers, but it's a very nonstandard description. They're capitalized, for one. Like a title rather than a job description. And for two—"

"That's technically point number five, Julian."

"No, it's sub-point two to major point three."

"Splitting hairs."

"Being exact," I countered, and he grinned, elbowing me gently in the ribs on my uninjured side.

"So, the Wreckers-with-a-capital are what? Pirates? Ghosts? Oh!" He sat up and bounced a little, patting my arm in excitement. "Pirate ghosts? I've only spoken with one pirate ghost, a rather snarky fellow in Newton Ferrers. he claimed to be Henry Avery but was much too late to have been him." Oscar clicked his tongue in remembered disapproval. "Ezra thinks the man was a tour guide who topped it while giving one of the West Country pirate tours and either didn't know he was dead or was very committed to remaining in character."

The idea tickled me, and I wondered what that said about me now, when the year before I'd have rolled my eyes and pretended I didn't hear that.

I *prefer this version of me*, I realized, not for the first time. *It's much less of an asshole.* "What happened to him?"

"Hm? Oh, well, he was dead so not much, I suppose. He was banging around in an older home, scaring the absolute daylight out of the owner, who was a friend of a friend of Grandmere's. He was one of my first clients."

"The ghost or the homeowner?"

Oscar tipped his head thoughtfully. "Both, I suppose, in a sense. The ghost—Henry, since that's the only name he'd give me—refused to leave, would never say why. I must admit, my adventurous heart hoped there was buried treasure or something like that, but I strongly suspect he was just afraid of what comes next."

"Aren't we all?" I muttered, flipping the page in the book to a line drawing of something tall, sharp-angled, and spidery.

Oscar fell quiet at my off-hand remark, folding his hands in his lap and staring at the page I had open.

"Are you?" I murmured. Oscar darted me a glance and, very gingerly, shrugged one shoulder.

"Not so much fear," he said after a brief hesitation. "Perhaps more akin to uncertainty. I know there *is* something next. But what it is? Haven't the foggiest. Is it the same for everyone? Will I see my loved ones? Or will I be in some void waiting for what's after *that* stop?" He shifted uneasily, staring at the open book on my knee. "What if what comes next, if you're not a ghost, is just gray nothing? An eternal holding pattern? I'm not sure I'd do well with that."

"And no ghost has ever told you," I said, repeating one of the first things we'd ever seriously discussed when I climbed down off my skeptical soapbox.

He reached for the book to take a closer look at the page. "I suppose I'll find out when it's my turn," he said lightly. "These look terrifying."

I hesitated, and when Oscar didn't say anything else, took the hint and moved on from the topic. at least for the moment. "This is allegedly a Wrecker. The author describes them in a way that reminds me of the concept of *genius loci* with a hint of landvaettir from Nordic mythology."

"Land spirits... So, the area itself produces a ghost?" Oscar asked, his frown making his brows furrow. "Or is it the spirit of someone who'd lived here and is just very protective of the land?"

"It depends," I said, stretching my sore leg out. The walking earlier had felt great for a while, but my body was screaming at me now. Every day it looked more and more like I would definitely need to learn how to accommodate this new kind of normal when it came to my mobility and physical endurance. Oscar shifted, dropping to the floor beside me and, before I could stop him, started to gently but firmly massage my thigh. "I know that's meant to be helpful but it's really distracting, too..."

Oscar's smile was small and beatific. "Orgasms are great pain relievers, I hear."

"Very distracting, though," I said, my voice shaking just a little. Oscar's smile grew, his hands sliding up the inside of my thighs to cup the growing bulge of my erection. "I... I suppose we could do with some distraction right now."

Oscar surged up as I leaned down, meeting me for a kiss. He kept his hands on my thighs, his thumbs moving in slow circles grazing the edge of my cock. "I'm very good at being distracting," he murmured against my lips. "Got an A level in it and all."

I smiled back, our kiss turning a little messy as neither of us could stop giggling for no particular reason. "I don't know what's so funny," I said, nipping his lower lip.

"Nothing," he breathed. "We're just happy."

I hummed in agreement, sighing when the tip of his tongue traced the seam of my lips. He made an enthusiastic sound as I opened for him and I reached between us to unfasten my trousers, popping the button while he worked down my zipper.

Oscar's tongue traced the curve of my cockhead as I leaned back, sighing at the rough, wet drag of fabric against sensitive skin. "Yes," I hissed. "Just like that."

He tugged the waistband of my briefs down just enough to expose the seeping head. "For me?" he murmured, and I nodded desperately.

"All of it."

"Mmm..."

He'd just closed his lips around the tip when Sandra pounded on the door. "Making dinner!" she snapped. "And don't you dare ruin that couch! It's original!"

Oscar rocked back onto his heels. "Shit."

"We can pretend we didn't hear her," I offered, already knowing it was no use.

"Tonight," Oscar promised. "I'll make it up to you."

"How about tonight, we both—"

Sandra's knock came again, this time with the rattle of the doorknob. "Open up, gentlemen!" she ordered. "This is a historic home! This is *not* appropriate! I will terminate your stay immediately if you're violating the integrity of the soft furnishings!"

The door popped open before Oscar or I could get to our feet—we were too busy swallowing our urge to laugh like grebes—and Sandra strode in with all the fire and fury of Boudicca descending on the Romans. She stopped short, seeing us fully dressed, and instead shifted her glare to the book open on the table. "You removed it from the library."

"Yes," I said, pushing gingerly to my feet. "I wasn't aware we weren't allowed to read any of the books in there." She narrowed her eyes, stepping closer. "It's unharmed," I added. "I'm aware of how to handle old books."

Oscar shifted to stand behind me, clearly using me for a shield. His fingers twisted into the back of my shirt, and I could feel a tremor race through him as he pressed close.

"It's just some light reading," I said, shifting to keep myself between the pair of them. I didn't like the way she was looking at Oscar. I know that sounds ridiculous, but she was staring so hungrily at him, so intently that it made me want to throw a coat over him or something, protect him from that weird look in her eyes.

"We don't understand most of it," Oscar said suddenly. "The pictures are interesting, though."

I opened my mouth to correct him—we might not understand much of it, but we were definitely getting the gist—but the pressure of his foot atop mine stopped me. Admittedly, I felt a warm glow inside at the realization we'd reached the stage in our relationship where we both agreed on who to lie to and about what, all without saying a word about it.

And it also made me a little worried for what that said about us as people but not enough to really dwell on it just then.

Sandra rocked back on her heels, her jaw working as she stared at the book, then shifted her hard glare to me. "I would have thought you would understand what you have there," she whispered, voice harsh and shaking. "You, of all people!"

"I do understand," I soothed, but it was lost on her. "Sandra, we were just looking at the book. It won't happen again." It would absolutely happen again but next time I'd be more careful.

She glared so hard at us, I was surprised we didn't burst into flames. "See that it doesn't. This is not yours," she seethed, waving the book at us. "You have no right to it!"

The door slammed in her wake, and we were quiet for several long moments. Finally, Oscar spoke. "That was way more intense than I think the situation called for," he muttered.

"No argument here. What the hell is so special about that book that she's treating it like it's her own child?"

Oscar shook his head, his face scrunching as he fought a yawn. "No fucking clue, but it makes me wonder if she's hiding something about it."

I snorted. "Like what? Her precious monograph hidden in the pages?"

He shook his head, yawning again. "Christ, I can barely keep my eyes open," he muttered. "I might need to lie down a bit." He trudged toward the sofa and sank down with a groan. "What's that," he asked, as he slumped to one side. "Is that a receipt or something?"

A thin piece of paper lay on the floor at my feet. I scooped it up and huffed when I saw what it was. "It must've fallen out of the book," I muttered, hanging it to Oscar to see. "It's got some of those sigil designs on it."

"Huh."

Sandra's clattering steps sounded outside the study, so Oscar shoved the paper into his waistcoat pocket and gave me a sleepy, slow wink. "Get me in an hour?"

"Promise."

"JULES! MY FAVORITE skeptic!"

"Ezra, are you drunk? It's half past ten in the morning!"

Ezra snorted. "Not where I am, thank you very much." He paused, then added, "Oh, shit, wait, it *is!* Harrison! It's not even noon and I think I'm pissed!"

There was a scuffle, then Harrison's much less bubbly voice came over the connection. "The breakfast buffet had mimosas." He sighed. "He said he thought it was regular orange juice, but after the second one, that excuse ran out of steam."

"How many did he have?"

"Somewhere between four and seven." Harrison sighed. "They weren't very strong, really, but it's still alcohol, and Ezra's kind of lightweight when it comes to drinking. Hold on a sec." He muffled the phone, but I could hear him gently scolding Ezra that just because he felt too warm didn't mean he could take off his pants in the hotel lobby and yes, he was positive they had air conditioning on.

"Sounds like your hands are full," I said when he came back on the line. "I'll let you go—"

"No, it's fine. He's sitting on one of the sofas. We were going to take a tour of old homes in a few hours so we're having sober up time right now. Water, food, and a lot of fresh air." He paused. "Is it safe to guess that something wrong, given that it's you calling Ezra rather than Oscar doing it?"

Truth time. "I wouldn't say *wrong*, just... weird. And Ezra's known him forever, so I thought maybe he might have some insight into the situation."

Harrison lowered his voice, the background noise changing just a little to let me know he'd moved somewhere away from Ezra's tipsy rendition of *Modern Major General* that had some nonstandard lyrics. "What's going on? Is this a legal situation or medical?"

"Neither. I mean. Maybe medical? I'm not entirely certain." I gave Harrison a précis of what had been going on—Oscar's exhaustion, what he had claimed about the body swap incident. "I know I'm working on being more open to the supernatural, but Harrison, this is beyond seeing the ghost of my dead best friend. This is..." I trailed off.

"Weird," Harrison supplied succinctly. "Real fucking weird."

"In a word, yes."

He was quiet for a long moment before sighing. "I gotta be frank with you. Ezra could answer but he's likely to do it in a dramatic fashion and insist on coming to Broken Palm immediately."

"He could try, but the ferry's not going to run again for a few days. We're getting the outer bands of Hurricane Nelson, apparently."

Harrison muttered for me to hold on a sec and there was a rustling sound. Then Ezra's voice came down the line. "Jules. Honey. Babe. Dude. I made Harrison give me the phone because it's mine so all the words in it are mine. And I think I might be more drunk than not. Do you know mimosa's *aren't* a grandma drink? I thought they were. Like fucking... lemon shandies or something, you know? Something weak. Like, what's that word my mum used? A tipple."

"Ezra, it's fine," I said quickly. "Don't worry about it. Oscar's fine. I just got worried over nothing. Thought he was too cold."

There was a long pause before Ezra replied. "You called me... because you thought Oscar was too cold."

I winced. Yeah, it sounded absolutely ridiculous, but I was fully committed now. "Yeah, just... weird being on our own," I said, forcing a laugh. "Guess I got nervous. Y'all have fun on your old home tour."

Ezra huffed. "You're lying to me, Julian Weems, and I don't know why. It's not close to my birthday, so it's not about a present. And Oscar's birthday is coming up, but I have a suspicion this isn't about what to get him."

"It's nothing. I'm fine. he's fine. We're all fine here. How are you?"

He snorted. "Alright, Han. When I sober up later, we're having words. Give Ozzy a kiss for me."

I hung up, equal parts of embarrassment and frustration making me feel too warm and unsettled.

"Reggie," I muttered. "If you can hear me, I could really use advice right now. Or, you know, some sparkling insight into what's going on."

Nothing.

He'd been quiet since Savannah and I felt in my heart of hearts that he'd made his peace, or whatever it was that meant he was done haunting me. Maggie was healing, taking his ashes on those trips they'd always planned but never gotten to take. I'd seen the light, so to speak, and admitted there are some strange things in the world that can't be explained away. And who knows how many other things were on his to-do list that kept him here. Or if he even had one.

You know who else might know? Who else has far more experience in the paranormal and, despite their flaky exterior, actually knows what they're doing?

Fucking Heinrich.

I groaned softly, tapping my phone against my forehead. *If I call him, that means everyone in the world is going to know by the end of the week. It'll become one of his stories to tell his clients, I bet.*

There were easily a half dozen reasons I could think of that would cause Oscar's periods of seeming absence, the exhaustion and his claims about the body swap. None of them were to be treated lightly. It'd only begun yesterday, but things seemed to be escalating in such a way that rang alarm bells right in my ear.

"I could really use an ear here," I muttered. "Reggie, just so you know, I'm fine with you haunting me for the next thirty or so minutes if you're not too busy."

I knew the chuckle I heard was just a product of my imagination, but damn it if it didn't make me smile.

The vibration of an incoming call startled me out of my spiral.

CeCe had either the best or worst timing.

"Hey," I answered. "How's New York?"

"Ugh."

"That good, huh?"

"If I ever say I'm getting married again, remind me of this."

"Cec, I'm sure your next husband won't be a murder-abetting asshole. I mean, the odds are low, anyway."

"Sometimes one twin will absorb the other in utero. I'm sad that I didn't even try."

I snorted. "What's up, favorite sister?"

"New York is defying the laws of physics in that it both sucks and blows simultaneously. Well, not the entire state. Just this specific part of it." She sighed and I knew, without seeing her, that she was slumped to one side, her face set in a scowl that looked a lot like mine would. "Jacob is doing his damnedest to bankrupt me, claiming anything earned during the marriage is half his despite the prenup and the fact I kept my business earnings and investments separate from his." She hesitated, then said, "He's also claiming rights to *Bump in the Night*. Apparently, his attorney—one of them, anyway—found some hinky wording they're trying to exploit in the contract where he signed the show and company over to me."

My stomach did a slow roll, anxiety and anger mixing into an unpleasant acid boil. "That should be impossible for him to do, though," I started, and she made a frustrated sound that was definitely mingled with a profanity or two. "I suppose you already knew that, though," I muttered. "Which makes sense..."

"It's a delay tactic, but so long as he and his lawyer are making the threat, mine needs to follow up on it so everything is being pushed back by at least two months."

"Shit."

"In a word..."

"What about the murder trial?"

"That's another fun fact to know and share: Mark Thomas has an absolute feral shark of a legal team. They're suing Annie's family for defamation since they spoke about his involvement in her death before it was made officially public," she said wearily. "And..."

"And what? You can't just pause like that and not follow up. Not unless you're being eaten by a honey badger or something. Are there honey badgers in upstate New York?"

"I wish they were. I'd lure one to my hotel, tame it with this leftover Thai food, convince it to do my bidding, then turn them loose on Mark and Jacob."

"I'd absolutely help you lure a honey badger into your vengeance plot if I were there."

She sighed. "This whole fucking week's been a nightmare," she said, sounding small and tired. "I regret almost all of the choices I made that led me to think getting married was a good idea."

"It's not your fault the guy you married didn't exist," I said. "The Jacob Grant you thought he was, was just a front. He made him up."

"Don't say that too loud or his lawyer's going to claim Jacob's innocent of any wrongdoing because he's not the man named in the charges."

"Well," I drawled, "If they go that route, it also means he has to drop his attempts to get money out of you because he's not the man on the marriage certificate or the prenup."

"Touché."

"I have my moments."

"So talk to me, favorite brother. My twin senses were tingling. There's a disturbance in the Force. Something, something, Dark Side…"

"Ezra called?" I shook my head, even though she couldn't see me. "I *just* got off the phone with him less than thirty minutes ago!"

"Texted. I think he's drunk but figured I'd check on y'all anyway, just to be sure. What's going on with Oscar that's got Ezra in a tizzy? And why are you so calm if he's so het up? And oh my god, a hurricane? Seriously? I saw on the news it's heading right for y'all! Are you okay?"

"It's just been a strange day all around." I curled up on the armchair by the room's window and told CeCe a bare-bones version of everything so far, starting with Hurricane Nelson apparently deciding to head our way instead of bouncing off the mainland further up the coast, and ending with Oscar's strange new quirks.

"Good lord," she muttered. "Where's Oscar now?"

"Napping, downstairs in the study. He just looked so tired, I didn't have the heart to suggest hauling himself up to bed for a nap."

"Seriously, up until this year the most havoc you ever wreaked was the time you told Mother her toast points were dry during her Spring Fete. Now you're seeing ghosts, fighting murderous ex boyfriends… Jules, I think Oscar might be a bad influence on you."

"Ha fucking ha. And I'd think having a relationship that got me fired and blackballed from teaching for the foreseeable was far more havoc wreaking than telling Mother her canapés were bland."

"That's not entirely true, though. About the being blackballed from teaching."

The silence was heavy, expectant.

"Who told?" I finally asked on a sigh. "I know it wasn't Oscar."

"A Professor Norman Charles contacted my office to verify you're legit. Lee passed the call on to me after apparently info dumping all over the poor guy about your being on vacation, and we had a nice chat. He's very keen to get your CV officially and set up a time to talk. Is that… is that something you want?"

The insecurity in her voice pained me. It reminded me of the time we were in fifth grade, and she had her first run-in with a bully aimed her way. *But what did I do, Jules? Why do they hate me so much?*

"I don't think it is," I said carefully, weighing the words on my tongue. "They seem eager though." And it was true—I didn't *think* it was what I wanted, but the temptation, the pull, was stronger than I wanted to admit. The idea of leaving what I was starting though… It gave me a twinge of anxiety. Oscar might say we'd be okay, and I might be excited to dive back into academia again, but how much of that would last?

NRE, Reggie's memory whispered. *That new relationship energy. More guys have fucked themselves over thinking the sidepiece is their one true love, but once that NRE wears off, the realization that they fucked up a good thing just for a rush of dopamine and a blowjob kicks in and they're totally screwed.*

Okay, he'd been talking about a mutual friend who was a serial monogamist and on his fourth engagement in two years, but I felt the comment could stand for this too.

"Mmm. I just want you to know," CeCe said in a rush, "that you don't have to stay. I'll have Harrison figure out a way for you to break your contract if—"

"Hey! Slow down! I never said I wanted to leave, alright? The offer is flattering. And... okay, tempting." More than I'd like to admit, really. "But I'm happy, Cec. I'm excited about this new part of me, I love working with Oscar and Ezra but if you tell Ezra I said that you're getting one of those cheese and salami gift baskets for every birthday for the rest of your life."

"I'm lactose intolerant."

"Exactly. But no, I'm not leaving."

Not yet. I didn't think.

"Okay," she said slowly. "Fuck, I need to go soon and meet with Tamara and Peter about this bullshit defamation suit Jacob's trying to make stick. But listen, about the Oscar situation... Maybe you need to talk to Lisa."

"Lisa? I was thinking Heinrich."

"Lisa," she said firmly. "Heinrich went through nearly the same sort of meat grinder as Oscar. He was Violet's bestie. He might *think* he's giving you helpful insight but it's going to be pretty much Grandmere-lite. Lisa's going to have a different perspective, different suggestions."

"I'm not comfortable with that," I said flatly. "She's a nice woman but—"

"But it was just a suggestion," CeCe said, exasperated. "And I thought you realized she was nothing like her TV persona. Shit! Look, I gotta go. I'm calling you tonight, alright?"

We said our goodbyes, and I hung up, groaning as I stretched out my legs and let my aching hip relax. I hadn't accomplished a damn thing since leaving Oscar in the study. Grabbing my cane, I shoved to my feet, determined to tell Oscar that, as 'fine' as he claimed to be, I wasn't going to leave him alone all evening.

Not when this place didn't feel safe in the slightest.

"Doctor Weems," Sandra called as I reached the foyer.

Shit. "Yes?"

"I'd like to bend your ear again, if I may? I have some more thoughts regarding part of my monograph. Since you've seen *Rites and Rituals*, you might be in a position to help me smooth this out."

She was smiling hopefully, and I almost hated to turn her down, but not enough to actually give in and ignore Oscar just for the sake of politeness. "Ah, well, my area of specialty is in burial practices and—"

"And that's perfect," she cheered, smiling so big her face looked unreal. "You might be able to help me fill in some of the gaps I've found. I'd credit you, of course."

"That's very kind, but maybe this can wait till after my vacation with my boyfriend is over? We're really here to relax and spend some time together."

Her smile dimmed a bit, became sharper as she folded her arms and glared at me. "Are you saying you don't miss being able to speak with a peer about your area of expertise? Sharing intelligent conversation with an equal, someone who has actually made something of themselves rather than gone the path of least resistance?"

The snap of my temper was damn near audible. Her refusal to take no for an answer, her insistence on getting me on my own... Her pressure was a violation, and I was done being polite to keep the peace. "Sandra," I snapped, "that's uncalled for. Move out of my way!" I started toward her, but her hand on my chest stopped me from pure surprise more than force. "Remove your hand."

"Oscar's a very nice man, I'm sure, but you're wasted on that show, Doctor Weems. You belong in research. I've read some of your work. It's brilliant. Your thesis on the symbolic necrophagic rites in rural America was inspired."

Words literally failed me. I was torn between *you read my thesis* and *what the actual fuck is going on here.* Before I could muster so much as a peep, though, the study door opened and Oscar stood, glaring at Sandra, lips twisted in a disappointed scowl. "I think that Julian is fully capable of deciding what he is and isn't suited for, Ms. Cochrane."

"Oscar, hey," I started toward him, my heart lightening. "I was coming to find you."

"Doctor Weems," Sandra interrupted, "I have a laundry list of things I need to do this afternoon. I just need a few moments of your time."

"Just a few?" Oscar asked blandly. "Are you willing to give up a few more minutes of our holiday, then? I suppose I'll just go wait quietly in the corner?"

"Oscar, what the hell? I'm not—"

"Thank you," Sandra barked. "We won't be but a minute."

Oscar threw up his hands. "I'm going to walk into town, get some fresh air."

"Oscar—"

"No, it's fine, Julian. I need some time to be uninspired. You enjoy chatting with Sandra."

"Goddamnit," I muttered, pushing her hand away. She shrugged, giving me a tight-lipped smile. "Oscar!"

The front door closed firmly in his wake and Sandra sighed. "He'll be fine. The storm's hours away. He needs to blow off some steam. Now, let's talk business."

Annoyance spiked hot and hard in my stomach. "I'm afraid I don't know anything about running a B&B," I said. "So, I'm not sure what kind of professional matters we could discuss." I huffed a breath, closing my eyes for a moment before turning my gaze back to her with a tight, apologetic smile. "I'm sorry. That was uncalled for. It's been… stressful, lately."

Rage darkened her expression for a heartbeat, then she jerked her chin again and her bland, polite lines were back in place. "I've been writing something about Honey Walk and Broken Palm Island. The unique history of the place and how it came to be, despite the challenges the colonists faced trying to form their society here."

The grip of my cane dug into my palm to the point of pain. I wanted to use it to force her back but, you know, assault laws. "Please move out of my way."

Her glance flicked down to my hand on the cane, then back to my face. Her smile sharpened. "Just a few questions, Doctor Weems."

"Christ. What are they?"

"Are you familiar at all with the witch trials of Winnsboro County, South Carolina?"

What the fuck? "Only in the loosest of senses. That isn't my particular area of expertise, but I recall they occurred over a century after the more infamous witch trials in New England, and they were about sick cattle."

She nodded. "Four people were killed after being accused of witchcraft."

"Well. That's tragic and terrible. But I'm not sure I can be any further help regarding that particular topic."

"Think of that as a warm-up."

I found myself moving back into the room almost without realizing it—she leaned toward me and I stepped back before I could stop myself. Planting my feet and cane, I took up space until she edged back a fraction. "I'm not in the mood of a quiz, Ms. Cochrane. If you don't mind?"

"Your specialty is death and burial customs and rituals, particularly in the American South."

"That's not even a question." She was stalling me for some reason, and it was not a good one whatever it was. Panic started to seep in around the edges as realization dawned that she was trying to keep me from going after Oscar. "Why can't I leave?"

She ignored my question. "I ask about the witch trials because I'm curious as to whether you've seen any burials of alleged witches in your research, and how they compare to the Tibbins' burials here on the property."

I blinked. "The Tibbinses were accused of witchcraft?"

"No, but they weren't exactly witches. They'd have been accused, though, if anyone outside of Broken Palm ever knew."

Thunder rattled the windows hard. Deep in the house, something crashed just like we'd heard two nights before.

Sandra didn't bat an eye.

"What are you getting at?" I demanded. "Move or I'll—"

"Call the police? For asking you questions? You're not being a very good guest, Doctor Weems. Though I've heard how well your previous hotel stays have gone. That poor man in Colorado, and that show you recorded in New York." She made a face like something smelled foul. "It all seems so... suspicious."

"That's not what happened," I snapped. "I don't know who you're talking to, but a simple search online will show you that's a gross misunderstanding of what happened."

"Ms. Cochrane," I said slowly, firmly, "I don't know what you're trying to do here but I'm concerned for your wellbeing." Not entirely untrue—she was being misleading, asking nonsensical questions, being aggressive... "Now. Please move."

She shook her head, grinning, and stepped back with her hands held out to her sides. "You're not being held against your will, Doctor Weems. I just wanted to talk, professional to professional." Her smile was sharp, angry as she backed away. "I can see I misunderstood your interest in this work. I'll leave you to your afternoon."

Before I could think to ask her about using the van or getting a ride into town to find Oscar, she was gone, the back door slamming in her wake.

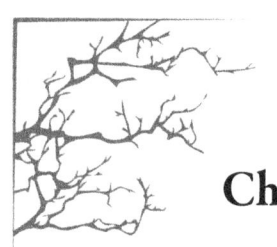

Chapter 5 – Oscar

I'm sure I looked ridiculous, speed-walking into Rosie Sands, but I didn't care. Anyone passing me on the road might think I was a ghost, I mused, dressed as I was and moving so fast. The thought gave me a bitter twist of amusement as I strode toward Delia's Café, one of the few businesses open on the main street aside from the grocery and Pirate Pete's. The others had boarded up in preparation for the hurricane, and I had no doubt many of the shopkeepers and residents had taken advantage of the last ferry run before the storm to go to the mainland for extra safety. Not all of the homes on Broken Palm were sturdy, centuries old beasts.

Delia glanced up as I stepped into the café, her scowl close matching my own. "I'm about to close."

"Ah." I stopped short. "I'll just—"

Ray-Don blustered into the café, pushing me forward out of the doorway. "Hey there, Dee. Lemme get a burger and fries. Been boarding up shit up and down the road all day and I'm starvin'. What're you having, Oscar?"

"Oh, she's closing, I thought?"

Delia gritted her teeth when Ray-Don laughed. "She's open till six! Who told you that?"

"Oh, must have misunderstood," I murmured. "I'd like a cinnamon roll, please. And tea, if you have it."

"Got coffee."

"Alright, then. Coffee."

Ray-Don chortled, elbowing past me to lean on the counter while Delia ducked back into the kitchen. He didn't seem interested in talking to me, instead calling out to Delia the details of his morning, expounding on this shop or that house, who was ready and who was being, in his words, a damn fool.

I closed my eyes, resting my head against the back of the booth as I waited for my sugar and caffeine fix, the exchange between Julian and Sandra playing ad nauseum in my thoughts. *Is that how it'll be whenever he meets someone from his milieu? I'll be the joke, odd little man who talks to invisible friends.*

"This island is cruel to the dead."

Opening my eyes, I sighed. "Virginia."

She was still washed-out pale, even more so now that she was away from her perpetual path along the beach, but anger or something like it sparked in her eyes. For a moment, I thought I could see their true color, a deep brown like coffee or damp earth. "This island is cruel to the dead, and it will count you among our number if you persist in your foolishness."

"Are you warning me off?" I murmured, curious. "It sounds like you're warning me off. About what?"

"So many of us are waiting for our turn to cross," she rasped. "But we're caught here. Because it was unnatural, what happened to us. We weren't ready. It wasn't time. We were *stolen*." The overhead lights flickered and the chime over the door wailed a sound like a dying robot cat. "I can't stay." She sighed, fading a bit more. "But you're strong, Oscar Fellowes. They talk about you; they whisper your name. We all do. And this island will be as cruel to you as it was to us."

Fucking dramatic ghosts. Christ.

"Here ya go." Delia dropped the plate with the singular cinnamon roll in front of me then sloshed a cup of dark, burnt-smelling coffee beside it. "You know I think you're full of shit."

"We've barely met," I said pleasantly. "Usually, it takes people at least three visits before they come to that conclusion. Well done, you."

She glanced back at Ray-Don, who was watching us curiously. "You're not going to stir shit up on this island, Oscar Fellowes. We got enough mess to deal with as it is, outsiders coming in and thinking they know us and can tell us what to do. Fuck. Off."

"What the actual fuck?" I muttered, staring after her as she stormed back to the kitchen. "We're not here to do anything other than have a vacation!"

"Ignore her," Ray-Don urged. "She's having a bad day." He saluted me with his glass of water. "Enjoy your treat there, Oscar, then get back before it's too late, hear?"

"This entire town is a shit-show," I muttered, taking a long sip of my coffee and grimacing at the bitter taste. "Fucking hell."

Ray-Don lingered at the counter, eating his burger with a deliberate slowness that made me think he was waiting to see what I would do, where I was going. So, I nibbled my roll, sipped the terrible coffee, and just to be contrary ordered a second cup. Delia brought it with a bit less ire the second time, setting it in front of me and muttering an apology about a stressful day. She was back in the kitchen before I could reply.

The second cup was no better than the first. I barely made it halfway before the acid reflux kicked in hard. *Perfect. Shitty mood, shitty coffee, shitty esophagus. Wonderful day all around.*

And I was a shitty boyfriend there, wasn't I?

Acting jealous of Sandra wanting to talk to him... Where had that come from?

No, that was a ridiculous question. I knew exactly where it'd come from. It was because I felt so easily dismissed by Julian at that moment—and a few others. But... But had it been dismissal? Or just my stunning sense of inadequacy that came with not knowing how to navigate the so-called normal world. The world where people didn't regularly talk to the dead and did things like have conversations about common, non-dead interests.

I knew the answer, and I didn't like it.

I closed my eyes and tried to focus, to will myself to get back up and head to Honey Walk before the storm that was brewing offshore came along. The thought of returning just then was anathema—I didn't want to face Julian yet and running into Sandra would either end in bloodshed (imaginary, purely in my fantasies) or... well, frankly, me sulking in the bedroom. I might be bold as brass with spirits but with the living? I hated confrontation. Ezra tended to take the lead when it came to that facet of our lives.

The damn door chimed again and the two teens—Kelly and Marilla, tumbled in on a burst of wind and dampness.

Ray-Don hefted himself from the stool and, cutting a hard glance my way, stalked over to Kelly. "Get the boat tied down? What about the lockers?"

Marilla sighed. "Mom says we gotta get back. We just wanted to drop off your keys."

"I still got you till five," Ray-Don scolded. "Your mama knows that. Now go get the shit tied down or you ain't getting paid when I sell the lot."

Kelly hesitated, glancing at me as if he wanted to come talk. I was relieved when he groaned and acquiesced, stomping out with Marilla. Ray-Don nodded to me, adjusting his cap as he headed for the door. "Remember what I said," he called to me as he opened the door to the windy street. "Not a long time left."

Delia's stares made me distinctly uncomfortable, so I paid my tab and left a generous *please don't poison me next time I order food* tip and headed out onto the pavement. A few intrepid tourists from the other end of the island, judging by their sporty get ups and a few t-shirts emblazoned with *Tibbins Quay Gold and Sport Fishing Excursions*, milled around Pirate Pete's, looking at the specials posted in the window: *Hurricane Sale! Get it now before it all blows away!*

The storm was impending, but people seemed to be at the excited, thrill-seeking stage just then. Afraid of what would come but feeling bold enough to exercise a little hubris, apparently.

Though I had little room to talk. I was out for a stroll as the storm inched closer, risking life and limb because I had hurt my own feelings over my boyfriend having a different area of interest than me. Maybe 'risking life and limb' was an exaggeration—I kept checking for updates on my phone and so far, all forecasts were for Nelson to only glance the area and keep moving, not settle in for some movie-level destruction, but still... I glanced at the weather app I had open again and frowned. *Does that little swirly symbol look closer or am I just freaking out? Or both?*

Maybe it was the mulling about history and Julian's (former?) line of work that led me to the museum, but I only know I found myself on the front steps before I realized where I was going. A cheery faux-gaslamp glowed near the door and a small sign read *Open... for now.*

A crackle of lightning gave me all the impetus I needed to duck inside and hope I wouldn't be immediately kicked out. "Hello?" I called softly. "You have a visitor."

Nothing save for the sound of the rain picking up again outside.

The lights were dimmed in the entrance and, beyond that, all seemed dark. *I should go,* I thought, turning to let myself out. Before I touched the door, an overwhelming feeling of exhaustion came over me and I let myself collapse onto the bench beside the stairs, barely able to keep my eyes open. "This can't be good," I muttered. "Shit."

It was like falling asleep in a blink. One minute, I was wide awake and the next, I was watching the dream unspool. A man I recognized as Jeremiah strode into the museum's foyer, a man nearly his equal in size rushing forward to meet him. They argued, their words muffled as if they were behind thick glass or I was under water, the distortion making it hard to tell tone or content. Judging by the way they jabbed fingers at one another, though, at how red-faced they were red-faced and their necks were bulging, I knew it was terrible.

And I knew, without having to see it happen, someone was going to die very soon.

Even as I thought it, the man Jeremiah was arguing with lurched toward the table under the massive portrait of three dogs and a deer, snatching up a letter opener and slashing at Jeremiah. The fight was brief, surprisingly so, and Jeremiah fell to the floor, eyes wide and expression one of great offense.

The man who stabbed him staggered back, shook his head and bolted. The scene dissolved and a soft voice beside me murmured, "My husband was afraid we'd be banished from the island. Or worse, he would be and then I'd be alone."

"Eliza?" I whispered.

"No... I assume you mean my grandmother, Eliza Noonan. I am... was, maybe... They called me Darla."

As I looked at the misty shape, she took on more definition. Not much, but enough to see she bore a resemblance to Eliza's ghost, though she looked different enough not to mistake the two of them on sight. "My husband," she said, gesturing toward the sight of Jeremiah's dead body on the floor. "He lashed out in anger when Jeremiah Tibbins sold the parcel down the way. I told him it was no matter, that we'd still have our home, our little corner of the island. But some of the others were furious with him, furious for allowing others onto our island. For letting them close."

She sighed and for a moment I smelled seaweed, burned wood, and something cloyingly floral. "He was so afraid, my Terrell, but when the others knew what he'd done, you'd have thought he was a conquering hero." She turned to face me more fully then and, for a moment, her appearance slipped. She wasn't a fresh-faced young woman from more than a lifetime ago. She was dead, corrupted, her eyes milky-blue and sunken, lips black and split. Then she was wholesome and smiling once more. "This island isn't kind to the dead," she murmured. "I can't show you much more. But you needed to see. To understand what Jeremiah Tibbins is about, especially as he has his sights on you to help him take what we denied him."

"What do you mean, what you denied him?"

Her smile was grim in her pretty face, dark teeth in rotting gums set in the milkmaid complexion. "His lifetime. It was only fair," she added, her voice a watery waver. "It was only fair! He ruined our livelihoods! We had a *chance* and when he sold that land—" She coughed, choked on something her spectral form remembered from her living one. "He said it was to help the island, that we were doomed without outside money coming in, but he was wrong. Terrell told me so and he'd never lie to me. Terrell was… he was a smart man," she finished, staring off at something I could not see as her form melted like sugar in hot water.

A tremendous bang startled me awake. The lights were off in the entryway, and I was alone in the dark, no longer even remotely sleepy. "Hello? Who's there?"

"I should be asking the same," Ray-Don muttered, lumbering into view with his toolbox in hand. "I came to batten this place down for the duration."

"I wanted to see the museum before it was closed," I extemporized. "I suppose I was more tired than I expected and accidentally dozed off."

He grunted. "You're one weird dude. Come on. I'll drive you back to Honey Walk." He stood aside to let me pass and I couldn't help but notice the cloying floral odor that clung to his clothes. "You sniffin' me?"

"Allergies," I muttered, hurrying my steps as a worm of fear started nibbling away at my calm.

Chapter 6 — Julian

If there had been a way for us to safely leave the island right at that very second, I'd have taken it and swallowed the cost, the guilt, and the anxiety.

We were unsafe, and I couldn't put my finger on the exact nature of the threat, but I knew it came from Sandra.

I kept myself ensconced in our room, trying Oscar's phone at intervals but receiving no reply. *Maybe I should call Ezra. Fuck, no, he's on his own getaway and Harrison would have my hide if I got Ezra riled up and ruined their week. CeCe? Shit She's neck deep in her own problems right now.*

... Lisa?

No, god, what am I thinking. The stress is getting to me.

I didn't have long to dither over who to reach out to because my phone chimed with an incoming call. **Unknown Number** flashed on the screen, but I answered it anyway, thinking it could be Oscar calling from someone else's phone or even CeCe calling from a hotel or something.

"Doctor Weems?"

"Er, yes?" *Please don't be the police. Please don't be an ER.*

"This is Jim Tomlinson at UUC. How're you today?"

"Ah! Jim! Hi there. I'm," I hesitated. "I'm on vacation for the rest of the week," I finally said, not technically a lie. "I decided to take my boyfriend to Broken Palm after hearing you talk about it."

"Oh, damn, and that hurricane and all..."

"Well, to be fair, that wasn't on the map when I reserved a stay at Honey Walk."

"Honey Walk, huh? So, how's Sandra doing?"

Something about his tone, a little too casual and curious, made my hackles rise. "You know Sandra?"

"Mmm. She used to work here." He paused, then in a carefully casual tone, asked, "Is she doing okay? Her departure wasn't exactly on the best terms, and I've wondered how she's holding up."

Those hackles were well and truly raised now. "Wait, she worked there? Y'all aren't trying to get me to take her position, are you?"

"God, no. She worked in research applications mainly, taught a few classes to meet university requirements. She was a fantastic researcher, really great with getting into the meat of things. But when her partner passed away suddenly..." He trailed off. "Well."

"I... well, I can't imagine but lord, how terrible. So, she took a leave."

"Er. No. She was strongly encouraged to take some time to heal," he said, his cadence telling me he was repeating a scripted line the university gave regarding her absence. "She went off the rails, frankly. Look, we're all about researching paranormal shit here, you know? But she threw herself into some ethically questionable research." He paused and, on a sigh, admitted, "Necromancy mainly. She got obsessed with some niche cult practices and... Well, she started getting a little *too* Stephen King for the university's liking."

My thoughts were spinning so fast I was surprised smoke didn't come out of my ears. "*Necromancy?*" was all I could muster after a moment's sputtering. "Jesus..."

Jim sighed again. "How's she doing, really? We still worry about her. The department tried to reach out to her not too long ago, but she had some very, ah, pointed things to say regarding her enforced leave of absence and several of our mother's more personal habits."

"She's very intense," I said diplomatically. "Intense and taciturn."

"Huh."

"Hey, you didn't call for us to talk about Sandra," I said, trying to shake off the creeping dread that was wrapping itself tightly around me. "How can I help you?"

"Well, the powers that be are *really* pushing for you to do this damn interview," he chuckled. "They seem to think I can sweet talk you into it."

"Jim..." I paused, uncertain how to go on. I didn't want to burn that bridge but at the same time, I wasn't anywhere near ready to leave the show. Or Oscar.

"Look," he said, "don't answer me. Think on it. And if it's no, it's no. But if it's no, just as an FYI, there are other options. Research openings come up all the time, especially if you come to us with something we haven't seen before."

We made small talk for a few more minutes and finally he had to go. I hung up, a weight pressing down on me as I shoved my phone in my pocket and grabbed my cane.

I opened the door to find her glaring at me from the other side. "Oscar's back," she snarled. "He's in the study. I told him not to track the water on the carpets. Take him down a towel and some clothes."

She turned and stalked away, leaving me to follow her orders and hurry down the stairs.

Oscar was waiting, already having shed his coat, waistcoat, and cravat, shivering slightly by the banked fire. "Hello," he murmured.

"I'd throw myself into your arms, but I don't think that'd work well for either of us," I said. "Towel?"

"Please."

He started to dry his hair, wincing as the curls sprung wild and free. "Fantastic," he muttered. "Now I'll look deranged on top of everything else."

I reached out and gently tugged one damp curl. "It's cute."

He glared at me as he shed his shirt, but it had no real heat to it. "I'm annoyed with you, and I shouldn't be."

"Ah?"

"Mmm. I've convinced myself you're going to get tired of being with someone who barely got any A levels. You're going to miss academia and you're going to resent me for holding you back."

"Do you really think that about me?" I asked, barely above a whisper. "Oscar, have I done something—"

"No," he burst out. "Yes. Maybe? I don't know. No," he said, tossing the towel aside and shedding his pants and underwear without preamble. "Hearing you and Sandra talking, it stung, alright? Seeing how excited you got about the things she talked about, how eager you were to just jump in there, help her with her monograph..." He sighed, clutching the dry boxers I'd brought down to his chest. "Maybe I was envious she could share part of your life that I'd never understand. And I felt... inadequate. Disposable, even."

My heart *ached*. "Oscar, no... I mean, look, there are things you know and do that I'll *never* be able to be part of. No matter how many years I work with you, I'll never be what you are, know what you know, do what you do. And there will always be that line of demarcation I can't cross. And do I hate it? Hell yes. But it's just something we have to acknowledge. We're not the same people and I think I'd be miserable if we were, you know? I love *you*, not in theory or conditionally. I love you. As is."

He sniffed, eyes wide and shining as he stared back at me. "This is very *Bridget Jones,* isn't it?" he suddenly asked.

"Oh lord. Please tell me I'm Darcy and not Daniel."

"Definitely Darcy," he agreed, and tugged his clothes on quickly so we could kiss in the open study.

"This is not the place for that," Sandra snapped from the open door. "Respect this space if not me, damn it!"

She pulled the study door closed behind her and, a few moments later, the sound of clattering and slamming pots came from the kitchen.

"What," Oscar said slowly, "the hell was that about?"

I gave him a brief recap of the odd encounter outside the bedroom, wondering if maybe she'd overheard my call. He listened, his frown growing deeper with each passing word it seemed. "Maybe she is really socially awkward," I allowed, "but I've been around dozens, if not more, socially awkward people in my life—hell, I am one—and the encounters have never left me feeling threatened like that one did."

Oscar shook his head. "I don't know what's going on but I'm not feeling great about staying," he admitted. "I'm sorry. I know you planned this getaway for us and—"

"And we can have a do-over later, somewhere maybe a little less... fraught. I'll feel better when we're back on the mainland."

He nodded. "I doubt we'll be able to leave with the hurricane though."

"No, not till it passes. And even then, only if it's not done too much damage. If the dock is trashed..."

Oscar huffed a tired sigh. "My dearest, we are *hell* on hotels."

Chapter 7 — Oscar

Ray-Don arrived just after we'd finished dinner. He pounded on the door to be heard over the storm, not letting up even once. When I opened it, he startled. "Expecting someone else. You look... different," he said distractedly. "Like you changed up something. But"—he shrugged— "it's been a long day. My eyes are tired, ain't what they used to be. I need to close up the hurricane shutters. Might be some bangin' sounds but it's just me. Didn't want to scare y'all." He held up a metal toolbox and gave it a rattle. "You got supplies? It isn't supposed to be too bad but if we're cut off from the mainland, that means no grocery runs for a day or two and I'm already closed up for the duration."

"We're fine," I said, hoping it was true. "Um how do you know it's not going to be a bad one?"

"'S only a cat two," Ray-Don sniffed. "Gonna go right over us, if we're lucky. This island's been here forever. It ain't goin' anywhere." He paused, then grinned. "We might, but Broken Palm will be fine."

He cackled, all too pleased with himself as he trundled down the porch to start on the set of wooden shutters I'd taken to be aesthetic only.

Julian tugged me back into the house, closing the door against the spitting rain and, after brief hesitation, turning the lock. "We need to check the supplies, make sure they're actually useful."

I followed, unable to shake the feeling of being watched. "I know you're here," I murmured as Julian rummaged in the hall closet, pulling out a large plastic tub marked *Hurricane Supplies—Box 1* in black marker letters.

"What?"

"Sorry, talking to someone else."

Julian looked up at me, frowning. "Anyone I need to worry about?"

I shook my head. No one he needed to worry about, no. Julian stared at me an extra moment, then resumed his rummaging.

A soft sigh and the sound of voices murmuring teased me, pulled me down the foyer until I reached the door to what looked like an office, but an old one. Nothing modern about it: an old desk that probably weighed more than any car I'd ever been in, dark bound books lining the walls, a blotter with yellowed paper, and an actual ink well with a nibless pen took up most of the room. It smelled of dust, age, and old paper with the barest hint of damp and some dusty floral. The voices, though, were coming from everywhere in the empty room. "Hello," I murmured. "I don't mean to eavesdrop, but you're a bit loud."

The voices stopped but a cold almost electric sensation spread up my legs, around my torso, settling behind my neck. A funny pressure wrapped around my head, and I had the distinct sensation of being smothered. No, I realized. Of being examined somehow. The pressure wasn't painful or predatory, more... curious, I thought. I didn't have Ezra's empathic abilities, so much of the nuance was lost on me, but the way the energy moved, gently pulsing and sliding, was almost calming. After a moment, it eased and the soft murmur of voices resumed.

I'd been dismissed, found uninteresting.

Fine, two (or more, as the case may be) could play at that game. My pendulum was upstairs, in our room, and I was reluctant to leave lest the spirits move on, so I walked to the desk, listening as the voices grew more agitated in tone. They were muffled, as if far away, the words indistinct but the rhythm suggesting an urgent conversation of some sort. The pen beside the inkwell wasn't just nibless, it was broken. And the well was dry as a bone.

"Honestly, I don't know what I was thinking," I muttered. "A still-usable well in a three hundred and something year old house?"

A soft click sounded and movement caught my eye at the corner of the desk. A generic ballpoint pen, the sort businesses by in gross-size bundles, was rolling toward me. White with a maroon cap, the side of the pen was emblazoned with the name and address of the Tibbins Quay Adventure Diving—*Specializing in Shipwreck Tours! See The ONLY Natural Reef in the Carolinas!* "Thank you," I said, brandishing the pen at seemingly thin air. "I'm guessing you already know what I'm about to do."

The voices fell quiet again, but the presence of the spirits were more palpable now. If I opened my awareness just a bit more, I had the impression of them standing closer. Indistinct bodies, three or maybe four spirits, playing at being casual as they paid attention to what I was doing. "You should feel honored," I said with a small smile. "I don't usually do this, but things are very strange here and I'd like to know more. And I feel like you'll give me a more honest answer than Ms. Cochrane might." Popping the cap off the pen, I took a moment to smooth the blank blotter page, age making the paper crinkle loudly in the office. "You don't need to try to take over my body," I warned. "Merely guide my hand. You'll find I'm very amenable to communication. I'm one of the lucky living who can hear, see, and interact with you, and I have spent my life trying to help spirits. So, know that I will not be afraid of you. I will not try to harm you in any way." I took up the pen as if ready to write, then held it poised over the paper.

And I waited.

And waited.

And... got very bored and annoyed.

"Look," I sighed. "There's a hurricane, which is not something I'm used to. I understand wishing to be dramatic, but might I ask you to be aware some of us do not have all of eternity?"

The voices were rushing then, a rapid-fire whispered conversation next to me. A few words were clear: *Now, best possible, storm. Time for it. Tell her.*

Well. That wasn't concerning at all.

I tapped the pen on the blotter page. From the corridor came the sounds of Julian hitting something with his cane and I hoped it was a spider and not an intruder. The heavy thuds of Ray-Don working the shutters in place thumped like a monster's pulse against the growing sounds of the storm. But the whispering voices were louder than all of that, rushing like an incoming tide right beside my ear.

"You may not need help," I said, "but if you would like to convey a message to anyone, I'm able to do it for you."

A cold prickle shot down my hand, like a larger one covering my own. My arm jerked and, after a moment's instinctual panic, I relaxed into the movement. The ghost holding my hand moved the pen across the blotter page, tightening their grasp when the ink did not come at first, jerking my hand up and down to make the ballpoint roll. The whispers were quiet again, and the ghost using me to write did not try to do anything other than move my hand. I was tense, braced for something worse, for some attempt to take more from me, but after less than a minute, they were done. Sensation returned to my cold fingers and the ghosts retreated. I laid the pen on the blotter. "Thank you," I muttered. "I have no idea where you were keeping that but here you go."

The pen gave a little wobble, but it didn't vanish into thin air or levitate away to some ghost's pencil case in the ether.

"What're you doing?" Julian asked from the doorway. A dusty cobweb decorated his hair, and his shirt looked a bit worse for wear. "Were you, ah, talking to *someone*?"

I shook my head, then nodded. "Maybe?" I glanced down at the blotter and frowned. "Julian, where's that book?"

The ghost hadn't written a message in words. Instead, it was an image, one that I was fairly certain I'd seen in the *Rites and Rituals* book.

Julian moved closer to peer at the sigil and frowned. "That doesn't look good."

A curving line over three triangles, interspersed with an X between each triangle and the next, with a twisting symbol in the middle that looked unlike any language I'd seen or heard was in the center of the page. Gingerly, Julian worked the blotter page loose, tearing one of the aged corners with a wince. "Are they still here?" he asked.

"I can't feel them. Or hear them." I paused, stretching my awareness further. "We're not alone in the house but this room is… it's empty, but it's somewhere they stay often. It feels like there's a residue, if that makes sense?"

"Like ectoplasm?"

"Nothing tangible. More like… Hm." I shook my head again. "Have you ever come into a room immediately after an argument or gone somewhere that usually holds a lot of people but it's empty when you're there? That strange feeling you get that you just missed something big?"

"I think so," he said slowly. "Maybe?"

"Well. That's how it feels when a space is haunted but ghosts aren't currently in residence. As if they've left traces of their energy all over the place."

Julian nodded thoughtfully. "This room is 'theirs' then?"

"I don't know. Not yet, anyway. I just know I followed the whispers here while you were checking the supplies—are we good there, by the way?"

He nodded. "Whoever set up the boxes did a great job. I want to make sure the rain barrels are good to go but other than that..." He trailed off. "We're alright."

Ray-Don's banging stopped, and, for a moment, we stared at one another, waiting for it to resume. When it didn't, Julian held up one finger and hurried into the corridor, leaving me to follow.

For a man with a still-healing broken pelvis, he was fast.

I caught up to him at the front door, where he was hanging half-out into the dark evening, staring at the ladder Ray-Don had left propped against the porch rail. "He's gone?" I asked.

Julian nodded. "Looks like he left in a hurry, too. Ladder, toolbox..." He stepped out, motioning for me to stay back. "I'm going to see if he's fallen or something."

"His truck's gone," I pointed out, raising my voice to be heard over the snapping wind. "Maybe he had an emergency at the store?"

Julian made a reluctantly agreeable noise in his throat. "Maybe. Let's check the upstairs windows to make sure they're secured too."

I made *him* stay back this time, going upstairs to verify the shutters were in place over all the windows I could find. The familiar sensation of being followed as I walked down the corridor made me roll my eyes and sigh. "I'm going to look up that symbol," I promised. "I'll figure out what it means, alright?"

"I already know."

Jeremiah appeared before me, solid-seeming and scowling. "I know what it means," he reiterated. "But you need to. It's important you—" He paused, glanced past me, and pressed his lips into a thin line before vanishing.

"Doctor Weems said you were up here," Sandra said, coming up the stairs at a clip. "I wanted to do a final check before the storm made landfall."

My stomach clenched in anxious fear as Sandra came into view at the top of the stairs. Compared to her earlier mien, she was positively cheerful. A small, true smile graced her lips, and her cheeks were rosy as she reached the top of the steps. It was unsettling and set off a thousand warning bells in my head. The cool brush of Jeremiah's presence settled beside me, and I fancied, for just a moment, he was trying to help me, maybe protect me.

Or maybe that was just wistful thinking because all I wanted in that moment was to *not* be stuck between Sandra and the dead end of a corridor.

"He's in the kitchen," she added. "I'm not sure if we'll lose power but it's likely, so I brought over some things that didn't need to be reheated, and the old camping kettle and coffee pot from the cottage." She stopped right in front of me and her smile grew to positively beaming proportions. "I have to apologize for my behavior earlier," she said. "I was waiting on some news and was afraid it would be bad. But," she paused, her gaze flicking over me greedily, "the news is excellent. And I realized I was taking my anxiety and upset out on you and Doctor Weems. Between my mood and my rather unfortunate tendency to just be terrible with people..." She trailed off with a self-deprecating shrug. "I do apologize. I know that I can't make up for any discomfort I've caused y'all during your say but I hope the remainder of your time is pleasant and I can at least offer my sincere apologies for any upset."

I nodded slowly. "That's... a lot," I said. "I appreciate your candor and explanation. And I'm glad your news is good."

Sandra's gaze roamed over me again and, for a moment, I wondered if she was trying to pull me, cornering me upstairs away from Julian and trying to ingratiate herself with apologies. But when she met my eyes, she darted her gaze past me, eyes widening ever so slightly. "Mr. Fellowes, as I said earlier, I looked you up after y'all arrived. I... I have to ask... Is Jeremiah Tibbins here with us?"

"I am," the man—Jeremiah Tibbins now—said. "And she knows it. She's testing you."

Sandra's face didn't change but something about her demeanor chilled just a bit, enough to notice. On the surface, she was still smiling and a bit deferential but the way she stood, the way her hands curled into loose fists at her sides... "He is," I said. "And he says that you know."

A bark of laughter escaped her. "How would I know that? It's not as if he speaks to me."

He grunted an annoyed laugh. "Sandra, for the love of god—"

"Are you fighting?" I demanded, glancing between Sandra and the ghost of Jeremiah Tibbins. "Do you two know each other?"

Sandra stiffened. "Do I know who?"

"Ms. Cochrane, I don't appreciate being tested," I said sternly. Typically, I brushed off such things, but this one felt *weird*. It was beyond *Oh yeah, if you're a medium, how's Elvis doing* or demands to tell them their dead gran's name in order to prove I really could speak with ghosts. This felt far more intimate, more exploratory.

"I'm not testing," she snapped. "His ghost is supposed to haunt this house, waiting for his lover to return, and I wondered..." She glanced past me again, her smile well and truly gone. "It's a stupid story," she muttered. "Like anyone would wait for their *one true love*, you know?"

Jeremiah sighed heavily. "For god's sake, woman!"

Oh my god, I'm in the middle of a lover's spat and one of them is dead!

"You said Julian was in the kitchen? I should check on him. His hip," I said, making a vague gesture at my own. She glared as I edged past her, toward the stairs. Jeremiah Tibbins remained in the corridor, his gaze fixed solely on Sandra Cochrane, neither of them paying any mind as I hurried down the stairs.

Julian was indeed in the kitchen, where she said he'd be. He'd made a sandwich of cold cuts and pickles from the hamper Sandra had brought over, another one sitting on a plate waiting for me next to a bottle of soda and an empty glass. "I didn't feel like dealing with making sweet tea right now," he said. "But figured we could use the caffeine boost if we're digging into that book when Sandra's gone." He paused mid-chew. "What's that look on your face?"

"You will never believe me," I muttered, taking up the seat across from him. The sound of heavy footsteps sounded overhead, followed by lighter but no less angry ones heading in the opposite direction, toward the stairs. A few moments later, Sandra strode through the kitchen without a backward glance and snapped her fingers for Lenny, who emerged from his spot in the shadows by the pantry and followed her out the back door, which she slammed in her wake.

Julian raised a brow. "Anything to do with that?"

"Okay, just... keep that open mind you've developed, alright?" I told him about the encounter upstairs, watching as his eyes widened to near comical proportions and his sandwich was forgotten.

"So, you're telling me she's dating a dead guy?"

"Well," I hedged. "A ghost, but he definitely died at some point before they started dating. Or whatever it is they're doing."

"Can ghosts do that?" he asked, face screwing up in thought. "I mean, with the living? Or, hell, with each other even?"

"I have no idea. I admit it's something that I wondered when I was younger, but I've never had the audacity to ask them."

More stomping upstairs, then the sound of something crashing.

I knew whatever it was, we wouldn't find it on this side of the veil.

"Jesus," Julian muttered. "I'd think being dead meant no more lover's spats. And how do you even get into a romantic relationship with a ghost? Is it some sort of weird crush? Like a limerence thing?"

"Limerence?"

"Mmm. Like those people who get obsessive crushes on pop stars or actors. They're convinced it's love, or some other deep connection. People experiencing it are convinced there's a connection between them and the object of their obsession, and the opportunity to prove it would make everything in their fantasies come true."

"That sounds dangerous," I muttered, popping a crisp in my mouth. "Like those people who murder their favorite singer because they didn't answer fan mail or something."

"Something like that. Usually it's not so extreme, just horribly awkward and embarrassing for the person experiencing it. But other times it can be…" He paused, turning his attention to the ceiling where the sound of creaking floorboards told us someone was pacing. "It can be a bigger problem."

Chapter 8 — Julian

The house quieted after lunch. Whatever had been creaking above us settled and the storm outside grew heavier. "At least the power's still on." I sighed, making my way carefully back down the stairs after changing into something dry and comfortable. The storm had made the temperatures drop considerably, between getting rained on and the house's already cold nature, I was shivering. Oscar gave my ensemble of a sweater, long-sleeve t-shirt, and fuzzy pajama bottoms with my thickest socks (a gag-gift from CeCe one birthday—they had her face emblazoned all over them. Joke was on her because the fuzzy material made her look like a Muppet covered in hair.)

Oscar waggled his phone at me before resuming his search. "I texted Ezra to see if he knew of any legit online sources to dig into the sigil situation, but he hasn't replied. So, I tried my own hand at it and, truth be told, I'm not as good as he is but I think I might have found something."

Propping my cane against the end table, I took up a spot beside Oscar on the sofa. He snuggled into my side and held the phone between us, open to a website I'd never heard of but seemed to be nothing but user-submitted stories that reeked of Main Character Syndrome. "This here," Oscar said, indicating one of the top posts. "They're an undergrad student at LSU doing some project on sympathetic magic and posted to this folklore board asking about sigil use. They ended up with some examples that look a lot like what we found."

I skimmed the entry, then read it again and frowned. "The response mentions something they call homebrew sigils but gives no examples."

Oscar sighed. "It's the best I could find, really. But see the picture they attached? It looks very similar to the style we saw in the book and on that paper."

He wasn't wrong—it was uneven, tip-tilted, and if I looked hard, I could see the shapes of interwoven letters.

"So..." Oscar trailed off, both of us glancing at the window as a particularly violent lightning and thunder combination made the windows rattle behind the shutters. "I don't suppose you know anyone in your academic corner of the universe that has knowledge of symbols and the like?"

He sounded both hopeful and wary, not quite meeting my eyes as he fidgeted with the hem of his waistcoat.

"Tomlinson," I admitted. "But I can start poking around on some databases, and in some academic journals."

"Tomlinson. From University of the Upper Coast," he reiterated.

"Right."

He'd said it conversationally but there was a hint of something in his tone. Hurt, maybe? Caution? I closed the book and laced my fingers with his. "Oscar, I'm not leaving."

"I didn't think—" He sighed, closed his eyes, and ducked his head against my shoulder. When he spoke again, it was muffled. "Okay, I thought maybe you might. But I wouldn't blame you, you know? You're a researcher. A scientist. And they're offering you an opportunity to return to that life."

I shifted then, ducking my face down so I could look at him, kiss him on the lips as he started to speak again. "And who says I want to?"

"I can tell," he whispered. "You're interested."

"Interest doesn't imply intent."

He frowned. "I'm being ridiculous, I know, but—"

"Stop," I murmured, stroking my fingers along his jaw. He pressed his face into my palm and closed his eyes. "We're figuring us out both as the show and as people. Things have gone so fast—"

"Are you... Is that bad?"

"No. At least I don't think so. But right now, there are things we're not going to agree on, things we're not going to understand about one another. And we may never do. But the important part is we try, and we accept that sometimes we're just going to not get it, why one of us is interested in something or believes in one thing or another."

"Like your love of that godawful mustard," he muttered, trying to lighten the weight of the moment.

"I stand by my condiment choices. And..." I trailed off, kissing him again. "As intriguing as that offer is, I can't see a way to do it and remain on the show with you, and I would much rather remain with you."

Oscar's face was warm with his blush, pressing against mine as we leaned in together for a long, quiet moment.

Upstairs, something rattled, then a heavy thud sounded again and again and again.

"Shit," I groaned, pulling away reluctantly. "The shutters!"

Oscar closed his eyes, took a breath, and marshaled himself, pushing away gently and getting to his feet. "I'll go check. I wish we could track down Ray-Don to fix it since I'm about as handy with tools as a fish."

"That's a weird analogy."

"I was going for something without hands, and it was either a fish or a caterpillar, then I started picturing a caterpillar with a wee tool belt and all those feet holding hammers and spanners." Oscar grinned sheepishly. "Rather adorable, really."

I snorted. "Go check. I'll start digging around for some ideas on these symbols."

Oscar bent to give me one more kiss, then headed for the stairs, leaving me with my laptop and the sound of a growing storm outside.

The first several searches were fruitless. Plenty of symbology and leads on witchcraft and folk magic in the region but nothing like what I was seeing with the sigils in the book. It wasn't until my fifth or sixth search, when I accidentally clicked on the wrong link, that I found a lead.

Create your own sigils! Financial security, love, happiness, success, protection and more! Simple instructions to craft your own!

"Jesus," I muttered, moving to back page but then pausing when I noticed the twisting symbol on the top of the page.

I glanced at the door; Oscar was still upstairs, swearing at the shutters from the sound of things, so I scrolled down past the eye-searingly purple and green header to the alleged article.

Hey, guys, gals, and nonbinary pals! I love love love making my own sigils and I'm always amazed when I meet other witches who think it has to be some arcane knowledge or difficult magicks! It's super simple and you don't need anything fancy to do it, but if you want to use your favorite oils and herbs it's totally cool!

"Oh my god," I muttered. "Am I about to do this? Take advice from someone who doesn't know punctuation aside from exclamation points?"

Yes. Yes I was.

So the easy-peasy-pumpkin pie way to do this is get you a piece of paper (any kind will do!) and a pen, pencil, marker, paintbrush—

"We get it, a writing implement! I bet you're the sort to post recipes with three pages of backstory before you get to the actual ingredients, aren't you?"

I scrolled down until I found the actual directions about five paragraphs later.

So this is so so so easy, guys! Write out your intention, then mark out each repeating letter. Like if I wrote Protection And Business Success, I'd mark out the c's, the u's, the s's, the n's, and the e's. Then take the remaining letters and weave them together!

The example given was so similar to the twisting designs on the sigils in the book that I had to scroll back to the top and start again. "Are you fucking kidding me?"

No. They were not.

I clicked on one of the other tabs, a staunchly academic journal geared toward anthropologists specializing in the study of magical symbolism. "Seriously, people," I muttered. "Get your shit together. I just got this from Raven Moon Goddess Pixie Pink who may or may not have a PhD but is definitely the head of the Rainbow Cloud Fey Love Coven in Omaha."

"Are you alright?" Oscar asked, pausing in the doorway with rain-damp hair and his cravat askew. "Fixed the shutter by the way. It wasn't latched properly. I don't think he even got 'round to the back of the house."

"Talking to myself," I admitted. "Come see."

Oscar headed over, letting out a low whistle when he saw the site I had open. "That's definitely an eye-catching color combination."

"Keep reading."

"Shit…"

He scanned the page in silence another few passes, then fished the folded-up blotter paper from his waistcoat pocket. "We'll never be able to sort out what they were making this for," he muttered. Smoothing the page out, we both huddled over it on the end table. "Is that an O?" he asked, tracing a particularly large loop with the tip of his finger.

"Maybe. Or a Q."

"That looks like part of an S," he noted. "Maybe a B?"

I shook my head. "The way it's drawn, it's hard to separate the letters out individually. And even if we could, that doesn't guarantee we'll be able to sort out what they were making the sigil for."

Oscar nodded, troubled. "What about the others?"

I pulled out the paper with the sigils I'd been able to copy from the book before it disappeared. "I wish I'd just thought to take pictures," I muttered.

Oscar patted my shoulder. "There, there. You know I love me an old-fashioned man."

"Oh, hush." He laughed, and I hid a smile as we started examining the first sigil on my page. "Could be an R. Possibly a Y here."

"It's a T, I think," he murmured. "Fuck me, this is bizarre."

I nodded. "I admit that I'm not extremely familiar with folk magic of this specific area, but it doesn't seem to fit the expected patterns of a developing magical system. It's like a hodge podge of things, but there's never any joining, like you'd see with a developing tradition. It's not uncommon for communities to add in bits and pieces from cultures adjacent to theirs as people marry into the group or travelers bring in new ideas, new methods of doing things, but this"—I tapped the book distractedly— "it reads like they were throwing things at this Wrecker idea to see what stuck."

Oscar smiled faintly. "Isn't that how traditions happen though? In real life, outside of the textbooks I mean. Gran likes to use these ornaments, Mum prefers that food, Dad hates fruitcake, so Brother moves out and invites the family over for a holiday with Gran's ornaments, Mum's lasagna, and Dad's lemon meringue pie, Brother's kids carry that tradition on to their families later. Nothing in the common local tradition about it but it's theirs, thrown together from a mix of likes, dislikes, finding what works..."

I sighed, tilting my head in acknowledgment. "In a sense, yes, but—"

"But," he said, leaning in to kiss me again. "Sounds like the people of Broken Palm came up with their own way of doing things."

"There's something off about it, though," I complained.

"I think," Oscar murmured, taking the book from my hands and setting it to one side, "you're focusing too much on the mundane."

"So, if I just clap my hands and believe, it'll make sense?"

He kissed the tip of my nose. "To badly paraphrase the Bard, there are more things on heaven and earth... than dreamt of in your philosophies."

"I don't think Shakespeare meant necromancy."

Oscar drew back. "No, but I think that's what we're looking at here."

My stomach gave a slow, oily sort of lurch. "When I spoke with Tomlinson last, he mentioned that Sandra was let go from her contract at the university. One of the reasons was she had become obsessed with necromancy and was using university resources to dabble."

Oscar let out a long, slow sigh. "And you're just now telling me this? Julian, it's important, in the future, for you to tell me, the *medium* who talks to *dead people* if necromancy could even be remotely involved in a situation, alright?"

I nodded. "So... Have you ever dealt with this sort of thing?"

He shook his head, expression solemn. "I've been accused of it, but mediums don't raise the dead. We just speak with the ones who are already here. I've never met anyone who could truly raise them. I—" He frowned. "I think I need to call Heinrich."

He snorted. "We'll just get a rambling story about some ghost he allegedly encountered while at Clyde's this evening. I think maybe..." He frowned at his phone. "Hm. Lisa?"

"What about her?" I asked narrowing my eyes. "Isn't she filming in California, anyway?"

Oscar smiled faintly, tapping his phone against his palm. "Yeah, Alcatraz. And I thought you liked Lisa?"

"I don't hate her," I admitted, and Oscar laughed. "What?"

"You like her. She's the absolute opposite of us and entirely legitimate and you like her."

"Maybe," I admitted. "When she brings me that really good coffee."

"Arse."

"Oh, yes please…" Oscar laughed as I went in for a kiss, unable to stop myself from smiling against his mouth. "Upstairs?" I suggested. "Further to walk but less likely to be interrupted."

Oscar nodded, and took my hand, leading me up to our room.

Sometime later during our tumble in the sheets, the power flickered, and someone stomped up the stairs. "Just the ghost," Oscar muttered against my neck. "He won't bother us."

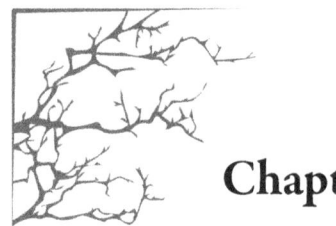

Chapter 9 – Oscar

Julian snored like a man possessed.

I was certain people could hear him over the sound of the storm.

The wind had picked up, then the rain, so loud that I worried the roof would fall in. Julian assured me it was nothing compared to what would come with the actual hurricane, effectively ensuring I wouldn't get to sleep any time soon.

When not fearing for my safety, my thoughts fixed on the sigil we'd found.

It was gone midnight, but we still had power, something Julian had seemed surprised about when he'd gotten up around an hour before to use the bathroom. "It won't be on long, I bet," he yawned before crawling back into bed. He shifted beside me, flopping one arm over his head and the other off the edge of the bed as he fought the urge to roll over in his sleep. I took the opportunity to slip out of the bed and shuffle to the armchair near the room's small fireplace. The temperature had dropped, but I was certain it had nothing to do with the weather. The snap of the chill, the way it buzzed along my skin and made my senses prickle. It was a ghost.

More than one, actually.

The whisperers, I thought. Jeremiah had been quiet since the altercation with Sandra in the corridor, and Sandra herself had been absent. So that left the ghosts who were apparently keen on having meetings throughout the house to discuss whatever spectral business needed seeing to. I pulled out the blotter paper from between the pages of the book, where Julian had left it on the side table and smoothed it over my knee. The chill wrapped around me, stealing my breath for a moment. "Do you mind?" I murmured. "I'm working here."

A soft chuckle sounded from near the hearth, and the sound of footsteps moved down the corridor.

Outside, the storm rattled on, the shutters thumping as they fought against the wind, a soft whine of branches on the roof oddly animal-like.

Tea. I needed tea.

Pulling on my jumper, I made my way downstairs as quietly as I could which was really for naught as the storm outside covered any bumps and creaks I made going down the steps. The house itself felt still, almost empty, Sandra back in her cottage and the house battened against the storm. It was cold downstairs, and only part of that was due to the weather. The whispering spirits were frantic, the soft hiss of their distant voices teasing at my senses. I hesitated, then sighed; I wouldn't be getting any tea any time soon, I imagined. The whispers were coming from the library, so I followed them there, flipping the light switch as I entered. The whispers fell quiet as the light flooded the room, flickered, then steadied. "I know you're here," I murmured. "Don't be shy."

A soft shuffling noise came from my left and I watched as two books fell from the shelf. Picking them up, I read the names on their spines. The first, a green, cloth-bound book with worn corners and faded gold lettering, was called *A Treatise on Death Rituals in Appalachian Granny Magic*. It had severely foxed pages and was almost too thick for me to hold one-handed. The other, a slim volume bound in hard cardstock with embossed lettering, making me think it was homemade, was titled *Plants, Herbs, and Other Flora of Broken Palm Island: A Guide for the Discerning Practitioner*. It was thinner than many paperbacks I'd read, the spine barely wide enough for the title's lettering.

What the hell?

"Death and gardening," I said aloud, picking the books off the floor and setting them on the end table. "I already know about the ritual. We've seen the book." I waited, listening for the whispers to come back.

They were silent, but nearby. I could feel them buzzing along my skin like tiny ant-feet. "What am I looking for in here?"

The books fell off the end table, the death ritual book open to a sigil diagram labeled *To Return To Me* and the gardening book open on a picture of those yellow flowers I'd noticed around the island that I took to be some local sort of weed.

"Look," I sighed. "I'm not very good with puzzles when I'm this tired. Give me a moment or two, yeah? We'll get this sorted."

I headed for the kitchen, unashamed to turn on every light I passed. Dark usually held no fear for me but something about the night was feeling wrong, heavy.

Grasping.

As soon as I stepped into the kitchen, all hell broke loose for a handful of seconds. Crockery pots holding sugar, flour, and coffee flew from the worktop and hit the floor, clouds of their powdery contents floofing into the air. The tea kettle rolled to one side before banging onto the floor, denting badly. The cabinet doors swung open, then slammed closed, and the rack of teacups above the stove burst into ceramic shards.

Shaking, I smoothed my hands over my pajama top and affected the most bored tone I could muster. "That was uncalled for. Very rude of you to destroy property like that."

I eyeballed the mess, wondering if I could get to the broom cupboard without tearing up my feet or I could sneak back upstairs to grab my slippers. Before I could decide, the back door swung open and Sandra loomed, glaring and wet.

"What the hell did you do to my kitchen?"

"I..." Gesturing helplessly, I was at a loss for words. "Poltergeist," I finally settled on, unable to come up with a good fib and knowing she'd see through it even if I did.

"Fucking hell. We'll deal with this in a minute. I saw the light on and figured I'd grab whichever one of you it was to help me right quick. Some of the older plants near the graveyard need tying up. The stakes I used earlier aren't strong enough and I need another pair of hands."

I hesitated, but under her shrewd, sharp glare, I nodded. "Let me grab some shoes."

"No need. Take my gumboots off the porch. Hurry up—we ain't got long."

Sandra didn't say a word as we headed down the weaving stone path toward the graveyard. I offered a quiet apology to the library ghosts, promising I'd be back soon and to wait for me.

I wondered if they were who I felt moving with us down the path, into the rainy dark. Sandra was moving fast, her flashlight bobbing with each step. It made the shadows play oddly, disorienting me as the dark grew thicker the farther into the garden we went. "Here," she finally said. "That vine there. It needs tending to."

She nudged me forward, and I nearly tripped into a small, heavily canopied circle. The rain was barely reaching the ground there, the grass practically dry.

Which, I supposed, was a good thing because a small metal brazier was glowing merrily in the shadows. Smoke so thick and gray I could see it even in the darkness poured from the flames, the smell sickly sweet. Cloying, really. It burned my eyes and nose, tickled the back of my throat. I coughed, unable to stop myself, and once it started I found it impossible to stop. Unseen hands clawed at my waistcoat, my hair, pulling at me, tugging me down to the ground as I hacked and coughed. I tasted blood as I heaved for air, the ghost-hands pulling my head back until my neck twinged in pain. Pulling on my focus, I forced some of my power out, pushing at the ghosts until they let me up. But they were still close, so near that if they'd been living I'd be covered in their breath. It was impossible to discern one ghost from another—it was a tangle of spirit and anger and fear, pushing at me even as I pushed back. Finally, they eased just enough for me to roll to my knees, gasping.

"Breathe," Sandra ordered. I motioned for her to move back, to let me get some air, but she snarled, grabbing my cravat and pulling me toward the smoke. "Breathe in!"

She jerked hard on the fabric, cutting off my air for a moment. When she loosened her hold, I gasped out of reflex, inhaling a mouthful of the bitter-sweet-thick smoke. Everything felt hot and slippery as the smoke hit my bloodstream. Sandra caught me as I sagged, my muscles suddenly week. My tongue felt too thick, words unable to form but, I realized, I was too sleepy to care.

"Here," Sandra hissed, yanking at my neck again. She pulled my cravat off and someone else started tying it around my head and mouth, keeping me quiet. "We need to move fast. Tide's going out and I need to clean that shit up inside before the other one gets up."

Stop, I tried to say. *Let me go.* But the smoke was sweet and soporific. Everything was a gray hazy cloud, cool and soft and sliding through my grasp. But for that moment, I found I couldn't care. **

I woke on the beach.

What the fuck?

"Julian? Julian!"

People moved between massive fires, spitting in the rain and stinking of kerosene. The eye of the storm, I realized. A small reprieve from the torrential winds and downpour. It wouldn't last long. I had to get back... "Help! Hello?"

Figures moved in the firelight, ignoring me.

Except for one figure. Jeremiah Tibbins approached from the water, growing more solid the closer he got.

Jeremiah was staring at me oddly, eyes wide but lips pursed. "She really did it. She really..." He chuckled mirthlessly. "Well, damn."

Shaking my head took effort. Everything felt slow and heavy, even my eyelids. Grit made me tear up, stinging my eyes as the wind pounded the beach. "We should go inside," I said. "The storm—"

"The storm's always coming," Jeremiah muttered. "It never stops. Not in this place." He turned, staring out at the ocean, lips pressed into a thin line that disappeared into his thick beard. "I can get you close to the house, but tonight, I can't come in."

"What are you talking about?" I stepped toward him, then paused. It was far easier to walk this time—the soft, abundant sand wasn't dragging at my feet, slipping into my shoes. Just stinging my eyes and spattering my face as I tried to look toward the ocean, toward Jeremiah.

He jerked his hat from his head, raking his fingers through the wild thatch of blond hair that stood up like the seagrass at our feet. "Sandra. I told her to wait, if she was so certain. That the time would come..." He trailed off, turning to look at something over his shoulder. I couldn't see whatever he was looking at, but it unsettled him and he motioned for me to move. "Let's go toward the water then."

I started walking, feeling sluggish and thick. Had I been drinking? I never could handle my liquor. Not like Ezra.

Ezra... Why did I feel sad thinking of him? Was he okay?

Looking back toward the ridge of seagrass and sand, I saw Jeremiah much closer than I expected. He had a strange light about him, a fire-lit glow that made his eyes seem dark even while picking him out sharply against the darkness of the island.

"Why is it so dark? Where are the lights?"

Jeremiah didn't answer, just nudged me forward. "Stop here. Go no further."

We were at the edge of the beach already, the shiny darkness of wet packed sand like a sheet of glass stretching out before me.

He shook his head. "It's the middle of the night. The eye of the storm is overhead now." He gestured up at the sky. Overhead, the dark clouds had thinned somewhat, making it seem less ominous. They moved in a sluggish, slow spin, a hole in the sky larger than the island. "It's time." He sighed. He turned back toward the shore and walked toward dark figures coming down the rocky slope. The fires were burning high again, three of them now, laid out as points in a triangle. In the middle, someone bent low, scraping at the sand with their hands. The figures were person-shaped but strange. I couldn't make out features, just suggestions of them. They moved oddly, too fast at times and too slow at others. My stomach clenched with nausea, bile and acid climbing my throat in a numbing burn. "Is this..."

Jeremiah paused and looked back at me over his shoulder. "You're not meant to be here. But because you stand on the line between the two sides, you were able to cross into this." He waved his hand at the dark, shifting beach. The fires moved like oil on water, the people stretched and dark shapes on the sand as they all bent and scraped and dug. "I had hoped Sandra wouldn't push for this but now that it's begun there's nothing I can do to change her mind." He made a shuddering, rasping sound that mimicked a sobbing breath. "This isn't what I wanted. Not for me, or you. Not for any of the ones before... God, I am so sorry!"

Oh god... "Am I dead?" I whispered, touching my fingers to my face, my chest, checking for some sign of life.

But if I expected to see one, wouldn't that happen? I'd encountered many ghosts who had no idea they were dead, who bled, who gasped and cried and breathed. And many who absolutely knew they'd passed but still mimicked their living states just out of habit.

So, feeling my heart under my hand meant nothing, did it?

I stared around me, my thoughts a broken jumble I couldn't sort through just yet. Everything was *off*. Like watching the world through greased glass.

Jeremiah was the only thing that looked solid, living. And that jumble started to slip into place.

"I'm not supposed to be here," I murmured.

"All of us feel that way."

"What's happening?" I asked, part of me morbidly fascinated—this had never been seen by a living person! Hell, a living person had never been on this side of the veil... as far as I knew, anyway. But the rest of my brain was in full panic mode, my body itching to flee. *Where would I go though*, I thought. Behind me was the ocean, stretching wild and dark. In front of me were the figures on the sand, working their intent into the sand.

Julian's remarks about the land spirits pushed through my tangle of thoughts, about genius loci and landvaettir and the dozens—if not more—other examples of 'land spirits.'

"Are these people?" I murmured. "Or is it the island?"

"People," Jeremiah grunted. "Very definitely people. The Wreckers, though..." He jerked his chin at the ocean behind me. "They've never been like us."

Suddenly, I couldn't stand the thought of being near the water. I pushed myself forward, that sluggish drag against each step making me ache as I moved toward the fires.

"Stop! Fucking hell, you idjit!" Jeremiah moved fast, a dark blur in the night, grabbing my arm to haul me back toward the water. "They need you," he snarled. "They need to offer something to the Wreckers and you're it! Do you want to be taken?"

"Taken *where*?"

"Wherever's past that," he snapped, pointing out at the water.

Two massive ships darkened the horizon, full-masted and round-bellied. They were shadows against the strange glow of the hurricane sky, not moving with the waves, not making a sound. Between the two of them, a bright line stretched. Shining white-green and thin as thread, it trembled as I stared at it, slowly thickening until it looked about the width of my arm. "Is that... is that the crossing?" I asked, remembering what the book called it. "Where the Wreckers come from?"

Jeremiah nodded. "I don't know what's across there, just that some of us can go easily, but others can't even get close."

"Why not?"

Jeremiah sighed. "I don't know." His grip on my arm tightened and a strange look flickered over his features. Sadness, hunger maybe. "What does it feel like? When I touch your arm?"

"What? Pressure. Not like a living person doing it. Colder than the living."

Jeremiah grunted, closed his eyes and dropped his hand. "I can't even feel that. If you go, if you let them take you... It's your body Sandra wants for me. It'd mean your death, for me to feel again. And you... would be here, with the spirits who need you." His opened his eyes and stared out at the green light on the water.

The light was a steady pale green now. *Like the tulips I had once,* a soft voice murmured next to me.

I found some for you, when you died, another voice whispered. *I hoped you knew.*

I knew, I knew...

The dark figures around the fire had stopped their work and were facing the ocean now. The storm overhead had stopped turning. Everything felt heavy, pressing down on me. The speakers on either side of me were quiet but I could feel them next to me. Ghosts, I thought, but something felt off. "When did you die?" I murmured. "What's your name?"

"Diana Gleeson," the first one replied. "I don't remember. I know I was scared. I've been waiting here for such a long time. So long..."

"Johnathan Gleeson," the other voice whispered. "I don't know either. I don't remember much before I came down here."

Jeremiah spoke from behind me. "There are others. Here so long, they're worn thin with it. They know you're here."

Diana sighed near my ear. "The storm is stronger this time."

The light between the ships was bright, blinding if I looked too long. It reminded me of hospital overheads, the glare and flicker, more white now than green. Overhead, the storm was churning, the hole in the clouds closing. "What's going to happen?"

Johnathan's low chuckle was seagrass-raspy. "We don't know."

The light pulsed, obscuring the dark ships. The waves smoothed and the water became glassy-smooth. Overhead, the hole in the clouds finally closed and all was dark.

The fires were still, fractured like broken glass against the shadowed mass of the rocky slope.

The people-shapes were watching, unmoving. I could feel their eyes on me, or maybe they were staring out at the water. I turned from the light and started toward the unmoving fires. "I don't understand what's happening. I... Where's Julian?" I asked, peering at the shapes. "He was at the house, wasn't he?"

My head ached. Everything felt like so much jelly, wobbling and homogeneous. *He hates marmalade,* the wild thought burst from that muddled tangle. *He'd appreciate the jelly, though. It's got no bits in it.*

Where is he? The shapes were difficult to discern beyond being human-like. The glow from the unmoving flames showed the occasional flash of an eye, the curve of a jaw, but I couldn't make out features. More voices, soft and thin, rushing like sea foam on sand, stirred as I neared the cluster of dark figures.

Can he see us?
Isn't he one of those? The ones that see us?
Help! Hey! Can you hear us?
Hey!
Mister! Where are we?

Why can't I find Rilla?
Do you know where my dog is? I thought I'd see him after.
What time is it? I'm supposed to be home by dark. I think I got hurt.
Mister! Hey! Hey!

They were loud, bleeding together, overwhelming me as I reached the edge of the dug-out sand.

Sobs as fragile and delicate as tissue paper drifted from over the water. Creaking, snapping canvas.

Choking gasps, thick and desperate.

I tripped at the edge of the dug-out sand. The figures tensed, moving closer together. Something was in the middle of the triangle, something on the ground.

My head throbbed, knife-sharp pain exploding behind my eyes.

Hey, mister! Come here! Down here! Hey!
Please, please! Oh, god! Please help me!

Diana murmured, "I loved my tulips. Do you think they still grow?"

"I doubt it." Johnathan sighed. "It's been so long."

The fires flared bright, moving again, and the figures were suddenly clear. Sandra, Delia, Ray-Don. A very scared looking Kelly and Marilla.

And me.

The shape on the ground was me.

I wished I was witty enough to say something sharp and cutting, something morbidly funny.

I wished I was quick enough to put it all together. But my thoughts were slowed by shock and confusion.

I lay in the middle of a sigil, one of the ones Julian had found in the book. *What was that one for?*

Sandra and Ray-Don were staring out at the water, their mouths moving and voices distant and thick. Delia was busy with something between the fires, moving from one to the other, checking I assumed, adding something to them.

Kelly and Marilla were still, quiet. For a moment, I thought they were ghosts, but I realized the girl was crying, the boy comforting her. The old man was the one who saw me. His lips quirked sadly. *Sorry,* he mouthed.

Jeremiah's hands closed over my shoulders. I startled—*I could feel him!* He squeezed hard enough to make my body ache as he leaned in and whispered, "This is harder than I thought. But also... right? I feel good again. I feel again." He laughed softly.

"Jeremiah—"

"I've been wary for so long," he murmured. "I resisted this. And suffered for it, really. But it's hard to remember *why.* Why did I try to stop them?" He shook his head, frowning in confusion. "I thought it would be awful but right now, all I know is that I can feel again. I can *breathe* when I'm in your body. And *taste!*" He shook me gently, an expression of grim wonder twisting his lips into a smile "Maybe it's time," he muttered. "Maybe it's been long enough?" His grip on my arms intensified. I bucked, struggling to get away but unable to tear my eyes from the sight of my own supine form. "I wonder if you can reach into the light, or if you'll stay with us," Jeremiah mused.

He spun me around, back toward the water. I saw Diana then, and Johnathan. Pale against the dark sky, washed out by the years. Whatever definition they'd had in life was long gone, leaving them mere smears of faded color and the intense sadness and anger that came with some ghosts—loss, confusion, envy of the living, deep and abiding grief for their own passing and the years they never got to see for their loved ones. Others were there, too insubstantial for me to see but I could sense them moving along the sand, in the near water. And they were all focused on me now.

"You're not like us," Jeremiah continued. "You're not truly dead. You're a light shining in a dark house, a candle in a hurricane." He chuckled at his own analogy. "We'd hoped your gift would remain when we pulled you free, but it looks like it stayed with you."

I swallowed, my mouth and throat dry and hot. "Julian would love to know that," I muttered. "He'd make a note in his spreadsheet, I'm sure. *Medium's powers do not remain with body but follow the spirit.* Rather like car insurance, isn't it?" I was babbling, words pouring out as if I could stop what was happening through sheer force of chatter.

"I'll be sure to tell him," Jeremiah said, then shoved me hard. I didn't fall but rather found myself being dragged forward, toward the stark white glow between the two ships. Something was moving out of the light toward us, long and thin and almost arachnid in their shapes. I tried to scream but only burning came, like I had swallowed fire.

The light swelled, a cresting wave that towered as high as the clouds and made the ships stand in stark relief against the glare. They were solid and real, not just shadows in the night. People stood at the railing, waving and calling out in silent pleas for help. Then the wave crashed down and light washed over me.

Chapter 10 — Julian

I tried not to worry. Rather, I tried not to let my worry control me. But I lost that battle quickly, mostly due to the fact the weather was worsening again as the eye passed over, bringing the dirty side of the storm across the island and Oscar hadn't left so much as a note or voicemail. When I woke at bit after seven, his side of the bed was empty and there was no sign of him in the room or bathroom. By the time I made it downstairs, I'd convinced myself he was getting something to eat, or maybe in the study, and just didn't hear me calling for him and had, for some reason, turned off his phone. The wind rattled the hurricane shutters and, for the first time in a long time, I hated rain. "C'mon," I muttered, trying his phone again

This time it went directly to voicemail.

Great. So it was either off, or he was ignoring me. Or both, I realized, since it'd been ringing out to voicemail every call until then.

Or... I hurried to the study, where he'd been charging it, getting ready for the storm. He'd laughed when I suggested ways to forget about the damn phone for a few hours.

Shit.

It was there, sitting on the end table, plugged into its charger.

Somewhere deep in the house, something fell over and a door slammed.

"Sandra? Sandra, have you seen Oscar?" I called, hobbling back into the foyer.

Of course she didn't reply. And of course the foyer was freezing. I could practically hear Oscar and Ezra patiently explaining signs of hauntings to me again, as if I'd never read a book or watched one of those ridiculous paranormal investigation shows.

I often tried to avoid thinking of the ironic parts of my life. It's historically saved me a lot of headaches.

The banging sound came again. *Fine, want to play? We'll do this.* "Hey! Now would be a great time to actually *talk* to me, you know! I can hear you slamming around!"

Silence.

That weird sort where you *feel* someone listening to you, wondering if they've been caught out.

If you've ever been around kids for any length of time, you know the one I mean.

"I'm not like Oscar, but I'm willing to listen. He's not here..." I closed my eyes, gritting my teeth against the spike of anxiety, of annoyance, of hope mingling with frustration, and forced out, "I'm worried something bad might have happened. Please, if you know something... tell me. Please?"

Silence. Silence for so long, my ears started to buzz with it. *Maybe it's my old standby, hypnogogic hallucinations. Lord knows I slept for shit last night so having a particularly vivid—*

The slap of something hitting the floor nearby made me jump. It was followed by another two more slaps, all of them off to my right within the study. It took a moment's searching to see three books on the floor by the bookshelves.

Doesn't mean anything. They slipped off.
Who are you fooling?

I limped over and gingerly picked them up, laying them out on the sofa to see the titles and covers. Both were local histories, one about flora and fauna, and one about witchcraft..

"Okay." I sighed. "If this is a hint, could you be more clear? Maybe, I don't know, muster up at least a partial body apparition, preferably the part that can communicate clearly?"

This time, when no answer came after a minute, I knew I was definitely alone. The stillness was different, less fraught and watchful. Now, it was just the quiet emptiness of being alone in a strange house.

The wind gusted again, harder this time, and I forced myself into motion. There wasn't much I could do, so I chose the least worst, most viable option and went looking for the old yellow slicker I'd noticed when checking the hurricane supplies. "If anyone wants to tell me this is a bad idea," I said aloud, "now's a great time to do it."

Nothing. Of course.

I shrugged into the slicker and found a heavy old flashlight in the tub, the big square sort people take camping or hunting. It worked—I'd checked it earlier, but I gave it another test again just to be sure—and should be waterproof, if it was like the ones I remembered my grandparents having. Something thumped upstairs, and outside the wind screeched like a banshee.

"Okay. This is fine. This is all fine. This is for Oscar. He's out there," I muttered, cringing at my sad attempts at a self pep talk. "I love him, and I'll be damned if something horrible happens to him and I'm not there to help stop it."

My leg screamed as I made my way to the door, the howl of the weather almost enough to drive me back into the study to think of another way to do this.

But the mental image of Oscar, scared of the storm, alone… It was a powerful motivator. I yanked the door open and stepped out onto the rain-lashed porch before flicking on the flashlight.

"HEY, I HATE TO BOTHER you but I'm looking for Oscar."

Ray-Don was soaked to the bone, taking advantage of the lull in the weather to check the shutters on his store. The bright orange slicker he'd put on was unfastened and hanging, useless, from his shoulders as he gave a grungy nylon rope a hard haul to test whether it was secure. He glanced at me but didn't answer.

"Have you seen Oscar?" I called more loudly, hobbling closer. The trip into town had been hell, and I knew I'd be paying for it later, but with no sign of Sandra or her van, and an absolute dearth of rideshares or public transit, walking was my only option. "He was gone when I got up this morning. I was hoping maybe you've seen him in town."

Saying it aloud, I could hear how ridiculous that was. There was a hurricane due literally any moment, most of the shops had closed the night before and only Delia's Café and the grocery still had signs of life, and Delia's was closing even as I looked, the grim-faced owner flipping the sign to closed and stepping out to pull down the metal rolling door over the glass store door and windows.

"Ain't seen him," Ray-Don muttered, not looking up from where he was tying and retying the yellow rope around a cleat that had been bolted to the exterior wall beneath the window. "You should get back to the house, doc. This is just the farthest outer band of the hurricane. We're gonna be getting the real shit soon. Ain't no way you can be walking around in that, not with your bum leg."

The door to the shop opened and that teenaged boy, Kelly, stepped out, saw me, and made a startled sound before ducking back inside. A moment later, the door opened again and a girl around the same age stuck her head out, scowling. "Ray-Don, the freezer's empty now."

He nodded. "Go on in, then. Tell your brother I'll be up in a minute." The door shut firmly and Ray-Don grunted. "Some tourists down at Tibbins Quay had that hurricane shindig down on the West Beach," he said. "Gotta make sure nothing's left behind."

My chest ached with the effort to not shout, to keep from just grabbing someone and shaking an answer out of them. "It's just that I can't find him," I said as if Ray-Don hadn't spoken. "He's not in the house. I'm worried. Have you seen him at all?"

Ray-Don shook his head slowly, focusing on that damn cleat. "Not since I was by the house."

I nodded, then paused. The unsettled feeling my gut wasn't anything as esoteric as Ezra's empathic ability or even some shade of psychic power. It was paranoia, plain and simple, and having spent many years instructing students who were always finding new ways to get out of trouble by not quite lying but being creative with the truth. "When was that again? To fix the shutters, right? Not after?"

He pressed his lips into a thin smile. "Sorry. Haven't seen him since I left." Ray-Don gave the rope a tug and nodded, satisfied. "Best get back to the house before things get worse, doc."

I expected him to disappear into the store, but he stood there, not quite facing me. Waiting for me to move. To see where I was going, I was certain.

"I'm going to check the diner one more time," I said. "Maybe he couldn't resist the idea of some coffee."

"Diner's closed. Delia's not keeping it open during a storm like this. Go on back." He made a shooing motion like I was some sort of a dog or errant child. "It's safer if you're in the house, away from everything."

"Safer for who?"

Ray-Don shrugged. "Everyone. I'm sure your fella just went down to the cemetery or something. That garden's so overgrown, you can get lost in there if you're not careful."

"I checked. And Oscar's not a cemetery wandering sort." Ghosts tended not to linger at their burial sites, he'd told me before, not unless it was a murder or a burial 'out of place' and they wanted their bodies to be found, but that was not a frequent occurrence either.

Still, he avoided hanging around cemeteries as a matter of course. *You never know when someone is feeling dramatic,* he'd told me with that small smile and wink of his when we laid in bed, talking about the ins and outs of his profession one day not long before, but what felt like eons ago now.

"I. Cannot. Help. You." Ray-Don took a step toward me with each word, until he was so close I could smell the faint licorice tang off his skin and feel the heat of his breath on my face. "Go back to the house. Wait till Sandra comes and tells you it's alright to come out."

"Fuck this," I swore. "Tibbins Quay is bound to have a radio to reach the mainland. I'm calling for help."

"How you gettin' there, doc? You done walked all this way with your game leg, you gonna walk clear to the other side of the island then?"

If I have to. "There're more people in this town than you, Ray-Don. Someone will give me a ride."

His smile was small and sharp. "You think so, huh?" He chuckled. "Get back to the house. Your fella will be back at some point."

He went back into the store, the rattle of the security gate rolling down grating and painful.

"Shit!" My scream was loud enough to startle the handful of intrepid seagulls that had come out during the calm eye, pecking for whatever they could find in the parking lot and grass.

"Julian."

The woman was soft-spoken, her voice barely above a whisper but somehow still impossibly attention-grabbing. She stood on the sidewalk behind me, just a few feet away, staring at me with a strange intensity when I turned to face her. She looked a little familiar with her wide, blue eyes and dark hair in a cornet around her head, but I couldn't place her. "Yes?"

"You're looking for Oscar," she said, smiling just a little. "Is that right?"

I nodded. My first thought—*how does she know Oscar?* —was replaced by the realization she must watch the show or maybe just saw an interview with him somewhere. "Have you seen him?"

The woman smiled slightly, sadly, and turned to walk away.

"Wait! Damn it!" No matter how fast I walked, she was faster. She moved down the sidewalk toward the gate to Virginia's Walk with a speed that *should* have been a run but gave the impression of being just a regular saunter for the woman. She moved farther, faster, until I couldn't even pretend to try to catch up to her. As she passed Virginia's Walk, she paused and glanced back at me, gave me a small wave, and vanished.

"The fuck?" I shouted, not caring if anyone heard me. Hell, let them—it was a great summation of my feelings. A low rumble of thunder pushed my decision-making process, and I sighed. Honey Walk was just a bit farther ahead of me, and it would be beyond dangerous to keep running around the town while a hurricane was nearly on top of us, and no one knew where I was. "Goddamnit!"

I pushed on, fat drops of rain pelting down harder as I followed the path of what was likely the least helpful ghost ever in the history of dead people. As I neared the house, a flicker of motion caught my eye and I paused.

The porch light had just come on.

Someone was there! If it was Sandra, I would beg and cajole her to help me search for him. Hell, I'd even offer to read her damn monograph and offer advice if it helped. But if it were Oscar already back at the house... Well. I was torn between wanting to shake him and wanting to throw myself at his feet and meep piteously until he promised not to disappear like that again.

Wow. Stage five clinger alert. Awesome.

The last several yards to the door were painful on any level I could think of. I hesitated before pushing the door open, expecting the house to be empty after all, the light to be a figment of my imagination.

A panicked thought occurred to me—what if Oscar didn't want to be found? What if our disagreements were actually too much, and he was just done?

No, I thought fiercely. He wouldn't just walk off. Not Oscar. He'd want to have it out, to let me know... No, he was missing because something was keeping him from returning. Something was in his way otherwise we'd both be back at Honey Walk, safe and dry and waiting for the storm to pass.

I was saved from my dithering by Ray-Don, who flung open the door to glare at me. "Took you long enough, Doc."

"Did you make me walk back here when you could've *driven* me?" I demanded, my voice a near-shout. "What the hell?"

He grunted, shrugging. "You didn't ask." He stepped aside to let me in, as if he owned the place. It was through sheer force of will I didn't wallop him with my cane as I passed. The only thing that kept me from rounding on him was the sound of Oscar's laugh from deeper in the house. "Oh, thank god," I breathed, the words hitching on a dry sob. "When did he get back? Oscar!" I called.

Sandra appeared in the entry to the kitchen area, scowling as she approached me. "He's having a shower to warm up. He'll be down shortly."

I was shaking with relief. "Oh, god," I repeated. "Pardon me, I need past."

"Now, Doctor Weems," she said with the barest hint of a snide smirk. "I think it's best for you to go up to your room for a bit and let Oscar be. He's had a rough day and is very tired."

Something was definitely wrong—she was pressing in like a shark scenting blood. "What's going on? Oscar?" I called. "Are you alright?"

"He can't hear you, Doctor Weems," Sandra chided. "I've sent him to my cottage to use the shower there and get some rest. He's a mite unsettled about you, it seems. All that fuss earlier, he didn't take it too well."

"You don't know what you're talking about. Let me past."

"Now, Doctor Weems," she soothed. "Let's not go making folks upset. Wouldn't be good to start something up now, would it? When you ain't go nowhere else to go, and no way to get there even if you had?"

I looked between the two of them, all but hearing the slam of jail doors in my head. "Right," I nodded. "So. Upstairs, then."

"Just for now," Sandra said with a tight, fake smile. "Until things are... better."

They watched me go the entire way, and I had a strong feeling they'd be watching my door once it closed behind me.

Chapter 11 — Oscar

"I feel like I'm in a fluorescent bulb," I murmured, the glare of the white light sizzling along my neck and down my spine. It had begun happening faster, these flashes of light and change. Everything crackled for a moment, like standing in a ball of lightning, When the light faded, a cluster of tall, spidery shapes stood around me, shadows moving in the dark of Grandmere's library. The vast room that had been my grandfather's domain in life and kept as unchanged as possible after his death. It had been the single concession to lifelong mourning my grandmother allowed herself, the preservation of his favorite room in the exact state he'd left it the day he died.

But this version of the library was different—these figures had never been at Grandmere's home.

Wreckers. The name popped into my thoughts and burned there, but I pressed my lips tightly shut against speaking it aloud.

One of them detached from the others, slipping down the floor-to-ceiling shelves (*the section where he kept almanacs and local histories,* I noted distantly, wondering if I could read one or if it would be like the tea and biscuits, or would it be different because this was a real place, and I wasn't a real ghost yet). It moved toward me with a disjointed grace, stopping just a few feet away. I couldn't make out a face or any features other than spindly limbs and an elongated torso, nowhere near human but far from much else. It was considering me, I realized. Something about its posture, its stillness.

"They called you Wreckers," I said into the quiet. "Like the pirates."

The Wrecker shifted, a shudder moving along its limbs. I thought it might be laughing.

"Julian thought you might be like... oh, damn it, what did he call you? Genius loci. Landvaettir. That sort of spirit?"

The Wrecker didn't move, but it felt watchful. Waiting. Not threatening but curious.

"I've never had experience with a spirit like you," I said. "Only... the dead."

The other Wreckers moved forward as one, the shapes coalescing into one shadow before flattening, spreading out and becoming people—or appearing like people. A half dozen stood in a semi-circle before me, vague of feature and form, shining with the white of that light that had been dogging me. "We're one and the same," the Wrecker closest to me murmured. "Spirits of land, of flesh, we're all the same. The vessel changes, but we do not."

I blinked, stifling the urge to laugh with nervous energy. "Is that so? I've never heard that. I was under the impression the two things were different."

"Why should we be?" they said, gesturing at their cohort. "We've been part of the ether for longer than we weren't. It was our decision, long ago, to stay, to become part of the world rather than leave it."

The library seemed solid enough, real enough. I reached out to touch the spines of the nearest books, the memory of the smooth leather making my incorporeal fingers tingle. "Why the ships? That's you, isn't it? The ships?"

They nodded, then paused. "Some of us," they said. "I think... most of us." They turned toward another of their group and a silent communication passed. "Some of us have been there far longer. Created, perhaps? Or just so long gone that it is impossible to differentiate our existence from our departure."

"I'm not dead. Why am I here?"

"Because you came into the light, crossed the veil," they said patiently. "Some living might see hints of it, perhaps a faint shimmer here or there. And many humans can see spirits, communicate with some of us."

Another of the Wreckers spoke then, their voices like soft bells over the rush of seawater. "But you're closer than most. You're already on the precipice between the two states of beings." They lifted their hands, moving them as if weighing something. "Life, and death. It is part of you, more than in others we've seen."

"Is that why I'm able—"

"In part," the first one cut me off. "But others are able, too. You, though. You're closer to us than others. It's strange."

I realized, belatedly, their mouths weren't moving as they spoke. "Is this what happens when we die?" I whispered, something pulling on me, making me want to move, to fold in on myself. *My but the gravity is heavy out today...* "The light I saw, that I keep seeing... If I were truly dead, when I entered it—"

"No," the first one murmured. "It is different for all. Your spirit is only one part of your being but it is a secret part, even from the rest of you. Your ideas of the afterlife are small. Crossing into the light doesn't remove you from the world of the living. It merely changes your perspective. Your accessibility."

The second one seemed to nod. "Death is part of you, Oscar Fellowes. It is tangled into your very spirit. Not because you are a medium, though it is likely why you are such a prolific one. It is something else. It makes you more like the ghosts you speak to than not."

"What?" I jerked back at that notion. "I'm nothing like a ghost. I'm... Well, on a good day, I'm not having this conversation while my body is on a beach in a hurricane. But I'm definitely not dead enough to be a ghost."

The first Wrecker laughed, raspy paper over rough stone. "Think of it as a puzzle, Oscar. A puzzle for you to sort out before you run out of time." They were shifting again, pulling apart to become their spidery selves. Conversation over.

"Wait!"

They paused and the first one moved back into the human shape. "How do I fix this?"

They shook their head. "We've witnessed this for over four centuries, Oscar. A blink in our existence but a seemingly unending span for the living. When the first of them called to us, we were curious. Those of us who were there, that is." A soft rattle of chuckles raced through the Wreckers at that. "We aren't gods. We aren't all-seeing. We are merely very old."

I teased out the memory threatening to hide away from me. "Julian... The book he found. It said people summoned you to help them? When they lost someone... They were raising the spirits of the dead. And calling on you to assist them?"

The first one shook their head. "No. Not like that. We have been called by them, but what they do has nothing to do with us. We're not magical beings, Oscar," they chided gently. "But that doesn't mean the abilities they're using do not exist. Much like yours run in your family, and Ezra's in his."

"Ezra," I murmured, a faint pang of longing unfolding in my chest. "How do you know him?"

"You spoke of him, with Julian." They tilted their head, spreading their hands wide. "We're tied to the island, Oscar. We're part of everything there, even when we're quiet, when we're visiting our resting places, or just in the light of the ether. Your strangeness called to us, and we were curious."

"So you eavesdropped?"

"As you say."

The light began to brighten. I was leaving again, or maybe they were leaving me. "Wait, why are you here? With me, specifically," I added. "Just to tell me you're not the one helping the islanders do what they're doing?"

They regarded me with a cool, lengthy silence. The second one finally spoke. "In all of my time in the light, as a Wrecker to use the islanders term for us, I have never seen one like you. The very fact you survived what they did is singular."

"Others haven't," I muttered, a statement rather than a question.

"Just so. You're curious, in many senses of the word, Oscar Fellowes. And you may not remember anything about us when you return, if you return—"

"Thanks for the vote of confidence."

"But if you do, we hope it is the first thing you learned from us: spirits continue, the vessel merely changes."

"And your vessels? They're in the shipwrecks off the island?"

"Some of us. But others, no. There's no application process to be part of us, Oscar. We don't do background checks."

I snorted softly. "What do I do now?"

They shifted away, spreading out, elongating, returning to the shadows of my grandfather's library. "Find your way back."

I LINGERED IN THE LIBRARY for minutes, hours, days. Time had no meaning where I was.

And I startled myself when I realized I didn't care. I could stay here, just wandering the library until I grew tired of it. Then maybe see my old flat, scare the new tenants.

See Ezra—Even as the thought crossed my mind, I felt myself pulled, moving frictionless through a nameless space until I saw Ezra, sprawled on a generic hotel bed with a box of chicken wings open beside him. He was naked except for his socks, his feet resting on Harrison's bare chest.

Harrison, thankfully, still had sleep pants on.

I'd never be able to look him in the eye if I saw his junk, even if I was an almost-ghost when it happened.

Ezra picked one of the wings out of the box and sniffed it. "I think this is the habanero one. You want?"

Harrison made a face. "My indigestion is still trying to murder me after that ghost pepper chip bullshit you had me try. All yours, hon."

Ezra did a happy wiggle, and I knew it wasn't because of the chicken wing. I moved closer, drifting almost, not trying to walk but somehow moving all the same. The world outside the hotel window was dark, lit by strands of white faerie lights and wrought-iron streetlamps. *Ezra always loved New Orleans,* I thought. *I hope Harrison shows him a good time. One of us should enjoy their romantic getaway with their boyfriend...*

Ezra made a startled, pained noise and I turned to find him staring in my direction, eyes unfocused but definitely aware. "Oz?" he whispered. "Fuck, fuck, fuck. Nope, no. No. I won't allow this, you arsehole! Oscar Michael Fellowes, what the fuck is happening?" As he spoke, he scrambled to his feet, his nudity ignored as he stumbled toward where I stood. He passed through me, the sensation uncomfortable but not painful.

Harrison sat up, frowning. "Ezra, what's going on? Talk to me, baby. Take a breath!" He scrambled to his feet, tossing his tablet aside and grabbing Ezra by the shoulders. "Breathe with me, baby. In, two, three, four, hold—"

"Stop, stop!" Ezra twisted away, spinning to face me again. "He's here. I can feel him." He jabbed his closed fist at his own chest. "I can feel him in the room. Like a... Like when someone is... Fuck! Harrison, I need to call Oscar. Where's my phone?"

"You might not be able to get through," he said gently. "The storm—"

"Pick up, pick up, pick up," Ezra muttered, phone pressed to his ear, staring at the spot where I stood.

"Ezra," I said. "Can you hear me?"

He dropped the phone.

"Okay," I said. "Okay. This is good. Good news all around. Ezra! Shit!" I surged toward him as he buckled, eyes rolling up and body bowing. Harrison caught him, lowering him gently to the floor and positioning him so he would be safe while he rode out the seizure. It was an eternity wrapped in a few minutes as Ezra's body and brain worked against one another and Harrison split his attention between Ezra and keeping an eye on the time, phone clutched and ready to call 911 if the seizure didn't abate soon. Finally, Ezra's body relaxed and his eyes fluttered and opened.

"Oscar..."

"I'm not dead," I said hurriedly. "Just... kind of almost a ghost?"

Ezra let Harrison sit him up, leaning against Harrison's chest as he finally pinned my location with his gaze. "Do you promise me you're not dead? Is this like an Enoch thing or something?"

"No, it's just... A weird story," I sighed. "Very, very weird."

Harrison shook his head. "Baby, I don't know what the fuck is going on but I support you."

I laughed. "Definitely keep him around."

"That's the plan," Ezra murmured. "Now. Talk."

TO HIS CREDIT, EZRA had always been excellent at rolling with the punches.

Even when they packed a hell of a wallop.

"Right," he said after the second retelling, where he actually sat and took notes. "Okay. First things first. Call Julian."

Harrison waved his phone between his fingers. "Already tried. No service in the area, apparently."

I drifted closer to Ezra and he shivered. "Sorry," I muttered. "Still getting the hang of this."

"Hopefully you won't need to fully grasp the nuances of being a ghost because we're figuring this shit out."

"Can you try Julian again?" I asked. "I don't know if he even knows..."

"Still not connecting." Harrison sighed when Ezra asked him to try again. Harrison had no idea I was even in the room, just accepting Ezra's word on trust.

Goddamnit, I missed Julian.

"Can you, I don't know, go to him?" Ezra suggested gently. "See if he's okay? Like you came to me?"

I hesitated, frowning. "Possibly? Earlier, I just thought of you and here I am. But I've been thinking of him, too, and nothing."

"Try," Ezra suggested. "And if you don't come back..."

"I'm not dead. I promise."

He nodded, frowning. "I'll keep trying to call him and sorting this shit out," he sighed. "Harrison?"

"Already working on travel plans."

"Don't ruin your break just because—"

"Just because my best friend is a living ghost? Really, Oscar?" Ezra demanded. "Think that through."

I snorted softly. "Right. Just don't rush into anything alright?"

Ezra huffed. "Remind me later to kick your arse a little, alright? You're cockblocking the hell out of me."

"So the chicken wings were foreplay?"

"Don't judge our sex life."

Harrison glanced up. "Do I even want to know?"

"Not especially," we answered together. I closed my eyes then and... had no idea what to do.

Ezra was looking in my direction expectantly. "Well?"

"Well," I huffed. "I have no idea!"

Harrison was staring at Ezra like he was the most fascinating thing on the planet. "What's going on?"

"Oscar can't go to Julian."

"Why?"

"Yeah, Oscar. Why?"

"If I knew, I wouldn't be standing here getting verbally abused on what is possibly the worst day of my life!"

"He says he's having a bad day," Ezra relayed, a tiny smirk playing at the corners of his lips.

"I said more than that!"

"It's your word against mine, mate."

Harrison sighed, shaking his head as he laid back against the pillows. "I'm glad that, even in a crisis, you two don't change."

I shot him a double digit salute, though neither of them could see me.

After five more minute so trying, I was feeling worn. Not tired, just less substantial somehow, like the first day after a long illness. "I can't," I muttered. "Either I'm just not doing this right, or something isn't letting me."

"Possibly because you're not an actual ghost, just... displaced," Ezra suggested.

"Possibly," I allowed. "Has Harrison had any luck?"

Ezra relayed the question and Harrison answered me directly. "I'd have let you know, Oscar."

"I know, I know." I sighed.

"He knows, he knows," Ezra mimicked though not unkindly. He hesitated before adding, "Ozzy, maybe... We need to ask for help."

"We?" I huffed, exasperated beyond measure.

"We. I'm not letting you do this alone, you twat!" He shoved to his feet, starting toward my general direction before stopping mid-step. "Damn it! How can I hug you when you're incorporeal?"

I reached out, letting my fingers brush against his arm. He shuddered, closing his eyes and pressing his lips into a tight line before he gasped on a choked-back sob. "Stop that. It's freaking me out," he muttered.

"How do you think I feel?"

He shook his head, eyes still tightly closed. "I hate this, Oz. You're not supposed to be... ghosty and shit! We're supposed to be ghosts together, okay? In like ninety years!"

I nodded, though he couldn't see me. "We've got plans, yeah?"

"Yeah."

"Guys, I hate to interrupt but have you considered maybe calling in some reinforcements for this?"

We both looked at Harrison, who was now fully dressed much to Ezra's disappointment. Ezra had gone as far as putting on pajama bottoms but insisted that, even in a time of crisis, he was going to be comfortable. Harrison spread his hands in a *Well?* Gesture. "Like who?" Ezra asked. Then, "Oh! Oh, yeah, you're right... Oz—"

"I can only think of two people," I sighed. "And I don't want to bring either of them into this."

"Three," Ezra said with a small, pleased smile.

"Lisa, Heinrich, and... Jesse?"

Ezra shook his head. "Nope. Enoch."

"He's a child!" I cried. "He's, he's..."

"He's the most likely to be able to reach Julian or know someone who can," Ezra said. "And he's older than you were the first time you had to reach out to the other side, yeah?"

"We have very different abilities. He's in a bad place. He's not ready to do something like this."

"Sounds more like you're projecting, Oz," Ezra murmured. "I think Enoch would know best when it came to what he's able to do and ready to do, don't you? Besides, didn't you say he knew others with his ability, too? If he can't, maybe he knows someone who can."

"And bring even more people into this?" I groaned. "I don't know—"

"Ozzy, how much of a choice do we have?"

Harrison broke in then, a softly voiced warning. "According to local reports out of South Carolina, Broken Palm Island is one of a handful of locations without power or cell service right now. It's expected to be restored after the hurricane passes but they're not sure how long after. Anywhere from a few hours, given the small size of the area, to a day or two."

"Fuck my life." I sighed. "Alright. Let's get hold of Enoch."

And all it took was saying his name, thinking of talking to him, and I was gone.

Chapter 12 — Julian

The storm was still going, maybe weakening a bit, and I was alone in the room I meant to share with Oscar. Between the thunder and the sound of those damn hurricane shutters flapping loose, I couldn't hear, couldn't think, could barely keep from screaming in frustration, fear, and rage. My phone had no signal and despite the little voice in my head telling me I could do it, I knew walking to Tibbins Quay, even without my leg the way it was, would be one of the worst things I could do in that moment.

So think it through, dork.

My inner voice sometimes sounded like CeCe and it was both motivational and annoying.

*What **can** you do? You can't walk to Tibbins Quay. You can't call out for help. So stop obsessing over those. Focus on what you can do.*

Dork.

This would be easier if I was actually talking to CeCe, I thought, scrubbing my hands over my face. "Alright. First things first. The house isn't safe," I muttered, dropping to sit on the edge of the bed. Ray-Don and Sandra were aggressively odd, hiding something and acting like I was the enemy.

Which, depending on what they were hiding, was a possibility.

Oscar was not Oscar. Was he drugged? Concussed? Pretending?

Or was his earlier spell what he thought it was? Someone borrowing his body?

"That's not possible," I muttered, then paused. "Then again, I didn't think Reggie was possible until last month. Hey, Reggie, now would be a great time to visit. I need help."

Nothing. Not even a drop in temperature. "Asshole. Love you, though. Mean it."

I waited for an hour, maybe a bit more, until the house felt quiet. I didn't hear anyone moving around but then again, they could've been tap dancing in the hallway and I wouldn't have known. The storm's eye had already passed and now, the worst side, the 'dirty' side, was slamming over us and making the wind howl outside like a living thing. It would only be a matter of hours, most likely, till it passed but that still felt too long. Even then, it would still be causing havoc with debris, swells, and God only knew what else. *Play dumb*, I decided. *Play dumb and act like you're not worried about Oscar at all.*

I made my way back down the stairs with careful steps, stopping when I heard Ray-Don complaining just inside the study. "I don't know why you need me to help," he whined. "Soon as the storm lets up, you know it's prime time for me to head out there and start pickin'."

"I need you to help me," Sandra bit out. "Jeremiah, a little help here?"

Cold fingers gripped my throat, my stomach.

My heart.

I'm hearing things. That has to be it. I had too many painkillers. Maybe I fell in town, hit my head. Maybe I'm having a stroke. They did say that was a possibility, even this far out after a head injury. A clot is cutting off oxygen to part of my brain. I'm dying and my synapses are misfiring wildly and this is all part of my death throes.

They suck. I'd rather have something dramatic and definitely not this.

"I think we're fine without him. All he does is bitch," Oscar muttered, though the cadence of his words sounded wrong. Not like his usual speech pattern. Too slow, the words almost thick, like he didn't know how to navigate the shape and space in his mouth to make words happen.

"Christ," Ray-Don muttered. "I wish you'd put him in the closet or something. This shit's creeping me the fuck out."

Oscar unfolded himself from his spot on the sofa and stretched, sighing. No—Jeremiah sighed in Oscar's body. My stomach clenched hard, and I closed my eyes. *It's not him. It's not him. He's safe somewhere. He has to be.*

He had to be because if that was someone using Oscar's body, violating Oscar's body... A scream clawed at my throat as I watched him move toward Ray-Don with Oscar's legs, Oscar's sway of the hips, but without Oscar's grace. Without Oscar's *presence*. It was indefinable but something was missing. He looked, sounded, and moved like Oscar but one look could tell me whoever that was, they weren't him.

He was a shell, filled up by the wrong spirit.

Oscar's voice, slurred a bit as Jeremiah tried to navigate Oscar's voice, cut through the room. "Ray-Don, it takes two people. One to prepare the sigil, the other to prepare the body. This," the sound of a hand hitting bare skin, "is temporary. We need the final passage tomorrow, as the tide goes. Or don't you remember how to read?"

Ray-Don grunted in annoyance. "I'm just sayin'. He ain't fightin' you. The Wreckers opened up the light. We all saw it. He's gone. You don't need me a'tall!"

Jeremiah made an annoyed sound and Ray-Don muffled a yelp. "Christ, Jeremiah! Why you hittin' me?"

"Because you're useless, Ray-Don. You care about that ridiculous dream of treasure more than this. If this finally succeeds, don't you know what that means for us? Immortality, of a sort. Replacing the vessel when it breaks like so much pottery."

Oh my god. This is unreal... I sank down to sit on the tufted bench under the coat rack, sending up a silent prayer of thanks that we were not filming an episode here. *The clusterfuck would enter epic proportions,* I thought with a wild urge to cackle in panic. Instead, I slipped to my feet and made a bit of noise, stopping at the study door like I'd just come down.

Because I learned all my stealth tricks from old detective movies.

"Sorry," I muttered, sticking my head in. Jeremiah stared at me from Oscar's eyes, annoyed and wary. Sandra and Ray-Don just scowled. "I was thinking of making some sandwiches for dinner. Are y'all hungry?"

"No," Sandra snapped before anyone else could answer. "Get your food and go to bed. You need rest."

"Oscar," I said, smiling a hollow smile in Jeremiah's direction. "Want your usual?"

He nodded, the wariness fading just a little. "Please. I'll be up shortly." I nodded and backed out of the room, pulling the door behind me. Heading to the kitchen, I made enough noise to let them know I was in there, then waited. When no one came, I closed my eyes and took a breath. "Look," I murmured, "I know I'm not really cut out of this but I *have* had some run ins with a few ghosts this year. If you could, I don't know, have some pity on me and help me?"

In my pocket, my phone vibrated, startling a yelp out of me. Fishing it out with shaking fingers, an unfamiliar number flashed on the screen. Normally, I'd send it straight to voice mail but beggars, choosers, etc. "Hello?" I whispered. "Who is this?"

"Julian!" Lisa sounded far too cheerful for my crisis. "What's up? Oscar's not answering. I tried calling earlier and—"

"And," I hissed, "help! My phone's had no reception till literally this second. Listen to me, okay? Don't talk, don't joke. Just listen."

Lisa blew a raspberry at me. "Fine," she said. "You got five minutes. I'm about to go talk to the ghost of Al Capone a-fucking-gain."

"Oscar's been body snatched and I need to get his spirit back in his body."

She was quiet for a long moment. "Okay, just a sec. I'm gonna tell them I got cramps."

I was back in the bedroom with the door locked behind me by the time Lisa came back on the line. "I don't know how much time I have," I whispered. "They probably don't realize I've got reception, and I don't know how long it'll last."

"Walk me through this, alright? I got my brother Jesse on messenger right now. He's good at this sort of shit. Reads a lot and yada, yada, yada. If you weren't dating Ozzy-bear, I'd totally set you two up. You'd have a huge library and wear matching sweaters and argue about Proust or some shit while living in your happy gay cabin in Kentucky."

"I... Thank you?"

"No problemo. Now. Talk."

I hit the highlights, and Lisa listened quietly, tapping at her keyboard as I spoke. "And right now this taking a strong turn for some Bly Manor shit so if you have any ideas," I trailed off.

"Bly Manor? Wow. Dig into the classics, why don't you? I would've said maybe *Invasion of the Body Snatchers* or something. I mean, *Turn of the Screw* is cool and all but nothing like what you've got going on there."

"Lisa," I rumbled. "Focus."

"Julian," she mimicked. "I can multitask."

"Oh my god."

"Just a sec. Jesse's thinking. Okay, he says you need to make a sigil and put it on Oscar. Well, on his body. Seriously, dude? That's it?" She tapped on the keys some more. "He says Occam's Razor."

"Tell him he makes sense."

She grunted. "Well. I was gonna say the same thing. Cut 'em with a razor until they reverse the magic."

"That's not what Occam's Razor is."

"I know, but I like it when your voice does that high pitched disdain thing. Shit, I gotta go but listen, talk to me as soon as he's back, okay? Tell him I'm kicking his ass for scaring my Julie-boo."

"What the actual fuck," I muttered. "Lisa—"

The call ended and I swore again under my breath before switching to the text app to get in touch with Ezra with a quick summation of what Lisa and Jesse had suggested. Ezra's reply came just a minute later.

Do it. Not like we're swimming in options here.

And just after that, one more line. *He'll be okay. He's Oscar. He has to be.*

JEREMIAH CAME TO THE bedroom as the trees outside beat against the house, flexible palm trunks making them whip and creak rather than break. It felt like monstrous hands were trying to rip the walls away and for a wild second, I was almost glad Oscar wasn't hearing this. I rolled onto my back, feigning waking as he slowly approached the bed. "Sorry," I muttered. "Couldn't keep my eyes open."

He nodded. "Sleep is precious." He paused, eyeing the bed warily. "Sorry," he murmured. "I just remembered I need to brush my teeth."

I let out a harsh breath as Jeremiah hurried to the bathroom in the hall and I grabbed the folded piece of paper with my sigil on it. A twisted design of letter distilled from *This is Oscar Fellowes' body and you do not belong here.*

This would be a two-fold approach, I decided. If I used the right kind of pen, I could make the sigil almost like a stamp by drawing it on paper then pressing it to his skin. And if he came to bed in his clothes, I'd slip it into his pocket, I thought. If he was in his underpants, I'd slip it into his shoe while he slept, so it would be under his foot all day tomorrow.

It wasn't a perfect plan but it was all I had.

Jeremiah came back a few minutes later and hesitantly stretched out beside me, stiff and quiet.

So the big man is having a bit of a freak out from sleeping next to lil' ol' me? Good. Suffer.

"Goodnight, Oscar," I murmured, tugging the blankets up to my chin.

"Night," he grunted.

Neither of us slept for a very long while. Finally, his breathing slowed and deepened. I shifted to my side and waited. He remained still as I slipped my hand closer, thanking the powers that be that he wore trousers and not sleep pants or Oscar's underwear. I slipped the sigil into the pocket and... What next? Would it be instant? Did I need to say words? Was Jesse full of shit? How could it be this simple?

I hesitated and, grabbing the maker I used from the nightstand, carefully, slowly drew the same sigil on the curve of Oscar's ass showing where the trousers had slipped down a bit. He'd never see it there, I thought, and if the paper didn't work, maybe that would.

Jeremiah didn't stir. There was no flash of light, no sudden waking where Oscar looked up at me from his own eyes.

Just the snores of a man I didn't know in my lover's body.

"Oscar," I whispered softly. "Oscar, please be okay. I love you. Be okay."

I don't know how long I laid awake but when I opened my eyes, the sky was a wet dove gray and the bed beside me was empty, save for the paper with my sigil on it spread out and torn into pieces and a dark smear where the ink from his skin had rubbed onto the sheets.

Chapter 13 — Oscar

"Mind your tea, Oscar. That shirt is French linen and will absolutely stain."

"Yes, Grandmere." I set my teacup down gently on the saucer. Not gently enough, though—Grandmere shot me a reproving look as the China rattled together. Heinrich made a soft, quelling sound in his throat and she sighed, turning her attention to him instead.

"I've heard from Michel's cousin," she said, picking up a thread of conversation that happened before I arrived. "She wishes to visit."

Heinrich cut his eyes to me and pursed his lips. "Does she now?"

"Don't give me that tone, Henry," Grandmere sighed, exasperated. "You know my feelings on the matter."

"I know what you said but the fact you're mentioning her wish to visit tells me that you're not as settled on your decision as you like to pretend."

"*Tch*."

I was only half-listening, intent instead of slipping another biscuit from the plate before Grandmere noticed. Heinrich, bless him, nudged it just a bit in my direction when he reached for his own cup.

If Grandmere noticed, she didn't comment. I smirked, plucking one of the bourbon creams from the plate and hiding it under the edge of the second-best saucer I'd been given (Grandmere was *not* about to risk her China on a ten-year-old's clumsy fingers) as Grandmere adjusted the position of her gilt-handled teacup atop its matching saucer. "Charlotte has been a thorn in my side since before I even accepted Michel's proposal," Grandmere said coolly. "I don't wish to cast my lot in with her, no matter what she thinks her family is owed."

Oh, this was getting good. I slipped the biscuit from its hiding spot and palmed it, intending to engage in some forbidden dunking while Grandmere was distracted. Heinrich snagged a shortbread from the plate and dunked with a laissez-faire attitude I could only dream of emulating—he was impervious to Grandmere's cool stare and curled upper lip, popping the soggy shortbread in his mouth with a pleased smack of his lips. "You're being a bit of a bitch, you know."

Ohmygod!

Grandmere merely rolled her eyes, fidgeting with her cup again before tucking her hands into her lap with a grimace. "Michel knew how I felt about the entire *situation*." This time she was the one who cut her eyes at me.

I froze, bourbon cream halfway to my tea.

What happens next?

I don't remember.

Wait... did this even happen?

Light flared bright, white blurring out everything. A raspy, breathy sound left my throat as I tried to claw at my eyes, whether to block them or clear them I wasn't sure. But the light disappeared as quickly as it flared.

Grandmere was playing her piano in her dimly lit music room. We were at the house in Hertfordshire, the one that had belonged to her side of the family and not Michel's. Not something they had purchased together, either. The place was a rambling pile of different eras and smelled of orange wax, old books, and decades of strong tea steamed into the very wood and carpet around us.

Homesickness like I'd never felt slammed into me, knocking the wind from me as I watched her fingers—older than at tea—move over the keys. I didn't have to see her face to know that her eyes were closed.

"When I was a young girl, I dreamed of being a concert pianist."

Grandmere still played, but she was also beside me now. She looked different from when I'd known her in life. Her hair was still gray but more steel than snow now. Her face still bore lines and a few wrinkles but they weren't as deep. "Are you wearing pink lipstick?" I asked, oddly delighted to see such a bright color on her after years of only knowing her bare-faced or in what she called *mature shades.*

"Am I?" she murmured, her hand coming up to touch her lips but stopping before making contact. "Well. That isn't very surprising. I was happy here. This," she gestured at herself from the bright pink of her lipstick to the surprisingly figure-hugging dress and sparkling high heels she wore. At the piano, Grandmere played on in her green silk bathrobe, oblivious to the conversation behind her. *"Etudes-Tableaux* by Rachmaninoff."

"You used to play that to warm up," I recalled.

She smiled, watching herself play. "Ever since I was young. Drove my instructors spare with that one." Her smile was the same as the one I'd known but different as well. Softer, maybe. Less tense.

"Grandmere, where are we?"

"I'm dead," she said, shrugging. "You are less so. I must say, though, I don't know whether to be impressed with your audacity or disappointed by your temerity."

"Why not both?" Ah, there was the Grandmere I remembered, in that pinch-lipped frown. "I don't know what's happening," I admitted. "I was having tea with you and Heinrich a moment ago, and before that..." Where had I been? *Light, so much light. Sand? No, that doesn't sound right. Hertfordshire doesn't have a sandy beach like that. Someone was mad. Tulips?* One word popped out, sharp and clear. "Wreckers," I muttered. Grandmere raised her brows. "That word. Wreckers. I was... with them? No, that feels wrong."

"*Really*, Oscar." Grandmere sighed. "Focus, child. Focus on your abilities. You're allowing fear to cloud your natural instincts and powers."

I frowned. "I'm not *trying* to be afraid! What the hell is going on, Grandmere? You're dead, I'm..."

"Most certainly not dead," she supplied flatly. "And that is a problem, Oscar." She turned to face me more fully, the music she was still playing swelling louder until my ears ached with it.

Then, silence.

The white light was back but this time I wasn't alone. Grandmere stood with me, a blur of shape and color until the light turned off and we were at the home where she'd mostly raised me. Standing in the study, beside the freshly laid tea cart. "Now, Oscar. You pour," she ordered, taking up the armchair nearest the cart and gesturing for me to get on with things. She looked like the her I knew best—snowy hair, age lines around her mouth and at the corners of her eyes with a hint of exasperation in her movements. "Now, you've been complaining that I've kept things from you and hobbled your development as a medium. Don't," she said, raising one finger when I opened my mouth, "bother to deny it. Heinrich is a talker, and I'm not entirely ignorant of your muttered words thrown in my general direction."

She glanced at the tea service, then at me with a pointed tilt of her chin. Years of practice kicked in and I started pouring out our tea, doctoring hers the way I knew she preferred: no sugar, a single slice of lemon, no joy. She watched as I added several sugar cubes to my own tea and sighed when I clinked my spoon by accident. "There's no use reminding you that you're not a child and adding so much sugar to tea ruins the taste."

"No use at all," I agreed.

"Hmmm." She lifted her cup and sipped, closing her eyes. "I wish," she said as she set the cup down soundlessly, "I could taste. I remember what things taste like, mostly, but there's something to be said for being able to experience the sensation."

My own tea tasted of nothing. It felt like nothing—no heat, no liquid, just a cup of air that looked like milky, sweet tea. "Is this how the afterlife works for you?" I asked, setting my cup down with a pang of disappointment. "Shifting scenes, tasteless drinks, changing faces?"

Grandmere sighed, pinching the bridge of her nose between her fingers as she marshaled her thoughts. "This is not truly the afterlife," she said after a long moment. "Though I'm quite dead. You're not, however, and cannot cross the veil no matter how hard you throw yourself at it."

Shoved being shoved someone shoved me... Jeremiah. Jeremiah pushed me. Ships, dark ships on a storm... Wreckers. Wreckers, Wreckers, Wreckers.

"Wreckers. I remember Julian said they weren't ghosts..."

"Tell me what happened, Oscar."

"Wreckers. Jeremiah Tibbins pushed me at the light. The Wreckers were emerging from it."

"Where are you, Oscar?"

I glanced around the room. "Here. With you. Having air for tea and pretending like I don't want to scream and rip my hair out in panic and frustration."

"Where. Are. You."

Beach. Fires. People watching. Help, help...

"I'm not dead," I repeated slowly. "But I'm here... My... I'm on the beach. At Broken Palm. There was a storm I think..."

Grandmere set her cup down and gently dabbed at her lips with what I knew to be a linen napkin, at least when the room was real. "And?"

"And what?" I felt like I wanted to panic, like my breath should be coming in gasps, my heart racing but the sensations that came with having a body were distinctly lacking in my current state.

Maintain now, panic later.

That had been one of Ezra's favorite things to say when we were in school and it was exam time. Maintain our composure during recitations. Don't panic during the pen and paper portion. Go back home and scream into our pillows.

Seemed like a solid plan now, as well. "And," I said slowly, wrapping my fingers around the teacups handle and feeling only the memory of its texture against my skin. "And I'm scared," I sighed. "What's happening, Grandmere?"

She nudged the plate of biscuits toward me. "Take the bourbon cream. It was your favorite."

"Was?"

"It might have changed since I died," she said pointedly. "It's not as if you've had me for a visit since then."

"Grandmere, is now really the time for this argument?" I sighed. The bourbon cream was another ghost, the taste tantalizingly close but more like a faint itch in the back of my mind than an actual experience.

No wonder so many ghosts were in piss-poor moods. This would drive me mad if it were my eternity.

Grandmere made a disapproving noise.

"I said the loud part quiet and the quiet part loud?"

"Mind your manners, Oscar. Don't embarrass me."

I shook my head. "Thank you, probably. For the biscuit," I clarified.

She sniffed. The room pulsed, wavering around the edges, and she sighed again. "This isn't my home, Oscar. And you're not dead. This place will reject you as soon as it is able."

"Are you really you, Grandmere? Or is this... Am I imagining this?"

She didn't reply. Just picked up her cup and took a delicate sip before nodding at me to do the same with mine.

The cup didn't shatter when I slammed it onto the table, but I wished it did. "This is a nightmare. All of it! Julian and I were—"

Grandmere looked at me expectantly.

"Julian. Is he..." I trailed off, trying to remember. "I think I left him at the house, where we were staying. How long have I been gone?"

"Contrary to popular belief, we have better things to do than monitor every moment of the living's existence."

The room pulsed again and Grandmere set down her cup far more gently than I had. "We've wasted too much time with our posturing." She sighed. "I don't know if I'll be able to pull you back to me again in this place."

Everything felt like it was vibrating, the sensation of a heavy lorry trundling past my small flat's window. "What do you mean?"

"Just what I said, child! Where we are, it's not for you. It's barely even for me." She looked up as the room shimmered and melted slowly into the image I held from my parents' photo: the golden-lit porch steps, the summer-washed garden. Grandmere made a small sound of surprise, pressing her fingers over her lips before she gathered herself and resumed her air of cool control. "I know this place as well, though I never do come here."

"It's a memory of mine. Of a sort. A memory of that picture of Mum and Dad."

"No, this is real." She stood, the chair she'd been in vanishing back to the parlor I assumed. "It just hasn't changed much since they died. Here." She held out her hand to me. When I didn't take it, she rolled her eyes. "Oscar. Really."

"Sorry. Just you haven't tried to hold my hand since I was about nine."

"Well. You were a very self-sufficient child."

"Because I had to be," I muttered, following her to the porch. She dropped her hand and shot me a glare but didn't comment any further. "Is this where we take a Dickensian turn and you walk through walls, expecting me to follow a la *A Christmas Carol?*"

"Populist drivel," she muttered. "Dickens should never have attained the level of popularity he did. He was a terrible, cruel man who abandoned his wife and children." Grandmere glanced at me and rolled her eyes. "What? I'm allowed to have opinions on things outside of your experience of me."

"I know—"

"Do you though?" She pressed her hand against the door, and it appeared to open but the image was blurred—it opened under her touch but stood closed at the same time. "Come inside."

Hesitantly, I followed her through the blurred door. We were in a small entry way, barely big enough for the coat rack and the cluster of dusty boots by the door. If we'd been corporeal, we'd be bumping into one another. "I don't remember this place outside of the photo," I admitted.

She nodded. "You wouldn't. It was theirs before you were born."

"Then why are we here?"

"You tell me."

I looked around, staring at the dark staircase leading to the second story, the dimly lit sitting room beyond the entryway and shook my head. "I don't know."

"We go to where we have attachments," she said. "Do you remember that lesson?"

"Ghosts are attached to places, occasionally to a person," I repeated the words from my childhood, one of the first things Grandmere ever explained to me about hauntings. "That's why Henry VIII doesn't suddenly appear at the Brooklyn Zoo or The Gray Lady of Wroxham Hall remains on her staircase."

She nodded. "And you, for some reason, have an attachment to this place. A place you've never been in life."

"I dreamed of it, though. Because of the photo."

She made an approving little sound at that. "And what does that mean?"

"That I was desperate for a connection to my parents, who I barely remember in life and who've never visited me after?" My eyes wanted to burn but didn't. Instead, I felt a wave of sadness, deep and bitter and cold, wash over me. Overhead, the light burst to life, flickered, then exploded.

Grandmere sighed. "You were always so dramatic, Oscar. Really. Think this through."

"I'm not a ghost," I began, but she shook her head.

"For the moment, you're as close as you can be without being dead. This is not a case of astral projection or a bad dream, Oscar. You've been forcibly displaced. Your body is not your own, and you have nowhere to go."

"I was trying to find Enoch," I murmured. "He's the one I was looking for, not you." Cocking a curious glance at her, I frowned. "Why did I find you?"

The light pulsed, and she scowled. "Not yet, damn it! Not yet!"

"I need to find Enoch," I repeated. "He might be able to help me. Oddly enough," I chuckled. "Who'd have thought..."

The white glare washed over us, and I felt nonexistent. No weight to my limbs, no pressure of air and gravity. Everything was white and glowing. I tried to speak, to call for Grandmere, but no sound came out.

All I could do was fall.

"THIS IS AWKWARD."

Enoch stared at me, eyes wide. "Uh. Hey. This is my friend Theresa. Theresa, this is Oscar Fellowes. He's the best medium in the world, and also I think he might be dead. Are you dead?"

I shook my head. The girl beside Enoch, not much older than him, scrambled back from the edge of the tailgate they'd been sitting on and gave me an odd little wave. "Um, I'll let y'all... do whatever it is you do." She vaulted over the side and headed toward the low-slung blue house about a hundred yards away, nearly reaching the porch before she burst into a run.

"I didn't mean to interrupt," I muttered. "I don't know what I'm doing, actually."

Enoch grinned. "You picked a good place to practice astral projecting! I'm at a retreat for people like me. Theresa, she's real good at it. She wanted to give me lessons and all."

"Enoch, I think Theresa..."

He waited, eyes wide.

"You know what, she'll explain it to you later, I'm sure. Enoch, I actually need your help, if you're able?"

"Hell yeah!" He jumped to his feet, giving strong golden retriever vibes as he grinned down at me. "Do you need help practicing? I can show you what we did in the workshop last night. I got up early this morning to work on it, but Theresa and I got to talking and she said she'd teach me some stuff."

"Oh, my sweet summer child... Right. Listen, this is a lot, but I need you to really pay attention, yes?"

"Roger that."

Sigh. "Can you reach out to someone who isn't typically open to your abilities?"

"I mean... yeah. It's possible. Kinda rude, though. Like bustin' in on someone's conversation or something, I figure."

"Well, this is an emergency. I need to get Julian, but he's not answering his phone."

Enoch laughed. "This is a funny way to deliver a message, Oscar. Why don't you just email him?"

"Because he probably thinks I'm dead and my body is being used by someone else at the moment."

Enoch stared at me, his expression falling as he sat back down on the tailgate. "Alright. I might need more details."

ENOCH HAD A ROOM TO himself at the Crescent Moon Retreat Center for Exceptional Minds (good god). The place was crawling with ghosts, but they didn't seem to notice me at all, which could be good or bad. I was undecided just then. But ghosts or no, Enoch had been blooming since the last time we'd met. He talked a mile a minute and hopped from subject to subject like a rabbit, greeting early risers heading for the kitchen and the night owls just staggering to bed alike with enthusiastic, contagious cheer. We reached his room, and he opened the door with a flourish. "Make yourself comfortable," he offered, stretching out on the bed. "Sorry, it's just easier for me to do this if I'm totally relaxed, you know? Like, if I got too many things in my head, I start getting all scattered and might scare some poor ol' lady at HEB by popping in and asking her what she's making for dinner cause her cart looks like it's gonna be tacos and I love tacos."

"Enoch."

"Sorry, sorry. Mike—he's one of the counselors here—he said I need to work on my focus."

"Tell Mike he's right," I muttered.

"Okay. Let me see here. Julian Weems. Julian Weems..." Enoch smirked. "Paging Doctor Julian Weems. You've got a call holding."

"Oh my god."

Enoch cleared his throat. "Sorry. Here we go." He was quiet for a long time, his body sinking into a sort of stillness that was not sleep but something deeper. His eyes moved rapidly beneath their lids, his lips pressed into a thin line as he pushed himself into the astral plane or whatever they called it. After a long time, he dragged in a deep breath then let it out on a sigh. "I can't find him. There are a couple of lights on that island you mentioned, and I found that easy enough on my mind map, you know? But not Julian. It's like he's a blank spot."

"He'll love to hear that," I sighed. "You said there were other lights? Can you see who?"

He shook his head. "Just that some folks there, they got tendencies like us. Not totally normal human stuff. I don't know if they can talk like this or not but... want me to try?"

Reluctantly, I nodded. "Just be careful, okay?"

"Will do! Okay, let's see what's what."

An hour later, he'd weeded out a startled man in Tibbins Quay who thought he was having a stroke, someone else in the same area who knew exactly what was happening and shut him down in a heartbeat, and finally settled on a very bright light, one that was actually on the mainland but Enoch said had a line running to the island. "I've been practicing," he said proudly. "I'm gettin' real good at seeing connections now."

"That's wonderful," I said, trying not to sound exasperated. Something was happening, and I was feeling strange, unsettled. My being itched. I needed to move... "Enoch, I think... I think something's happening to me. I don't know if I'm going to be here longer or not."

He nodded. "Let me just try, okay?"

"Try but if I disappear on you—"

"I think I found someone. He's pissed, but he's listening."

I nodded. "Tell him—"

FOR AN ENDLESS BREATH, I fell. Color, sound, everything whirled past me. I braced for pain, for the end, for everything to fall in on me at once.

And then it stopped.

I felt nothing.

No, that was wrong. I felt fear. Panic. But it was from outside me. Anger, too. Envy.

Exhaustion.

I rolled onto my back and saw the open maw of light where the Wreckers stayed. The two ghost ships, their wrecked bodies flickering in and out, sometimes whole and sometimes rotting wood and barnacles.

Virginia moved forward from the group, a pale figure against the glaring light, barely discernible. She held out a hand, silently offering. I looked away, into the strangeness behind me, a place that was not living or dead.

And I saw me, stretched out beside me.

Jeremiah Tibbins stared back at me, his form shifting with my body, not quite fitting since he didn't belong. But he was trying. almost succeeding. The lines rising from the sigils in the sand shone gold and green, wrapping around Jeremiah and pressing him into my body like dough into a pan.

"No," I growled. "No!" Moving without a body was effortless when you weren't being dragged out of your flesh. I lunged at Jeremiah and felt the impact this time, the electric jolt of his spirit and mine passing through one another. He yelped and, for a moment, I knocked him out of my body. It was easy, slipping back home, into the vessel I belonged in. Popping in like a puzzle piece, I thought. Then Jeremiah was shoving his hands into my chest, curling and pulling, trying to move me out.

But this time it didn't work.

This time I couldn't be moved.

Someone shouting made him look up, and that distraction was all it took. I let myself settle in, spreading to take up my space.

And it *hurt*. Everything hurt. Jeremiah screamed, throwing himself down onto me, scrambling at my chest and throat.

And then...

Then it was over.

And it was dark.

And I was alone.

No, not alone. Someone was nearby. A thin presence. Like tissue paper held against a light. Almost insubstantial but just enough to make out the shape, the realness. They moved closer, a cool touch moving over my face, settling over my chest above my heart.

Who are you?

They didn't respond. More soft touches, more hands. I wasn't alone, wasn't truly back yet I didn't think.

Am I dead?

The tissue-paper ghosts pressed close, gentle as a feather. "I'm not ready," I murmured, the sound of my voice rough and low. Sand on rocks, boots scraped on asphalt. The pain in my limbs intensified, heavy and hot and pulsing. The ghosts drew back, their cooling touch slipping away, leaving heat and prickling pain in their wake.

"Am I dead?" I repeated, this time softer, my breath thin and difficult.

"Oscar," Julian whispered near me. "Oscar, be okay. Please?"

I tried to nod but couldn't move. Instead, I let myself float. Let myself be home, at least for the time being.

Chapter 14 — Julian

There's a condition called stress-induced or Takotsubo cardiomyopathy. People refer to it as dying from a broken heart or dying from fright. It looks like a heart attack, but it's not quite the same.

That's all I could think about for several moments when I woke up to see the sigil destroyed and the other side of the bed empty. My chest ached like a weight had been pressed onto it. *Like Giles Corey,* I thought in a fit of historical pique. *Maybe my death will become a tourist attraction too. The island can advertise a new ghost.*

Stop it. Think.

Think like someone who is somehow enabling body snatching. Got it.

I groaned aloud. "Shit!"

I swallowed hard against the rising panic—*How will I get Oscar back now?* —and forced myself to my feet. There is calmness in routine and making myself go through a hastened morning get-ready took the edge off the pressure under my ribs, but it did not fully abate. Hurrying downstairs, I confirmed what I already suspected. The house was empty.

Maybe?

"Hey," I said, voice reedy with nerves. "Um, so if any of y'all know where Oscar went, I'm listening."

Only the sound of the wind met my ears.

The sound of the wind and a tiny little *plink* of sound nearly lost under the roar of blood in my ears.

A seashell lay in the middle of the foyer, rocking gently on the ridged curve of its back, the shiny pink inside glinting in the glare of my flashlight.

There was no surface nearby with shells. And yes, I checked.

"Okay so this isn't going to be the most scientific response to things but I'm desperate," I muttered. "The beach?"

No response that I could hear.

"I *do* know someone who can kick you out of here," I muttered. "Just saying, if this is a cruel joke or something…"

Quiet. I sighed and nodded to myself. "Okay then. Okay. Beach it is."

THE STORM WAS STILL turning over us, but we were between bands, so I didn't have a lot of time to play with. The house had been grimly quiet when I left, slipping through the kitchen door and going around the side where Sandra had parked the minivan. The keys on the kitchen rack had worked and it started in one try. My leg hated the driver's seat, but it was better and faster than walking.

Bouncing down the long drive, I aimed the van in the direction of the small downtown area and the head of the beach trail. The storm had flattened several palms and ripples of sand and dirt covered the road in parts. The road was built high enough that it didn't have standing water yet, but as I reached the main part of town, I could see some of the yards and lower spots were flooded. Shingles, bits of siding, lawn furniture and other things that hadn't been secured were tossed around like a giant had a hissy fit and threw their toys to the ground. It took just a few minutes to get there, the storm still whipping and blowing but not as bad as the night before. I didn't bother locking it or taking the keys, scrambling from the van with my cane and going as quickly as I safely could to the path, flipping my phone on as I walked.

Before I even reached the beach, I smelled fire fueled by kerosene. The sharp tang of the fuel burned my nose and throat—*God, how much did they use?* Underneath the petroleum fug, the sweet smell of woodsmoke was starting to grow, cutting into the nauseating edge of the fuel. I pushed myself to go faster, the screaming pain in my hip and leg numbed only by the sight before me. Oscar—or Jeremiah—was on his back between the three bonfires again, this time spread out like he was welcoming the tide, arms flung wide and eyes open to the sky. Ray-Don scraped something into the sand at his feet. Reviving the sigil, I realized. Digging in deep to make it last. Sandra was already dragging stones to fill in the trenches they'd made, keeping the sand from spilling back into the ruts.

Ray-Don stopped mid-action and pulled his clunky phone from his jacket pocket. Shouting at whoever was on the other end, he walked down the beach a ways, leaving Oscar's form prone and vulnerable.

I moved faster, slipping the last few feet but managing to stay upright. "Oscar," I panted. "Oscar, listen to me. Oscar, it's me. I know you're here. Help me, okay? Push him out. Or whatever it is you need to do. Do you hear me?"

Oscar's body bowed and he screamed, eyes rolling up in his head as he clawed at his chest, his throat. "No," he rasped. "Stop! No!"

"Oscar!" I was almost at his side when he went limp, eyes closing, and limbs flopped to his sides.

"Don't!"

I whipped my head up to see Sandra stumbling down the beach toward me. In her haste to get to the beach, she was clad only in a bathrobe, a threadbare nightshirt, and oversized sneakers that belonged to someone much larger than her. She tripped on the sand, her breath heaving as she staggered closer. "Stop," she shouted. "You're going to ruin everything!"

"I know!" I snarled. "Get back!" Grabbing one of the still-burning pieces of wood, I brandished it at her. She drew up short and stared first at my makeshift weapon, then at me.

"Seriously?" she demanded. "Seriously?"

"Stay away from him," I ordered. "You're killing him! Who else have you done this to?"

"No one who hasn't agreed to it," she shouted over the wind. "My students, they volunteered," she added on a wild laugh. "They wanted to know, too. They said it was good, that what I was doing..." She shook her head. "They were weak. They got scared. They ruined everything!" The hurricane was past us but the weather was still dangerous, high wind trailing after the storm and the tide higher and rougher than normal. There's no way I'd be able to get Oscar off the island any time soon, but I wasn't going to just let them use his body, force *him* out and kill him.

"Oscar never agreed!"

"He drank the tea," she said, moving closer. "He chose to do it. I picked him, knew he'd be perfect. He was already so close to the other side it was easy. He didn't even fight."

I shoved the torch at her, and she stopped, hands spread. "This is murder."

"No." She smiled. "There's not a single jury in the land that would convict me on that charge. Not over this. Not when Oscar appears before a judge and says he has no idea what you're talking about, that he's fine. You're a scorned ex who can't handle the fact he's breaking things off with you to live with me now."

"Jesus Christ," I muttered. "Before I met you," I said to Oscar's prone form at my feet, "my life was 98 percent less dramatic."

Sandra's nose wrinkled and she shook her head. "He's not here," she said. "He's gone. That's what the Wreckers do, Doctor Weems.

They open the veil for the spirit to pass. When the colonists did it, they attributed the veil opening to genius loci or even some mythical sea spirits. It was ghosts, Doctor Weems. *Ghosts.* Those sea spirits, those Wreckers they were just shipwreck victims, gone before they expected. Jeremiah told me," she added fiercely. "He found out. He learned, after his own death. The Wreckers don't cross, but the veil waits for them. It's always thin here, waiting for them. And it doesn't discriminate. A spirit is a spirit, whether the body is alive or dead. And Oscar's been gone since yesterday, since you found him on the beach. If fucking Ray-Don had done his job and stopped babying his incompetent friend, you never would've found Oscar."

"Okay, Scooby villain, now tell me the rest of your evil plan."

That was possibly the wrong thing to say. She howled in rage, leaping at me and knocking me back before I could sidestep her. I went down hard on my ass, pain shooting through my hip as I landed. She clawed at my face, missing by mere centimeters as I managed to shove her off me, my torch sputtering in the sand just out of reach. "I love him," she snarled. "You won't take him from me!"

Her hands weren't strong enough to choke me to death, but it was damned painful and inconvenient, her thumbs pressing in just hard enough to make me gag as she screamed wordlessly in my face, her weight on my chest pressing me into the wet sand.

"He's *mine*," she shrieked. "He'd been waiting so long for me! So long!" Her cries broke into sobs, her grasp weakening enough for me to push her off and aside. I struggled to my feet, my cane too far to grab without her stopping me. I sent up a prayer to whoever was listening that she didn't try to tackle me again—I wasn't sure my hip could take it, that I'd be able to get back up. Sandra rolled to her knees and scrambled to stand, sand and tears and snot and blood streaking her face and hands. "When I came to the house, I was so alone. So. Fucking. Alone. I'd lost... I'd lost Paul," she snapped. "Just gone. They kept telling me it was a mercy. That it was so fast, and he didn't have time to really suffer but he *suffered*, Goddamnit, and I had to watch him. I couldn't help him. Nothing I have ever learned or done prepared me for losing him. For not being able to stop him from dying." The sound she made was pitiful, painful. A deep, shuddering sigh that seemed dragged from the depths of her heart. Raking a shaking hand through her hair, Sandra shook her head, sniffed, and turned her hard, shining gaze back on me.

I pressed my lips into a tight line, keeping back the words that bubbled forth naturally. An offer of sympathy, a murmur of commiseration. That'd do none of us—her, me, or her dead—any good now. In fact, it'd probably make things worse.

"When I found the original copy of the founder's book, I nearly killed my assistant." She sniffed, a distant smile tinging her features. "If she'd brought it to me just a month before, maybe. Or even a week. But they embalmed him. Do you know what that does to a person, Doctor Weems? You do. You do."

"Sandra," I said, trying to sound soothing but my voice was shaking too much for it to be believable. "What you're trying to do, it's murder. Do you understand that?" My stomach lurched at the thought. It took everything I had and then some to keep from retching on the sand at her feet, from throwing myself at her and begging, pleading for her to stop.

If it came to it, I decided, I'd offer myself. I couldn't let this happen to Oscar, and maybe she'd take me instead, even if it was just to shut me up. Give him a chance to flee.

"When I came here, I found Jeremiah. He was alone too. For so fucking long. He understood the pain. He knows. He knows..." She shook her head, focusing on me once more, the small smile disappearing as her tenuous grasp on everything crumbled further. "When he found out I knew about the book, that that's what led me here, he was overjoyed. I made him happy. The first time he'd felt happiness in decades. Decades! And knowing I was going to bring back the old ways, the ways of his family? Jeremiah needs me. I can help him. I couldn't save Paul, but Jeremiah is still here. He needs me. I need him."

"Sandra, no," I rasped. "Jeremiah doesn't want this. This isn't helping him! This isn't going to bring you any peace. It's—"

"You wouldn't know!" she screamed. "You wouldn't know!"

"I've seen the museum," I shot back, grasping so hard at those straws it was a near physical pain. "He died because he tried to help this place, right? The story says he was killed, but it wasn't an accident, was it?" The display had been vague in that way museums could be when trying to make the truth palatable. And I knew, without being told, that Jeremiah's death had been a vengeful one. That his ghost wasn't hanging around because he loved the place so much but because he *hurt*.

Oscar would be so proud, I thought wildly. If we survived, I'd have to tell him.

"Fuck you, Julian Weems. You don't know the first goddamn thing about this pain. About the peace I can give Jeremiah, the peace Paul was denied. Ray-Don and Delia, they're pathetic little suck-ups. They thought I'd be able to do some table shaking bullshit and find the treasure their ancestors hid. They didn't understand. The treasure wasn't some stupid pirate hoard. It's this, it's what I'm about to do," she shrilled, jabbing her finger at her chest. "I'm the one who saved the ways! Ray-Don only knew part of it—his dumb ass was too interested in that fucking salvaged garbage! And Delia—she knew, she knew the ritual, but she'd never been brave enough to do it. *What if it doesn't work? What if I kill someone?* Pathetic! But me?" She shook her head. "I knew where the real important shit was. In that book."

"Sandra, you're talking about a dead man here," I said, trying to sound calm and reasonable. "He didn't even know you when he died. He wasn't waiting for you. What you're doing is hurting Oscar. He... He has people who love him and who he loves, too. He's still alive to share that, Sandra. Jeremiah isn't. He's using you. He's greedy. *You're* greedy, and selfish! You both want something you're not entitled to!" I hesitated, then added, "Paul is gone, Sandra. I don't know what you think this ritual will get you, but it's not Paul. Jeremiah isn't him. He can't step into Paul's place, no matter what you think will happen next. Let Oscar go. Hell, let Oscar go so he can *make* Jeremiah go. You don't deserve this, Sandra," I said, wincing as soon as the words were out, knowing she was going to pounce on those and twist them the wrong way.

She shook her head, sobbing openly and wetly. "No," she hissed. "You don't deserve the knowledge. Someone like you, you're lost. I was lost once. Blinded by what they tell us about magic, about spirits, about what comes next. I thought maybe heaven, you know? Hell. But it's worse than that. When you're like Jeremiah, there's nothing. Just years and years of waiting for something that never happens. Jeremiah told me. And the Wreckers, they help us, you know? When they open the veil to come across, the volunteer's spirit goes across. No one is hurt."

"It doesn't have to be like that for Jeremiah," I said. "Oscar can help him cross over. I've seen him do it for others."

"No," she growled. "No, you're lying! He wouldn't do that for Jeremiah!"

"Sandra," I said, trying to keep the panic from my voice as I reached out toward her. "Sandra, he would. Oscar cares about the spirits he works with. He cares about their living loved ones. And he wouldn't refuse to help just to hurt you. Or Jeremiah. Is this really what Jeremiah would want?"

She jerked away from me, baring her teeth in a feral growl of pain. "You don't fucking know! You don't know what it's like to be alone! For everything you thought you had, for your entire *world* to be taken from you!"

"And I don't want to!" I cried. "Sandra, please!" I glanced at Oscar's body. Or was it Oscar-proper now? I didn't know—he was breathing, or his body was, but was Jeremiah gone yet? Was Oscar safe? Sandra was ignoring me now. She made a broken, choking sound and was dragging one of the larger pieces of driftwood through the sand, muttering under her breath between sobs. She was tracing out a sigil between the smoldering fire remnants, distracted. I hobbled forward, scooping up my cane and moving to Oscar's side. "Oscar," I whispered. "Fuck... Can you hear me?"

"No," Ray-Don said, making me whip around to find him swinging on me with one of the pieces of driftwood. "But I sure can."

I pushed away as hard as I could, rolling onto my back with a pained cry. Ray-Don missed me by mere inches and was swinging again by the time I pushed myself into a sitting position, scooting back like a worm. "Ray-Don, you don't want to do this."

"Oh, fuck off, doc," he groused. "I want my birthright, okay? What's due me as a Noonan!"

"Murdering me is what's due to you?" I demanded. God, it hurt to get up, but I tried, struggling into a crouch and pushing up on my good leg, staggering to one side as Ray-Don swung again. I was slipping in the wet sand, my body not wanting to cooperate with my brain as Ray-Don snarled and took another swing, then another. Every swing he took put me another step closer to the water, which was rushing closer and closer with each gushing wave. "Ray-Don," I tried again. "Listen to me. Sandra *will* get caught. People will miss us when we don't go back in a few days."

"You died in a tragic accident during the hurricane," he said, the words sounding as if he were repeating something he'd been trained to say. "It's rare, but it happens."

"We're on TV," I reminded him desperately. "You don't think people will want to come see where we disappeared? Do some sort of investigation? Ghost hunting shows will be all over this island, hoping to talk to the spirits of a famous medium and... Well, mostly him, okay."

Ray-Don hesitated, glancing at Sandra. "No," he said after a heartbeat, taking one more swing at me before I stumbled, my leg collapsing out from under me. "They won't. Not when your body washes up on the mainland."

He threw his weapon aside and closed the distance between us, raring his foot back for a kick as I tried to roll away.

WHY AM I WET? FUCK, *everything hurts...* I tried to open an eye but got sand in it for my trouble. "Shit!"

"Stay still," someone whispered beside me. "You got a goose egg but I think you're okay. Your friend looks like shit though."

I lolled my head to one side and finally got one eye pried open. The ferry boat captain kneeled beside me, watching something past me.

"Hey man. Doctor Weems, right?"

"Yeah?"

He offered me a small, tight smile. "I'm Cap. Hey."

"Hey... Is she—"

He nodded. "Hey. Um, you know a kid named Enoch?"

"Enoch?" I muttered. "Uh, yeah. Why?"

He shook his head. "Fucked up shit, man. Stay here, okay?"

"I don't think that'll be a problem."

He stood and started moving along the dark edge of the beach toward where Sandra and Ray-Don were raking the sigils into the sand, filling them with something from a large kettle-like container. I looked around to see Oscar stretched out beside me—we'd been moved and were near the thick ridge of seagrass at the base of the beach path. Oscar was pale and breathing, but again too still. "Oscar," I murmured. "Please wake up. Please tell me it's you in there. Please, baby?"

He made a small noise but was otherwise unresponsive.

Shouting rose from the beach, and I pushed to one side, straining to see what was happening. Cap had grabbed Sandra by the arms, pulling them behind her back and lifting her off her feet. Ray-Don swung at them, aiming for Cap but hitting Sandra hard enough to make her cry out. Cap tossed her to one side as easy as a puff of cotton and started kicking at the sand sigils. Ray-Don shouted wordlessly, rushing at him. Cap sidestepped, his voice carrying on the wind. "You got no right to my family's book, you assholes! What the hell have you done?"

Sandra staggered up, grabbing one of the burning sticks and swinging it in an overhead arc that Cap easily ducked under, hitting her midsection with his shoulder. She went down hard, gasping on the sand, hands fluttering as she tried to catch her breath. Cap shoved to his feet and started dragging burning pieces of wood through the sigils, cursing as he moved. "Help me," he shouted. I staggered up, lurching toward him to destroy the designs in the sand.

Something that felt like hands scraped at my face, so cold it burned. "Get away from him," I shouted, not sure if I meant Sandra, Ray-Don or whoever was trying to claw at me and make me stop. I kicked at one of the deep-gouged lines and a howl went up. At first, I thought it was the wind, but more joined in and a tangle of voices emerged. So many it was hard to discern individual words. So close it drowned out all other sounds, the sheer volume making my ears ring even as I kicked at more of the sigil.

The howling was a raw and guttural sound as I scraped away the outer edges of the markings, dragging my cane across the smaller lines to obscure them. I wasn't sure how much I'd need to destroy to make sure it would fail, so I kept going, my breath sawing in and out of my lungs as I tried to move faster. Cap shouted in pain as Sandra managed contact with one of the smoldering logs, the sound making me jerk my head up to see what was happening. Sandra shrieked, a sound of triumph and pain as she lunged at him. Cap was injured but fast, sidestepping her then bringing his leg up to catch her around the knees, sending her to the ground. Oscar's body heaved weakly, like he was trying to sit up or even just take a deep breath. I went to his side, collapsing onto my good hip. There was no way I could be deliberate in my movements now. Everything hurt, and my panic was too great. "Oscar, baby, can you hear me? Listen, just hold tight, okay? Hold tight. We're here. Please be in there, Oscar. Please? Let me know... Say something. Anything. Oscar?"

"Help me here!" Cap shouted, and I looked to see he'd managed to pin Sandra to the beach, but she was strong and fighting hard. I half-lurched, half-crawled toward him. "The toolbox," he snapped, nodding at the metal box open where Ray-Don had left it. It was farther than I wanted it to be but needs must. "There's rope in it. Under the top caddy."

I didn't know why Ray-Don had a bundle of fresh hemp rope in his toolbox, and I didn't even want to being to imagine what he'd planned to do with it. I threw it to Cap, and soon Sandra was trussed on the beach before Cap moved to Ray-Don, securing him alike.

It felt like miles before I reached Oscar's side again, afraid to move him, afraid of the incoming tide.

Afraid this was all for nothing.

Cap kneeled on the sand, chest heaving as he watched the waves pull the charred wood away from the shore. The clumped sand, soaked with blood, kerosene, and whatever concoctions Sandra had made, was dark under the cloud-covered sky the carved sigils no more. In their place was plain sand, looking for all the world as if a giant had reached down and scooped up great handfuls before throwing it back down. "I called the emergency folks before I headed over," he muttered after an interminable span. "Said some people were tryin' to kill a tourist. Didn't figure tellin' them the truth would get me very far."

"You... you know the truth?"

Cap nodded. "I'm the last of the Tibbinses. This shit"—he nodded at the destroyed sigils, at Sandra and Ray-Don— "is why I left when I was sixteen. Lied 'bout my age, worked some odd jobs, joined the Army... Never wanted to come back till I heard through the grapevine that Sandra Cochrane was obsessed with Jeremiah Tibbins. The first one, that is," he said. "I'm the fifth one."

"Seriously?"

"Mmm hmm." He glanced up, squinting at the dawn-bright clouds still spitting rain. "Head's up. This is gonna kick up a lot of sand right in your eyes."

THE POLICE SEEMED PLEASED to be able to use their shiny new helicopter to arrest Sandra Cochrane and Ray-Don Jennings. Oscar had rallied and, for a horrifying moment, I wasn't sure if he *was* Oscar. But he looked at me, and I knew. I knew he was in there, that he was real. And I buckled over my knees and sobbed until Cap patted me gingerly on the back and muttered, "Get it together. They think you're on something, man."

The cops asked a million questions, ready to dismiss it as some drug fueled hurricane party, but seeing Oscar's injuries, and Sandra screaming how he was 'hers' and I had 'ruined everything,' led to the pair of them being taken back to the mainland. Ray-Don had muttered an admission about theft, about helping kidnap Oscar during the storm, and that was him gone.

Oscar refused medical transport, insisting he'd be fine with some rest.

"If you're sure," the young officer muttered, anxious to be gone from the weird people on the beach.

Oscar scrubbed his hands over his face, resting against my knees where I was sprawled on the ground. "Very sure. I just want to go back to bed for the next week." He sighed.

"Might not be a bad idea," the cop agreed. Cap went and got his truck, bringing it as close to the beach path as he could. Between the cop and him, they got Oscar up the path to the truck, me following at a slower pace.

The ride back to Honey Walk was quiet. A few people were already out, cleaning up after the storm, removing shutters and generally starting their day. Most of the tree branches and heavy palm fronds that had fallen on the road were already pushed to one side, but in a few places trees and limbs crushed roofs or stood jagged, broken in half but not completely severed. A few homes already had tarps over holes in their roofs, but more than one had a family outside looking stunned, staring at the damage left by Nelson. "I didn't realize this many people lived here," Oscar murmured. "It seemed like just Sandra, Ray-Don and a few others…"

"Most folks this end of the island work down at Tibbins Quay," Cap said. "Or the mainland. They're only here on weekends or holidays, or work shift hours. It's not lively like it used to be but there're more folks here than not."

Oscar nodded, lacing his fingers tightly with mine. "It's not what I expected."

Cap snorted. "So I gather."

"How do you know Enoch?" I asked as we pulled into the drive. "You mentioned him earlier…"

Cap and Oscar exchanged glances in the rearview mirror. "I'll tell you after I get some tea in me," Oscar said. "I need fortification for this."

I laid my hand on his arm, drawing his attention. "Maybe water for now, until we're sure whatever tea you're drinking is safe?"

Oscar's eyes widened briefly, then he nodded. "Water then. At least till the mainland."

Chapter 15 — Oscar

Enoch was entirely too pleased with himself. Even over the wobbly video link, his beaming pride was near palpable. "And then I was able to tell Cap what was going on because he was the only one that was open. Kind of like using Omegle but for people with the Gift."

Cap being the taciturn ferry pilot. The descendant of Jeremiah Tibbins. Jeremiah Tibbins V, or Captain Tibbins to his former military mates. Now just Cap, at least to an excited teenager from rural Texas who was slowly coming into his own with his abilities. Cap who was, in Julian's words, pulling a Boo Radley and trying to somehow melt into the shadows behind the open bedroom door while avoiding all eye contact.

"Thank you," I murmured, catching his eye. "If you hadn't come, I'm not sure I'd have cared much for what would happen next."

He made a funny little choked sound. "I, um. I don't know about all that. Your friends there, they were pretty much on top of things."

"You called Jeremiah to you. And you stopped Sandra," I added. "She was close, Cap. Closer than I care to remember."

Cap's weathered cheeks turned ruddy as he found the carpet suddenly worthy of all his attention. "I've lived here most of my life, 'cept when I was in the Army. I never thought..." He trailed off. "Well. I never thought."

I nodded. "Everyone here knows about the Wreckers, and about your family."

He nodded. "I grew up going to the shore, you know? I mean, not much else to do here. Wasn't till I was in middle school an' going to the mainland every week to stay with my Aunt Bitty so I could go to school that I found out other kids didn't see stuff like that. Didn't talk to their dead family."

"Or the ghost on the path," I murmured. "And the one in the garden. What happened then?"

He shrugged. "I shut it off. Stopped taking part. Drove Mom nuts, really. Said I was breaking tradition and hurting my great-grandma's feelings. She'd been dead fifty years by that point so I figured it wasn't much hurt involved." He smiled awkwardly, twisting his fingers in the hem of his t-shirt. "When I heard 'bout the goings-on starting up after Mom died, I was just getting out after my twenty years and..." He shrugged. "I didn't want to move back here, not after a whole life of it, but I couldn't just ignore it, you know?"

"So, you stepped in like Jeremiah did," I said. "To keep an eye on what was happening and try to protect the people here."

He nodded reluctantly. "For all the good it did," he muttered with a tinge of bitterness in his tone. "That Cochrane woman still nearly—"

"But she didn't," I said with a small smile.

"Shit." He sighed gustily. "I let that Cochrane woman nearly kill you. When she answered my ad looking for a caretaker, she said she was researching the history of the island for some university job. Hell, she even tried to turn down my money, said she just wanted to be able to do her work while living on site. I was so blind though. There were all sorts of things that should've warned me she wasn't right, you know? I was just so glad someone else was taking care of the place and I didn't need to set foot inside, and that nearly got y'all killed. Don't argue with me," he snapped when I started to do just that. "I should've put it together sooner. No one's that interested in the old family pile. No one is that obsessed. She stirred up shit that should've stayed down. Hell." He raked his fingers through his hair, turning the sandy brush of his hair into a bird's nest. "I should sell out to those resort people, you know? Let 'em turn this whole damn thing into a fucking golf course or something."

I sat up straight, pierced by concern and—yes, I admit it—annoyance on behalf of Jeremiah, Ray-Don, hell, everyone on the island who had worked to keep the Wreckers at bay for so long. "Cap, that would be the worst possible idea. It seems easier, I'm sure, but if you give it over to them, then what will happen when they start destroying the homes, the buildings, all the places the people of Rosie Sands have been working that ritual for years?"

He shook his head harder. "I can't keep up with this, Mr. Fellowes. My family started something that's never going to end if I don't yank it out by the roots."

"That's the problem," I said. "The roots aren't just deep, they're tangled with other roots. The Wreckers, the first settlers, the settlers roots in the old colonies.... And, Cap, tearing away one part of it will only upset the ecology of the rest."

His face was red with anger, with frustration, and maybe a bit of sadness. "So *I* have to stay here, get buried here like all the rest of 'em? I don't want to be the one at the end, Mr. Fellowes." He wilted in on himself, closing his eyes. "I saw my family let this island suck them dry. I saw the entire town wither away to almost nothing, letting the goings-on eat away at them until all that's left are just a handful of folks, trying to keep back monsters my ancestors stirred up!"

"They're not monsters," I murmured. "They're just ghosts. Strange ones, maybe stronger because of... because of their history, but just ghosts."

I couldn't bring myself to say magic—magic brought to mind tricksters, hoaxes, bad telly programs with thirty-year-olds playing teenagers throwing fireballs and having complicated affairs.

"Uh, hey..."

Enoch's voice startled us both. I looked down at the phone in my hand to see him looking back, eyes wide as he gnawed gently on his lower lip. "Sorry," I muttered. "Got a bit carried away there."

"No, it's just—Okay, can I see Cap, too? I feel weird talking about this when I can't see both of y'all."

Cap rolled his eyes but moved closer so we could both be in the frame. "Hey, Enoch. Nice to put a face with a voice in my head."

Enoch cackled. "I'm getting so much better at this whole astral projection thing. I got to practice with this girl—Patrice—she's part of the group Mom used to be part of, folks like me. Patrice is super smart, and she's got all sorts of tricks and tips to help make this easier and—" He cut himself off, blushing. "Anyway. I couldn't help but overhear what y'all were talking about and I have an idea for you, Cap. I mean," he stumbled, blush increasing until I thought he might actually pop on screen. "If you want."

Cap shot me a look—*What is he talking about?*

I shrugged. *Your guess is as good as mine.*

Enoch fidgeted, darting looks between both of us before taking a deep breath and, voice shaking only a little, made his suggestion. "So, there're a lot of people like us. I mean, in a general sense, you know? I know y'all don't do the whole"—he made a gesture near his temple, wiggling his fingers and widening his eyes— "thing that I do, but you've got your things, right?"

Cap's lips twitched in spite of himself, and I nodded. "Right," I said, smiling just a little. "What are you getting at, Enoch?"

"We form a group!"

There was a moment of silence, then Cap, in a mildly horrified tone, asked, "Like... a boy band or something?"

Enoch blinked, shaking his head. "What? No. I'm a terrible singer. I mean, I guess with auto tune it might work but, I mean, no offense guys but y'all are little old for a boy band. But that could be our thing, right? Unconventional and all that? Something for the moms—and dads," he added, giving me a nod. "Take their kids to the show, have some eye candy for themselves. That—"

Cap was making a funny sputtering noise I hoped was laughter, and I could practically see Enoch's train of thought derailing in real time. The time between meeting him and now had apparently been one of great changes for the boy. Not only was he talking fit to beat the band, but he was open and, frankly, obnoxiously cheerful. A real change from the withdrawn, frightened boy I'd met just a few months before. "Enoch, let's table that for later, hm? Explain your original suggestion to us."

"Oh! Right! So, when I was getting that, um, help for the stuff in my head? When I had to talk to people about Grandpa and Mom and... and what happened? It helped, you know? And those other people like me, the ones Mom introduced me to when I was little? It helps to talk to them sometimes about our abilities. So," he drew out, his grin growing to painfully large proportions, "my idea is we form a group. Like a mutual support group, you know? Mediums Anonymous or something? We all have stuff we can teach each other and sometimes it helps to have someone with similar problems to just like, listen to you rage, you know?"

Cap made a face, but... Damn it. Enoch had the seed of a good idea. I thought of Lisa's insistence that I needed to *network* and *meet some new friends*, of Sophia Gates and her gatekeeping of the community... How there was so much I didn't know still. Even after seeing Grandmere again.

Even after being across the veil.

Maybe Charlotte can tell you more, my thoughts whispered, the new emails that had popped up since regaining power and wi-fi suddenly heavy on my mind. *Maybe she knows something that will help.*

"That," I said carefully, not wanting to send him off half-cocked with the idea, "is definitely something we should talk about. Maybe decide who to start with—"

"Everyone!"

"I don't know everyone," I said with a dry huff of a sigh. "And we can't very well just post an ad about it."

"I got this," Enoch said with the sort of self-assuredness found mostly in teenagers and drunk people. "I'll message you," he added, then disconnected before I could sputter more than a few words of protest.

"Does he mean like a text or like..." Cap touched his temple.

"I'm not sure," I admitted. "Either way, I'm sure it will be effusive and require untangling."

Cap left after a few more minutes, needing to return to the ferry and meet with someone about repairs to the dock and the boat itself. His haste to return to Broken Palm had ended precipitously and, for the time being, the only way to or from the island was via the tourist trap's private launch at Tibbins Quay or waiting for someone to use their personal craft on the Rosie Sands end. Cap had a smaller boat and had offered Julian and I a ride back to the mainland when I was up to leaving. Judging by the way Julian was pacing our room, I was certain I'd be up to leaving fairly soon, if only to get him to stop wearing a track in the vintage rug. "I'll be good to go soon," I said, and he jerked his chin up, startled. "Did you forget I was here?"

He blushed, shook his head. "No, I just got lost in my own brain for a bit. It's been a lot. And, fuck, way for me to make this all about me." He sighed. "Can I?" He gestured to the bed, and I nodded, moving my legs over to give him space.

"I'm not an invalid," I murmured. "Just very tired. Cap can take us to the mainland with the tide. Ezra and Harrison are already on their way from New Orleans, and CeCe said she could be here in just a few hours. Heinrich—"

"Heinrich is already in Charleston." Julian sighed. "He's been texting me all morning. Apparently, Ezra is fast and loose with my number," he added with a glare.

I held up my hands. "Oi, take that up with him."

"Sorry, sorry. I just..." He sank in on himself, scrubbing his hands over his eyes then raking his fingers through his hair before finally exhaling a noisy, tired sigh. "I thought you were dead. *Twice*. And I don't... I don't know how to handle everything I was feeling, and I don't know what I'd do if you *did* die before me and—"

"And," I interrupted, laying my hand on his thigh. He wove his fingers through mine and squeezed gently as I continued. "And I didn't. I'm here. You're here. And by this time tomorrow, we'll be in Charleston."

Julian nodded, staring at our joined fingers. "I have to confess that I'm feeling very guilty right now."

"Oh?" I squeezed his fingers, curious more than nervous about what he could possibly be feeling guilt over.

"Ow!" He gently disentangled our fingers, shaking them a little as he shot me a wounded glare. "Testing your strength now that you're among the living?"

"Sorry," I muttered. "I... sorry."

He took my hand again, folding his fingers around mine this time and offering me a small smile. "I wanted to fess up," he started again. "When I knew you were going to be okay, all I could think was *get him to tell me everything so I can write it all down*. Research was the first thing I thought of, once I knew." He huffed, shaking his head. "I just... You were *gone* and I might never have known. I might have just thought you were acting weird, tired of me or something, and just never known. And all I could think once I knew you were really okay was *add that to the spreadsheet. Start a new one, interview Oscar.*" He cut a glance my way and murmured, "And I wondered if... if you saw Reggie. Or your parents? Or—"

I scooted up the bed, pulling on his hand until he moved with me, stretching out alongside me. "It's nothing to feel guilty over," I murmured against his temple, pressing a soft kiss with my words. "It's nothing for me to be angry over, either. What you're doing, it's important. And I think... I think maybe Enoch is on to something."

Julian tipped his face toward mine. "What? What does Enoch have to do with my spiraling guilt complex?"

I kissed him again. He scowled but kissed me back. "First let's make our travel plans, then I'll tell you about the boy band we're joining."

"Got everything?" I asked, following him out onto the porch. A truck that was more rust than metal idled in the drive, Cap sitting in the reclined driver's seat with his snapback pulled low over his eyes. The remains of Hurricane Nelson were evident in the streaky clouds overhead and the roar of the ocean still pounding the shore so close by, no longer the whispering hiss with the voice-like sibilance it had been just a few days before.

Maybe that's a good thing.

"I think so," Julian said, adjusting his grip on the cane so he could pick his way down the shallow steps to the front walk. "Everything should be packed up and right there in your sweaty hands," he teased, the humidity making us both more damp than we'd like.

"My hands aren't sweaty," I complained, shouldering the bags. "I have very nice hands, thank you very much."

"Mmm hmm."

He winked at me as we reached Cap's truck. Cap climbed out to help us arrange the bags and get ourselves sorted. "Y'all heard? Hurricane Nelson didn't do much to the mainland other than some street flooding, knocked out the cable for a bit so some folks got pissy they missed the season finale of some show." He paused to help Julian up into the front passenger seat before adding, "Gotta be honest with you, Delia and those kids are likely not gonna get any time, maybe just a fine since they weren't there for the, uh, big event and just are considered accessories."

"So was Jeremiah, technically, but you can't arrest a ghost." Julian murmured. At my startled look, he lifted a shoulder. "It's true."

"Sorry. I'm just still getting used to this new Julian-believes-in-ghosts development," I admitted.

He nudged me with his shoulder as Cap climbed into the driver's seat, sandwiching me between the two of them. "Well, it's only going to get worse." Julian sighed. "Better get used to it."

Cap started the engine, glancing up at the house for a long moment before shifting into reverse. "Feds came and got 'em," he said after a moment. "Ray-Don, he was sellin' shipwreck debris. The kids are both under eighteen and were helping him sell it on the down-low."

"Apparently, it's illegal to sell artifacts like that," he added with another shrug. "But since they're kids, they're not gonna get much in the way of trouble. Delia… She's just getting a slap on the wrist for causing a public nuisance when the cops were arresting Ray-Don." He reversed down the drive to the road, pointing us in the direction of the ferry dock. "I still own Honey Walk, but I'm never livin' there. It's mine, though. And I can't stomach the thought of anyone else… Anyone else getting caught up in it."

I nodded slowly. Since the night on the beach, I hadn't seen or heard Jeremiah or any other ghost. I knew they were there—I could feel them, sense their presence just out of reach.

Jeremiah was waiting, I was sure of it. Waiting for someone else to try, to keep up the family tradition. Sandra… I reached out as we drove past the beach path entrance. I could feel the flutter of awareness, of existence, but it was either too weak for me to discern or I was simply too far, or too blocked.

Grandmere at work again, I thought. *How long would it take to unlearn the ways she taught me and really understand what I'm capable of?*

And maybe she was. She was definitely being quiet again but, historically, that meant little when it came to Grandmere.

The journey to the mainland was long but not as quiet as I thought it might be. Debris from the island and mainland both littered the passage—mostly bits of trees, some broken wood from what Cap said were smaller docks, some fishing paraphernalia. The waters were choppy, leading Julian and me to stick close to Cap in the cabin... cockpit... bridge... whatever of his small cabin cruiser. Cap didn't seem bothered by any of it, navigating toward the mainland with a loose grace as he talked with Julian about historic houses and his 'line of work' before being on the show. Julian white knuckled the entire journey (and, to be fair, so did I), only unclenching when we were safely moored.

"Hey, so..." Cap called as we stepped off onto the pier. "I guess we should stay in touch? Or somethin'?" He fidgeted with the brim of his cap, staring determinedly at some bit of flotsam spinning past in the water. "For that Enoch kid's... thing."

Julian looked askance. "The boy band?"

I laughed. "The boy band." I fished one of my old business cards out of my wallet, and Julian added his own number and email to the back before I handed it over to Cap. "I know you're not very comfortable with your—"

"Gift," he muttered. "Ma always called it a gift."

"Well. If you'd like to talk, I'm available. Or..." I thought of Jesse, Lisa's brother. We hadn't spoken much but he had been kind, a calming presence really. *He'd be a great listener for an uncertain, scared, unwilling medium.* "I can find you someone."

Cap nodded, taking the card and giving us a wave as he hopped back onto the boat. He watched us till we cleared the pier and a gaggle of people came between us.

Chapter 16 — Julian

It was nice to be back home, even if only for a few days before heading back out on the road. Our stay in Charleston had been brief—hotels were price gouging (a fine tradition on the Gulf Coast in the wake of a hurricane, no matter how small), and we were, frankly, tired of everything. Returning to my apartment in Houston seemed like the best idea—we had just over a week until our next shoot, and Oscar and I had no desire to even try to have a do-over on our romantic getaway.

So, we went home.

Or to my home, anyway.

And we did jack shit for two days before work crept back into our lives officially. CeCe arrived from New York, frazzled and tight-lipped about divorce proceedings and forcing a smile for anyone who asked how she was doing.

Except for me—she was a terrible liar when it came to me. I don't know if it was a twin thing or I'd just known her long enough to see through her bullshit thing, but when she tried the *it's all fine* thing on me, all I had to do was stare back at her and she shook her head. "Later," she'd promised.

I was still waiting three days later, but I didn't want to push—whatever it was, she'd definitely tell me but the fact she was so mum about it was not a good sign.

On the morning of day three, she'd come over for breakfast, Harrison in tow. We crammed around the kitchen table in my tiny apartment near downtown while tucking into the box of kolaches and klobasneks Harrison brought with them. "Next episode, Morrisonville," she announced as if it were news to us.

Ezra rolled his eyes, selecting a poppyseed kolache with a small sound of pleasure. "Home of the haunted covered bridge."

"Popular folklore convention," I noted, nudging the box toward CeCe. "Is this the one with the goat man or the headless woman?"

She held up her hands, thumbs and forefingers extended as she pulled a face and said, in a rough, low voice, "The devil!"

"Oh my god," Oscar laughed. "Seriously?"

"Mmm. I figured we can hike up the viewer numbers with a few of those everything-is-a-demon episodes. How do you and Ezra feel about shouting at some imps and acting super jumpy? I'm thinking of adding in a too-loud soundtrack of piano stings to make things extra spooky," she said with a wink, well aware of the main conditions of Oscar and Ezra's participation in the show: complete openness about what they knew in advance and no creating needless dramatics.

Oscar and Ezra both shook their heads. CeCe nodded, handing Ezra their copy of the dossier, bits redacted so as not to give away too much. Discussion fell to which equipment we'd need, what accommodations had been arranged, what was there to do in the area on the one day off we had scheduled in, and Harrison nodded for me to slip away with him as the conversation moved around us.

I followed him to the narrow balcony off my living room, overlooking a tiny sliver of Buffalo Bayou. "If you squint," I said, "and lean way out there and look to the right, you can make out part of the Museum of Natural Science."

"Nice."

We lingered a bit, looking at the sliver of the city you could see through the trees and buildings on my street, talking about anything other than ghosts.

Just because we were believing a bit now didn't mean we wanted to dwell on it. Sometimes, it was good to remember that being alive was its own mystery too.

Inside, the sound of Heinrich arriving in full glory distracted us both, and we trailed inside. He was expounding volubly about the *charming little boutique hotel* he was staying at, one with oddly themed rooms and that catered to the artsy, more-money-than-sense set. "Allegedly, they have a *dungeon* room on the top floor! A dungeon! On an upper floor!" He clicked his tongue. "I'm very disappointed in their designer but I'll give them stars for the effort."

Oscar's lips quirked. "I don't think they meant that kind of dungeon, Heinrich."

Heinrich lifted a brow. "I know, lad. I know."

CeCe stayed a bit longer, leaving a stack of forms for us to sign about liability, NDAs, and other paperwork for the episode along with instructions about packing *actual cold weather clothes, Julian, and not just your professor sweaters and those sad emo boy flannels from college.*

Harrison and Ezra wandered off to my balcony for a close-together chat, leaning against the railing and occasionally touching one another's faces, hands, sides. Ezra caught me seeing them once and winked, making me blush in embarrassment before they resumed their private conversation.

Heinrich stayed longer, chatting with Oscar about things I knew nothing of, mostly stories from when he was a younger man and details of his stay in Savannah after we'd left. "I'm very impressed," he said, not for the first time. "I was expecting something sad and gauche, but they've done an excellent job of preserving the integrity of the ghosts there." Heinrich shot me a glance and smiled thinly. "What do you think of that, Julian? Respecting ghosts' boundaries and treating them like people?"

"Heinrich," Oscar said in a quelling tone. "Julian's done nothing wrong."

"No," Heinrich allowed. "But the cases aren't always going to be this straightforward, are they? There's not always a good ghost, bad ghost situation. There won't always be murderers and evil people seeking some sort of revenge after their bodies have ceased being useful." He cut his glare toward Oscar. "And your grandmother would like me to remind you that this situation in South Carolina is not only an exception to every rule, but quite embarrassing for all involved."

"Oh my god," I muttered. "Heinrich, I don't know what you're getting at here but I don't appreciate being accused of... What am I being accused of?"

He made his excuses to go then—apparently a charming young man name Geoff had asked him to some mixer at the art museum and Heinrich was going to be 'simply devastated' if he missed drinks with Geoff.

Harrison departed not long after, declaring an early day at the actual office in the morning, and a ton of paperwork to go through for Ghost of a Chance Productions. "With any luck," he said before brushing a quick kiss over Ezra's cheek and giving him a squeeze around the middle, "the paperwork will be in order and y'all will be able to sign off on your ownership by Thanksgiving."

"Cripes, that's strange to think about," Ezra muttered, glancing at Oscar as the door closed behind Harrison. "Do we need to change our visas?"

Oscar blew out a soft breath, eyes wide. "I have no fucking clue, mate. Who do we talk to about that?"

They drifted off together to talk about what to do next, tinges of disbelief in their voices over the turn of events actually coming to pass and left me to my own devices. It was oddly domestic, in our strange little way, and for the first time in a long time, I felt a comfortable sort of glow burning in my chest at the idea of being home.

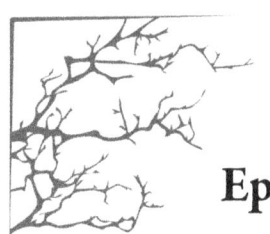

Epilogue — Oscar

"Admit it. You're happier to see me than you were spending time with Julian," Ezra said, stretching out on the sofa and flopping his feet onto my thighs.

Julian snorted but didn't look up from his laptop. He'd been head down in something for the past several days and, while I had my suspicions, I wasn't going to dwell on them, not until it was necessary.

"I don't know," I said, turning my attention back to Ezra. "How's your kissing? Is it better than Julian's?"

Ezra cocked a brow. "One way to find out..."

We both paused, glancing at Julian. He looked up from his computer and made a *go on* gesture. "Go on then. I won't stand in your way. Best friends to lovers... One of my favorite romance tropes."

Ezra leaned in as if he might go for it, and I puckered up. Then we both burst into giggles like we were twelve again and kissing was the silliest thing invented. "Alas, I cannot stand in the way of true love," Ezra said, flinging himself back onto the sofa with one hand over his eyes and the other trailing on the floor. "Oscar, we'll just have to go the rest of our lives wondering what if!"

"I don't know," I said, stretching my legs out to rest my heels on the coffee table. "Living with the mystery might be for the best."

Ezra snorted and rearranged himself on the sofa as if he were still twelve, all limbs and force and no regard for his spine's future happiness. "We'd never suit." He sighed dramatically. "Maybe in the next life."

I thought I hid my twinge well enough, but Ezra's pointed, sudden stillness and the silence from Julian's end of the room told me I'd been caught out. "It's fine," I muttered. "I'm not dead. No one died this time, so I'd say we're coming out ahead."

Another beat or two of quiet, then Ezra said, "It only counts if we're filming an episode. As this happened outside of filming, it doesn't affect our average of cadavers involved in an investigation."

"Damn," I sighed, forcing a small smile. "I'll have to try harder next time."

Ezra's phone chimed, and he glanced at the screen, a broad smile blooming on his lips. "Speaking of hard, it's Harrison. Don't wait up," he called, bouncing from the sofa and practically sprinting to the other bedroom.

Julian glanced up from what he'd been working on and smirked. "So he's distracted for a bit..."

I rolled to my feet, already unfastening the buttons on my cuffs as I headed for the bedroom. "Don't dawdle," I called. "We only have so long until Harrison has to hang up and get back to work."

It was a good while later, Julian and I laying lazily on a bed still damp with sweat and cooling fluid that would make me race to the shower if I thought too long on it, we stared at the ceiling with the old popcorn texture and let our minds wander into pleasant fantasies of *what if*. "If we lived in England," I said around a yawn, "I technically own Grandmere's house."

"Seriously?" Julian said on a startled half-laugh. "What do you do with it when you're not there?"

I shrugged. "Even when I *am* there, I don't live in it. Or any of her other properties. There's a service that comes out and maintains the grounds, and another that cleans the insides. There's a security service that keeps an eye on things as well."

Julian pushed up onto his elbow, fixing me with a bemused expression. "I'm about to be offensive here but... How do you afford all of that?"

"How do you think?" I asked, my face warming. Money wasn't something I liked to discuss, at least not when it came to obscene amounts of it.

"I'm guessing a trust created by either your grandmother or her late husband? Meant to protect their homes and properties?"

I blinked. "Actually, yes. Something like that. It's not out of my pocket. My parents had a bit of money set aside for me, meant for after I turned twenty, and I'm the sole inheritor for both of my grandparents..." Trailing off, I shrugged, looking down. "I prefer to make my own way as much as possible, but I admit it's been a great privilege being able to refuse money for séances and only accept gratuities or speaking fees and the like."

Julian stroked his fingers through my hair and gave it a little tug. "Why are you so nervous to tell me that? Are you afraid I'll want you for your money?" He said it teasingly, but I could hear a tinge of hurt in his voice. "You know I don't care."

I nodded. "But there have been times people have." Few and far between, thanks to my tendency to let Ezra be the public face of our enterprise and run interference when people wanted to get too close. But there'd been a handful of times, times when I thought a connection was real only to find they were interested in me for my real or perceived status, the fact I came from money. Almost worse than the users were those who assumed I was fake not because they didn't believe in the paranormal but because of my family, my background.

"Ugh," I groaned, rolling to press my face against Julian's chest. "Poor little rich boy, I know, I know. Out of all the things for me to fret over, this is the most ridiculous."

"Hey, stop that," he ordered gently, reaching to tip my chin up, to make me stop hiding. "You have your reasons, and that's it. I was asking because I'm nosy—I wondered how you and Ezra were able to scrape by in an expensive-to-live place like London is all. And now I know. Not a big deal." He dropped a quick kiss onto my forehead before asking, "And just for the record, if we *did* move in together—"

"When," I corrected, a thrill of excitement shooting through my veins. "When we do."

His smile was brilliant. "When we live together then, I would never make you use your grandparents' home just to have somewhere to live. There's a reason you don't stay there, and that's fine. Besides, somewhere of our own might be nice, you know? Somewhere just ours."

Somewhere without memories attached to it, things that made me angry, made me confused... I nodded. "When we're done filming this first season, let's... let's start looking for a place. We can figure out the where between now and then."

It was going to be a huge undertaking—Julian couldn't just pack up and move to England without miles of paperwork and approvals, and my visa was only good so long as we were working... "Shit. Ezra."

Julian sighed against me, pulling me closer. "Part of figuring it out, hon."

"Hon?"

"Hush. Go to sleep," he said, his smile curling his words.

He did, but I didn't. Not for hours. As tired as I felt, my brain wouldn't shut down enough for me to rest. What had happened on Broken Palm, the ease that Sandra Cochrane had over slipping into someone else's body, the Wreckers... I could still see their glowing shapes on the sand, stepping through the flames of Jeremiah's ghost fires. The hulking darkness of the ships foundering. The choked cries of drowning men would forever follow me.

As I tried to at least doze, shifting shadows made me jolt more fully awake. It had been nothing—the branches outside, moving across the security light's glow, but it had looked enough like a person moving to make me think of that shadow figure at the hotel, the way it had seemed so aware, so interested in me.

I closed my eyes, forcing myself to breathe slowly, to focus on my senses—I knew we were alone in the room. I could feel it. But that didn't stop my scared rabbit brain from churning out image after image, nightmare after nightmare.

Carefully, I slipped out from beneath Julian's heavy arm and padded to the sitting room. My laptop was still sitting on the glass end table, waiting for me to take it out onto the balcony overlooking the wedge of the museum district where Julian lived.. It was late enough where most of the shops had closed, leaving only glowing store signs over dark windows with only the occasional car going past. *Where are you headed at this hour,* I wondered. *All good children should be in bed by now.* Someone hurried past the donut shop across the street, darting toward the one thing still open on the street: the Pik-N-Go convenience store.

Maybe I should put on shoes and go get one of those slushies Julian swears are the best thing on earth. I watched a handful of young people—younger than me, at any rate—tumble out of the shop, clutching drinks to their chests as they slapped at one another with their free hands, voices raised without a care of the hour or place.

I thought of the Wreckers, the Tibbins family, nameless ghosts so worn and faded they didn't remember anything other than being a ghost.

Would that be me one day? Those kids? All of our laughing and fighting and crying and boring, quiet moments worn away to nothing? Or would some of us get to be proper ghosts or pass on without lingering in that strange between-state.

I thought of the Gleesons, on the beach with me. I'd asked Ezra to see what he could find on them. He'd come back with the names of a young couple who disappeared after telling relatives they were going to check out the island back in 1972, the two of them newly married and looking for a place to start a small business and build their life together.

When they didn't come home, when the police gave up looking, the family assumed the worst and, unfortunately, rightly so. Both of them still had siblings living, and I had plans to reach out to them soon. It had to be done delicately, though, and that was always the hardest part.

Would they be able to move on after that? Maybe I'd need to go back to the island and see if they were released. The idea sent a sharp chill down my spine, a residual pang of fear from what had happened, where I'd been.

Jeremiah Tibbins never got the chance to tell me what it was like, where he was. Or maybe that was by design—he hadn't been forthcoming in the first place, and at the end, when I was still on that side of everything, I hadn't been given enough time to ask.

The smell of burned coffee wafting from the convenience store dragged me out of my memory. I wasn't sure how long I'd been sitting on the chilly balcony, just that it'd been long enough for me to pass being mildly uncomfortable and slip into being actively cold. Still, I reasoned, maybe the cold would keep me alert for long enough to get this email out. Pulling up the message from Charlotte, I stared at the few lines again, weighing the choices, the possibilities.

"If you decide to go," Ezra's sleep-rough voice came from behind me, "you better buy two tickets because I'm going with you."

I huffed a silent, mirthless laugh. "Three—do you really think Julian would let me leave him behind?"

Ezra shuffled forward, his feet stuffed into his sneakers with his heels still hanging out and the hotel duvet draped over his shoulders. I scooted over to make room for him to drag up a chair and, after a moment's fuss, we were sitting next to one another with the duvet wrapped around both of us. "I'm not even going to ask if you want to see about turning this into an episode," he muttered. "I value my life."

"Thank you. I was having horrible visions of the channel getting wind of this somehow and pouncing on it as an opportunity for a special episode or something."

Ezra snorted. "Tonight, on a very special episode of *Bump in the Night,* Oscar learns the true meaning of friendship and love."

"But first, a word from our sponsor," I murmured, accepting the joint he proffered. "I'm assuming Harrison doesn't know you partake?" It was mild, not the skunky weed I'd been expecting from him, and I took a larger hit than I normally might have.

"He knows. And he says he's not a cop. And also," he took the joint back. "Where do you think I got this? His shit's better than mine. He uses it sometimes for migraines. I, um... I've been using it when I feel an episode coming on."

I sat up, the incipient buzz annoying now as I shifted to pin Ezra with a glare. "How many episodes have you had that I don't know about?"

"None. Since I've been heading them off at the pass, as they say." He took another long hit and handed it back to me. "It's not perfect, but it's helped. I haven't had a big episode since..." He trailed off, darting a guilty glance at me.

"I didn't mean for you to... to have an episode. If I'd known..."

He didn't reply, staring down at a new gaggle of people heading for the open shop. This one was far less exuberant than the other, moving as a solemn pack of dark-clad figures on their way to or from work, from the looks of things. No laughing, no joking, no raised voices. Just a quiet shuffle of people existing. I had a wild thought, wondering if they were dead, if they were ghosts stuck in a Sartre-esque loop of a mind-numbing jaunt to work every morning for the rest of their existence.

"Since Savannah, six."

"*Six?*" I hissed, remembering Julian was asleep just feet away. "Ezra—"

"The first time, Harrison and I had just finished—you know, finished—"

"Yeah, I get it," I muttered. "Stop stalling, please." Passing the joint back to him, I nodded at it. "It's nearly done."

He nodded, rolling it gently back and forth between his fingers, watching it as he spoke. "I felt the start of one of the spells as he was passing the joint to me and I took a hit automatically, you know?"

"Be rude not to," I said, rolling my eyes. "And it helped?"

He nodded. "The feeling just sort of faded. It wasn't one hundred percent gone, but it kept it from getting beyond just that unsettling sense of dread I get before a spell, and I didn't seize." He finished the joint, fishing in his sleep pants pocket for an Altoid tin to drop the roach in. "When I felt another one brewing a bit later, I asked Harrison for another joint. Same thing. It dulled it down enough that I didn't have a full-blown episode, and I'm still functional."

I nodded, leaning against his arm as we watched the grim group leave the convenience store and move as a flock toward the other end of the block where a crosswalk waited, leading to a bus stop. "Where were you when all of these happened? That's... Christ, Ez. Six? *Six?* In less than two weeks?"

"New Orleans," he chuckled darkly. "More ghosts per square inch than anywhere I've ever been. I can only imagine how you'd handle it. Lucky for me, I just got all of their feelings, good, bad, and indifferent." He cut a glance my way, a tiny smile curving his lips. "I used to think my empathic abilities were pants, you know? Like a weak version of yours."

"Ez—"

"Lemme finish, Ozzy. I'm having a moment here," he said, that small grin flashing into something larger and more amused for a moment. "Anyway. Where was I? Right, being shit. So. I've come to the conclusion that I've been self-pitying, you know? My abilities, they're not flash. They're not something people much care about, really. Oh, Gran's ghost is vaguely upset? *Phhht.* If you can't tell me what it is she wants, then fuck off."

"Ezra, it's not like that." I looped my fingers through his and gave a squeeze.

"Not to you, no. But me?" He shrugged. "Lifetime of being told I'm too sensitive, I'm too," he waved one hand back and forth. "Swishy. Too this or that. And no one to explain these abilities to me, you know? How they work, what to do with them. So, I've been riding that train solo."

"I want to help," I whispered. "But I'm not sure how. I don't have experience with your abilities. Mine are anything but empathic. Maybe—"

"It's okay," he said, his small smile back in full bloom. "Believe it or not, Enoch was able to put me in touch with someone who might be able to help. And since our world of weirdness is quite small, we already know them."

Whatever the expression was on my face made Ezra laugh. "No, it isn't Lisa. It's her brother, Jesse."

"And how the hell did Enoch get involved?"

"Apparently," he finally shifted, resting his head against mine, "he's been practicing his reach. And bumped into me."

"Did you tell him it's rude to go poking about in other people's heads like that?"

"Honestly, he just said hello, and I nearly had a heart attack since I thought I was hearing voices now. He's like a golden retriever, isn't he?"

I smiled at the comparison. "Eager, friendly, a little goofy and somewhat clumsy. Yep, that tracks."

We fell quiet for a few minutes, both of us riding the gentle buzz of Harrison's personal stash. Finally, Ezra reached out and tapped my closed laptop. "So, are you going to do it or not?"

"I'm undecided."

"Liar. You're very decided but afraid."

I grunted. "Anyone ever tell you that your perceptiveness is a pain in the arse?"

He chuckled. "Just you, dearest."

Ezra sat with me while I came up with a short email response to Charlotte, accepting her invitation to meet at her home in Paris in January. "Tell her there's three of us."

"I don't want to overwhelm her..."

"So, who are you not bringing? Me or Julian? Because you're *not* going alone."

"Sorry, Mum," I muttered, editing the email to mention I'd be traveling with my boyfriend and best friend/business partner.

"Oooooh, business partner! Aren't I fancy today?"

"Fuck off, Ez."

He laughed, pulling me in to kiss the top of my head. "Hey, Enoch's a pretty neat kid, by the way. Oh my god, did I just say that out loud? I'm turning into Grandad!"

I snorted. "It's the old man weed. And he is. I think I've been avoiding him out of some misplaced sense of decorum or something."

"Or, you know, being afraid."

"You keep calling me that," I mumbled. "I'm not afraid."

Ezra tugged my hair. "Everyone's afraid, Oz. Some of us just sublimate it into being giant dorks and smoking weed with their lawyer boyfriend at fancy hotels. Or," he tugged again, "their best friend who's had more ghost encounters than he's had hot meals."

"We do lead wild lives," I murmured. "Fuck, I thought I'd be able to just stay up till the sun was all the way up, but I don't think I'm gonna make it. You going back to bed?"

He nodded. "I'm riding up with Harrison, so I should get my beauty rest." He stood, tugging the duvet with him, smirking at my meeped protest. "Gotta stay pretty for my sugar daddy."

"Oh my god..."

He cackled. "He's not my sugar daddy."

"I know just... don't ever call him daddy where I can hear, yeah?"

Ezra smirked. "How about Sir?"

"I hate you. Go to bed."

Ezra kissed me atop my head again and headed back into the suite, leaving the sliding door open a smidge.

It wasn't until a third group—smaller this time—trundled into the convenience store and, a few minutes later, a cop car with lights flashing rolled up to park outside, that I went inside. Julian was half awake when I climbed into bed, rolling toward me with a half-snort, half-grunt as I snuggled against his chest.

"You're cold," he muttered. "And smell like weed."

"Ezra."

"Mm."

I closed my eyes, finally feeling the soft tug of sleep creeping up on me, but Julian had one more question.

"So, when are we going?"

I didn't bother to pretend ignorance. "January third," I murmured. "Houston to Gatwick."

He grunted again. "I need to make sure my passport is still good."

I nodded. "You don't mind that I assumed?"

"I'd have been mad if you hadn't."

We were quiet again, for a long time this time, before Julian murmured, "I've never been to a covered bridge before. I'm looking forward to this investigation."

I smiled, burrowing closer. "I'm glad."

Coming Soon: Ghost of a Chance (Medium at Large Book 6)

THE MIDNIGHT KNOCKING is pre-recorded.
 The bleeding walls are a fire hazard.
 The headless man on the bridge?
 Okay, that's actually a problem.

Things have finally calmed down for *Bump in the Night*. It's been months since they had a shoot go pear-shaped, and Oscar is finally starting to breathe a little easier. Ghosts have behaved, no one's been murdered (recently), and things with Julian are smooth sailing.

Until Norwich House.

Norwich House is one of the most infamous haunted houses in the country. But when Oscar, with Julian and Ezra's help, proves the hauntings are all a longstanding, money-making hoax, the owner of the house takes exception to their thoroughness.

It would all be a matter for legal until the man is found dead on The Devil's Bridge.

Oscar's aunt Colette must be right: He *does* have a curse over his head.

A good skeptic looks at evidence.
 A good skeptic keeps an open mind.
 A good skeptic definitely doesn't get caught on film fighting with a man who's found dead six hours later.

Between the easy run of things with filming, the renewed job offer from the university, and his relationship with Oscar finding its groove, Julian has every reason to feel good about life.

When the team's methods and intentions are called into question in the media by an angry hoaxer, Julian is confident the truth will take the heat off the team.

Julian has a history of being mistaken.

Between the social media avalanche, online tabloids, and the other ghost hunting team trying to poach their investigation into the brand new spirit at Norwich House, Julian is starting to rethink his newfound dedication to paranormal investigations.

Also by Meredith

YOU CAN FIND ALL MY books listed my website with links to buy at your favorite online retailers or ask your local booksellers to order you a copy if you prefer!

THE BEDEVILED SERIES
The Devil May Care
The Devil You Know
The Devil in the Details
Speak of the Devil (Summer 2023)

MEDIUM AT LARGE SERIES
Bump in the Night
Ghoul Friend
Old Ghosts
In the Spirit
After Life (Spring 2023)
Book Six TBA (Fall 2023)
Science of Magic Series
Data Sets
Fuzzy Logic
Discrete
Scientific Method (2023)
Marked
Nearly Human

Howl at the Moon (Winter 2022)
Book 3 TBA (Summer 2023)
In The Pines
Fetch (Spring 2023)
Witch Bone (Fall 2023)
Conjure (Spring 2024)
Damian Murphy's Pet Sitting and Murder Investigation
Book 1 Title TBA: March 2023
Stand Alones
Between the Lines
Shared World Series
Ring My Bell (Contemporary MM Fairy Tale Retelling, January 2023)

Leo (A Gaynor Beach Single Dads Romance, November 2022)

Final Days: The Calms (An apocalyptic romance with a HEA, October 2022)

Anthology

Easy as Pie*, a MM holiday romance, will be appearing in the **There Goes The Turkey** holiday anthology in November 2023.*

About The Author

Meredith (they/them/theirs) writes queer-centered stories with romance and happily ever afters. They write queer-centered romances in various subgenres including paranormal, speculative fiction/alternate universe, and contemporary. They firmly believe in happily ever afters and that pineapple definitely belongs on pizza.

For sneak peeks at upcoming works and other goodies, check out Meredith's website and social media.

www.booksbymeredith.com
www.facebook.com/groups/meredithsreadingranch[1]
www.twitter.com/meredithspies[2]
www.facebook.com/meredithspiesauthor[3]
www.instagram.com/meredithspies[4]

---

1. http://www.facebook.com/groups/meredithsreadingranch
2. http://www.twitter.com/meredithspies
3. http://www.facebook.com/meredithspiesauthor
4. http://www.instagram.com/meredithspies

Printed in the USA
CPSIA information can be obtained
at www.ICGtesting.com
JSHW022105020124
54699JS00001B/13